THE NECRO

Also Available from Valancourt Books

GASTON DE BLONDEVILLE
Ann Radcliffe
Edited by Frances A. Chiu

CLERMONT
Regina Maria Roche
Edited by Natalie Schroeder

THE CASTLE OF WOLFENBACH
Eliza Parsons
Edited by Diane Long Hoeveler

THE VEILED PICTURE
Ann Radcliffe
Edited by Jack G. Voller

Forthcoming Titles

THE MONK
Matthew G. Lewis
Edited by Allen W. Grove

ZELUCO
John Moore
Edited by Pamela Perkins

THE FARMER OF INGLEWOOD FOREST
Elizabeth Helme
Edited by Sandro Jung

THE NEW MONK
R. S. Esquire
Edited by Elizabeth Andrews

Gothic Classics

THE

NECROMANCER

OR THE

TALE OF THE BLACK FOREST

FOUNDED ON FACTS

TRANSLATED FROM THE GERMAN OF

LAWRENCE FLAMMENBERG,

BY PETER TEUTHOLD

TWO VOLUMES IN ONE

Edited with a new critical essay and notes by
Jeffrey Cass

CHICAGO:
VALANCOURT BOOKS
2007

The Necromancer; or, The Tale of the Black Forest
First published by William Lane in 1794
First Valancourt Books edition, April 2007

Library of Congress Cataloging-in-Publication Data

Kahlert, Karl Friedrich, 1765-1813.
  [Geisterbanner. English]
  The necromancer, or, The tale of the Black Forest : founded on facts / Lawrence Flammenberg ; translated from the German by Peter Teuthold ; edited with a critical essay and notes by Jeffrey Cass. -- 1st Valancourt Books ed.
      p. cm. -- (Gothic classics)
  "Two volumes in one."
  First published by William Lane in 1794.
  Includes bibliographical references.
  ISBN 0-9792332-2-4
  1. Black Forest (Germany)--Fiction. I. Teuthold, Peter. II. Title.
III. Title: Tale of the Black Forest.
  PT2372.K28G4513 2007
  833'.6--DC22

                                    2007002736

Published by Valancourt Books
P. O. Box 220511
Chicago, Illinois 60622

Typography by James D. Jenkins
Set in Dante MT

                         10 9 8 7 6 5 4 3 2 1

CONTENTS

PREFACE

" . . . when you have finished Udolpho, we will read the Italian together; and I have made out a list of ten or twelve more of the same kind for you."

"Have you, indeed! How glad I am! What are they all?"

"I will read you their names directly. . . Castle of Wolfenbach, Clermont, Mysterious Warnings, Necromancer of the Black Forest, Midnight Bell, Orphan of the Rhine, and Horrid Mysteries. Those will last us some time."

"Yes, pretty well; but are they all horrid, are you sure they are all horrid?"

Jane Austen, *Northanger Abbey*

The Necromancer; or, The Tale of the Black Forest (1794) is, of course, best known today as one of the seven "horrid novels" read by Catherine Morland and Isabella Thorpe in Jane Austen's satire of Gothic fiction, *Northanger Abbey* (1818). And yet, unlike the other six novels, which without Austen's famous endorsement of their "horridness" would have been completely forgotten, *The Necromancer* has continually re-appeared in print to fascinate and terrify new generations of readers. Following its initial publication by William Lane's famous (or, at the time, infamous) Minerva Press in 1794, the book resurfaced in Dublin the following year, and nearly half a century later was resurrected by William Hazlitt in his *Romancist and Novelist's Library* in 1840. During the twentieth century, the book was reprinted three more times, in 1927, 1968, and 1989, testifying to its persistent vitality and interest, even to modern readers accustomed to books much more "horrid" than anything existing in Austen's time.

And yet, the perennial fascination of *The Necromancer* is not easily explained. Certainly it has never been endorsed by the critical establishment, either then or now. One late eighteenth century critic declared his fervent hope that it was indeed a translation from the German, since he would be embarrassed to find such a book among the corpus of English literature. Twentieth century critics, including Michael Sadleir and Frederick S. Frank, have tended to view the novel as "incoherent" or "incomprehensible."

Nonetheless, despite (or perhaps because of) the novel's bizarre plot, it was eagerly welcomed by a late eighteenth-century English reading public suddenly enamoured of translations of German works. This interest appears to have been sparked initially by an impassioned speech given in 1788 by Henry Mackenzie, the famous author of *The Man of Feeling* (1771), who in remarks before the Royal Society of Edinburgh highly praised Schiller's drama *Die Raüber* (*The Robbers*). The play was soon translated into English and met with great success, and famously influenced notable writers such as Samuel Taylor Coleridge, who wrote to Robert Southey, "My God, Southey, who is this Schiller, this convulser of the heart? . . . upon my soul I write to you because I am frightened . . . Why have we ever called Milton sublime?"

This newfound fascination with German literature led to translations of a number of German works, most of them more or less Gothic, throughout the 1790s, including Schiller's *The Ghost-Seer* (1795), Carl Grosse's *Horrid Mysteries* (1796), and Christian August Vulpius's *The History of Rinaldo Rinaldi, Captain of Banditti* (1800). In addition to authentic German translations, authors and publishers capitalized on the popularity of German novels by publishing numberless sham translations, including three of the so-called "Northanger Novels": Eliza Parsons's *The Castle of Wolfenbach: A German Story* (1793) and *The Mysterious Warning: A German Tale* (1796), and Francis Lathom's *The Midnight Bell, a German Story, Founded on Incidents in Real Life* (1798).

The other dominant strain in popular fiction during the last decade of the eighteenth century and the first decades of the nineteenth was, of course, the Gothic novel, some of the most important examples of which are Ann Radcliffe's *The Mysteries of Udolpho* (1794) and *The Italian* (1797) and M. G. Lewis's *The Monk* (1796). *The Necromancer*, published in 1794, is significant then, in that it predates most (if not all) of the above-cited works. Given the types of fiction in vogue in 1794, it is difficult to imagine a more fortuitous novel appearing on booksellers' shelves than *The Necromancer*.

But if late eighteenth century critics experienced some difficulty in classifying the novel as an original English work or a German translation, they have not been the only ones puzzled by the novel's mysterious provenance. Indeed, until now the identity of the author-translator "Peter Teuthold" has remained unknown, and a number of speculations have been offered as to the author and source of the German original.

The novel is in fact a translation of *Der Geisterbanner: Eine Wundergeschichte aus mündlichen und schriftlichen Traditionen gesammelt* (which translates roughly as *The Spectral Banner: A Wondrous Tale Collected from Oral and Written Traditions*), published by Johann Baptist Wallishauser at Hohenzollern in 1792, and attributed to "Lorenz Flammenberg". Lorenz (or Lawrence) Flammenberg was in fact a pseudonym for Karl Friedrich Kahlert (1765-1813), author of a variety of stories and plays, none of which appear to have been translated into English. Interestingly, however, the English version of *Der Geisterbanner* adds a long episode (Wolf's trial) not found in Kahlert's original, but in fact adapted from a story by Friedrich Schiller. And perhaps still more intriguing is the fact that Kahlert appreciated Teuthold's addition so much that in 1799-1800, he republished *Der Geisterbanner* at Breslau in an extended edition, acknowledging Teuthold, and translating the Wolf episode into German and inserting it in the third volume of the revised novel.

The identity of the translator "Peter Teuthold" (pronounced "Toit-old") has long—until the publication of this edition—remained shrouded in mystery. The name is a pseudonym, drawn from German literature: "Teuthold" was the name of the armourer in the German national epic "Hermannsschlacht" ("Hermann's Battle"), and the morpheme "Teut-" stands for "Deutsch" ("German").[1] That no critic until now has been able to divine Teuthold's identity is somewhat surprising, given the "Translator's Preface" to *The Necromancer*, in which he states that,

> If the Subject of the following Tale should be thought interesting and amuseing [*sic*], the Public may expect a speedy Publication of a still more intricate and wonderful one, exhibiting a long Series of similar Frauds, perpetrated under the mysterious Veil of pretended supernatural Aid.

This plot synopsis describes another German Gothic novel, translated into English by P. (Peter) Will as *The Victim of Magical Delusion*, and published in 1795, the year after *The Necromancer*. However, de-

---

[1] I would like to acknowledge gratefully Norbert Besch, who provided this information.

spite Will's prolific work as a translator of German Gothics in the 1790s (he also translated Carl Grosse's *Der Genius* as *Horrid Mysteries* and August von Kotzebue's *Leiden der Ortenbergischen Familie* as *The Sufferings of the Family of Ortenberg*) and despite the similarities in style and composition among these translations, no one until now has identified Will as the translator of *The Necromancer*. The circumstantial evidence for his authorship just outlined is corroborated by Georg Christoph Hamberger and Johann Georg Meusel's *Das Gelehrte Teutschland oder: Lexikon der jetzt lebenden teutschen Schriftsteller*, which gives this entry:[1]

> Will (Peter): Prediger einer teutschen Gemeinde zu London, geb. Darmstadt. Unter dem Namen Teuthold gab er heraus: The Necromancer of the Black Forest, founded on facts . . .

Peter Will was born at Darmstadt in 1764 and later moved to London, where he served as a minister and also translated a variety of German texts, both fiction and nonfiction, into English. The grammar and style of his translations were frequently attacked by critics, but nonetheless, despite whatever shortcomings his translations may suffer from, Will deserves a great deal of credit for helping to popularize German literature in England and also for the influence of his translations on English writers, notably Matthew Lewis.

Given the frequent claim that the novel's plot is incomprehensible, it may be well here to give a brief outline of it, which may help prevent the reader from becoming too lost in the tale's winding diversions (although indeed this is one of the book's greatest pleasures!) The reader may wish to skip this portion and commence reading the novel and return to consult this summary only if he finds himself mired in confusion while reading.

The novel opens in the present day, where two friends, Herrman and Hellfried, meet again after a thirty year separation. They relate to one another the adventures that have befallen them over the last three decades, and Hellfried opens with his strange experiences at the town of "F—". While staying at an inn there, certain of his possessions mysteriously disappear, and one night he believes he sees

---

[1] Acknowledgement is due to Norbert Besch, who made this important discovery and communicated it to me only a week before publication of this edition.

the thief—the ghost of his mother. A strange old man also residing at the inn seems to be acquainted with the secret of these mysteries, and invites Hellfried to a necromantic ritual. During the ceremony, Hellfried loses consciousness and awakens inside a carriage, which overturns, breaking his leg. Here his story ends, and Herrman reveals that he, too, has had similar experiences.

Herrman tells how, while serving as tutor to the young Baron de R—, he travelled to a village apparently haunted by spectral horsemen who reside in an old ruin. A brave Danish lieutenant also staying at their inn proposes that they go investigate the ruin and the mystery of the phantoms. A number of adventures ensue, and finally, in the present day, Herrman gives Hellfried some papers, which he says will tell the rest of the story. Both of them, by now quite old, die, and the remainder of the story is told from the collected papers.

Part II of the novel opens with a letter from Herrman's former student, the Baron de R—, now grown, who some years after the earlier adventures, meets the Danish lieutenant, now a major. He writes to Herrman to send him another letter, this one from the lieutenant, explaining what happened after Herrman and the Baron left him after the adventure of the haunted castle.

The lieutenant meets an Austrian, who flashes back twenty years to tell how he knew then a sergeant named Volkert who was reputed to be a necromancer. The lieutenant tells the Austrian of his adventures at the haunted castle, and the two of them decide to go visit it.

Part III continues with Lieutenant B—'s letter to Herrman. Returning to the town of F— with the Austrian, they meet Lieutenant N—, who claims to have been visited by a ghost. Having been frightened by this phantom, Lieutenant N— is very relieved when he meets an old man who claims to be a necromancer. Lieutenant B— suspects the necromancer to be involved in the haunted castle affair, and the Austrian suspects it may be Volkert. They thus determine to capture him and force him to reveal the truth. However, at last they determine not to turn Volkert over to the authorities, and instead set him free, and the Austrian parts ways with Lieutenant B—. Soon after, Lieutenant B— is taken prisoner by bandits, but is spared by Volkert, who is one of their party, out of gratitude for previously having spared him.

Two years later, Lieutenant B— happens to arrive at a town where he finds a trial taking place, and he learns that those being tried include Volkert and Wolf, the captain of the bandits who had previously taken him prisoner. The novel concludes with the account of their trials, the very end of which is recounted in a letter to Lieutenant B— by a friend of his, P—.

* * * * *

It is the custom nowadays when a publisher reissues an old book to affix to it the appellation of "classic"; various such series today include "World Classics", "Pocket Classics", "European Classics", and many others, in addition to the present series of "Gothic Classics." But is it fair to label a book like *The Necromancer*, a book which few critics have succeeded in comprehending, and upon which even fewer have bestowed any praise, a "classic"? Undoubtedly it is an important novel historically, as one of the first German novels translated into English, and as an influence on more famous novels like *The Monk* and *Frankenstein*.

But in looking at the history of *The Necromancer*, we see that it is more than just a literary footnote. As we can tell from the progression of incarnations of *The Necromancer* — from part of a library of the best romances in 1840, to a Victorian-style yellowback in the 1927 edition, to a deluxe 1968 collector's edition, to a 1989 mass-market paperback geared toward late 20th century neo-Goth horror fans, to the present edition with its new essay on queer theory — the novel has had something new to say to each succeeding generation. For almost two hundred and fifteen years, readers from different backgrounds and different nations have continued to read *The Necromancer* and continue to enjoy it today as much as its first readers, who picked up a copy in 1794 for six shillings, did. In my opinion, this is the true definition of a classic, and *The Necromancer* certainly deserves the label. Enjoy.

JAMES D. JENKINS
Chicago

February 2, 2007

Queering *The Necromancer*

Jeffrey Cass

"There is nothing I would not do for those who are really my friends. I have no notion of loving people by halves, it is not in my nature. My attachments are always excessively strong...I would not dance with [Captain Hunt], unless he would allow Miss Andrews to be as beautiful as an angel. The men think of us incapable of real friendship you know, and I am determined to shew them the difference."

—Jane Austen, *Northanger Abbey*

"The hurricane was howling, the hailstone beating against the windows, the hoarse croaking of the raven bidding adieu to autumn, and the weather-cock's dismal creaking joined with the mournful dirge of the solitary owl, when Herrman and Hellfried, who had been united by the strongest bonds of friendship from their youthful days, were seated by the chearing fire side, hailing the approach of winter."

—Karl Kahlert, *The Necromancer*

THE NECROMANCER has fared better than the other "horrid" novels cited in *Northanger Abbey*, having been first introduced to the public in 1794 (Minerva) and then re-introduced to the public with subsequent editions by William Hazlitt in 1840 (*Romancist and Novelist's Library*, J. Clements), Montague Summers in 1927 (R. Holden & Co.), Devendra Varma in 1968 (Folio Press), and Lucien Jenkins in 1989 (Skoob). Oddly, however, little is known about Karl Kahlert, the original author of *Der Geisterbanner, eine Wundergeschichte aus mündlichen und schriftlichen Traditionen gesammelt* (1792)[1] or his English translator Peter Teuthold, who in 1794 published *The Necromancer: or The Tale of the Black Forest*. So little was known, in fact, that Montague Summers first thought that Teuthold's allusion to the German provenance for *The Necromancer* was fictitious and only later "reversed" himself in his book *The Gothic Quest*, nearly a decade after the publication of his edition of *The Necromancer* (Conger 2). According to Devendra Var-

---

[1] Translation: *The Necromancer, A Story of Wonders collected from Oral and Written Traditions*.

ma, Teuthold was a German refugee who used "Lawrence Flammenberg" as a pseudonym for Kahlert. Teuthold may have attempted to
profit from the popularity of *Sturm und Drang* literature in England,
notably the splashy arrival of Friedrich Schiller's play *Die Räuber* (*The
Robbers*), first published in 1781.[1] The real Lorenz Flammenberg was
from Freiberg and was something of an "antiquary" or bookseller
(Varma xv), having compiled a loose collection of stories under the
title of "Der Geisterbanner." In 1800, Flammenberg also published
Der Geisterbanner: eine Geschichte aus den Papieren eines Dänen,[2] con-
tinuing to cater to the popular taste of the German reading public for
horror and to profit again from Kahlert's stories.

Published two years after *The Necromancer* in 1796, and proba-
bly directly influenced by Teuthold's edition of Kahlert's novel, *The
Monk*, written by Matthew Lewis, illustrates that the British, too, had
developed a toothsome taste for terror, and the subsequent explosion
of Gothic fiction in the 1790s, with many cases of German settings,
became the literary landscape against which Austen situates her
novel *Northanger Abbey*. That the "horrid novels" are so prominently
featured in *Northanger Abbey* suggests a sophisticated readership that
was, as Michael Gamer has argued, "capable not only of understanding irony but also of treating their own reading experience with it"
(40). The sophistication of Austen's reading public additionally suggests that they, like Austen, had turned their attention to the "horrid" novels and were able to draw their own conclusions with regard
to the thematic and generic elements that *Northanger Abbey* gener-
ally shares with the gothic literature of the time. One might even
argue, as Tony Tanner does, that *Northanger Abbey* explores reading
and reading practices: "There is a good deal of defence of novels and
reading in this novel, so that it is in a self-justifying artefact" (44).

---

[1] Indeed, Syndy Conger demonstrates that the last part of Teuthold's version of
The Necromancer interpolates a portion of Schiller's *Der Verbrecher aus verlorene
Ehre* [*The Criminal of Lost Honor*] (1786), forming the final episode of the novel
and further indicating the influence of the German writer on English literature. Conger also argues for the influence of *The Necromancer* on Mary Shelley in the writing of *Frankenstein*. E.J. Clery has argued that the launch of the
Minerva Press in 1790, under whose imprint *The Necromancer* was published,
encouraged the very kinds of literary piracy that Teuthold apparently practiced
when he inserted Schiller's story into Kahlert's text.

[2] Translation: *The Necromancer: A History from the Papers of a Dane.*

While interpretations of *Northanger Abbey* have flooded Austen criticism, most have tended to the view that Austen calls into question the social and cultural value of reading gothic works. For many critics, her heroine, Catherine Morland, is too credulous, too willing to accept the supernatural existence of the gothic, and less willing to find rational explanations to the problems and mysteries of everyday life, preferring instead to concoct terrifying plots and conspiracy theories. Typical of this view is B.G. MacCarthy who suggests that "burlesquing the Gothic romance" becomes the overarching "intention" of Austen's novel (487). More pithily, Stuart Tave writes, "[*Northanger Abbey*] is a novel that takes the romance out of life" (37). While not untrue, views of this kind tend to oversimplify the complexity of Austen's representation of bourgeois reading preferences and, more concretely, of the gothic. In this vein, Anne Ehrenpreis properly asserts, "Catherine's folly lies not in indulging a taste for melodramatic fiction but in imposing its values on the life around her" (21), particularly since her eventual partner Henry Tilney clearly enjoys reading Ann Radcliffe's *The Mysteries of Udolpho*, "without mistaking romance for fiction" (22). While recognizing that "Catherine must learn to throw off her gothic illusion and cease to expect in life the trappings of villainy," Isobel Grundy argues for a Catherine Morland who "first and more importantly…must learn to throw off the social timidity which makes her vulnerable to the Thorpes' social tyranny" (205). Of course, overcoming "social timidity" does not entail a criticism of the status quo. Indeed, as Marilyn Butler argues, Jane Austen forecloses such a possibility in *Northanger Abbey*: "From the beginning, when [Jane Austen] takes up a typically conservative plot, she is writing defensively—fearing subversion, advocating the values which in times past justified the rule of the gentry. She never allows us to contemplate any other ideology" (108).

Along more metacritical lines, Rachel Brownstein offers a complex fiction, in which "*Northanger Abbey*'s take on tropes of fiction, kinds of readers, and modes of reading is too thoroughly riddled with ironies to allow one to categorize it comfortably as parody or pastiche" (37). Vijay Mishra goes even further: "Familiarity, ludic resistance, aleatory narrative, and parody—the playing out of games with texts—are the characteristics of Catherine's complex responses to Isabella's encyclopaedic knowledge of the Gothic" (47). "Horrid" books such as *The Necromancer* elicit, in Mishra's words, "the civilized semantics of the unspeakable, the sublime" (47). Brownstein and Mishra's unease at a comfortable categorization of *Northanger Abbey*, as well as the female characters in the novel who engage Gothic texts as sites potentially critical of social and cultural norms, suggests that subversive readings of the novel are not only possible, but desirable. They take place within intertextual interstices—bodies of gothic texts joining up with Austen's to reveal uncanny and uncomfortable, multivalent and "sublime" interpretive spaces. Not surprisingly, juxtaposing the above epigraphs within the context of this herme-neutical discomfort opens up a rather more interesting intertextual relationship than has been previously discussed between Austen's novel and *The Necromancer*, one of its "horrid" cousins. In the case of the passage from *Northanger Abbey*, Isabella's semi-coherent speech highlights the possibility that women should form intense relation-ships with one another, relationships that potentially rival or displace male-female bonds, which in the view of Marilyn Butler staunchly support a conservative ideology. To be sure, from Catherine's per-spective, women ought to defend one another from masculine pre-rogatives over women, from men who either deny the capacity of women to make and keep same-sex friendships or who deprecate their personal usefulness and sociocultural validity. Isabella's fiercely funny speech to Catherine Morland, in which she not only reveals that Isabella cannot love people "by halves," but that admirers must acknowledge the beauty of her friends as well, hints at the protection from paternalistic regulation that sororal relationships offer. They effectively shield women from the unquestioned dominance of male power, privilege, and prestige.

In addition, the passage from *Northanger Abbey* takes place with-in the context of Isabella and Catherine's discussion of gothic novel reading, specifically the "horrid" novels that have entered into much of the critical discussion of Jane Austen's presumed anti-gothicism, a set of books that includes Teuthold's version of Kahlert's novel, *The Necromancer*. The juxtaposition of the two cited passages indicates that Austen may have appropriated the theme of same-sex friendship from Kahlert's work, although for Kahlert the intensity of same-sex friendship among men establishes the homosocial links that drive masculine behaviors and perpetuate male power. Herrman and Hell-fried are not only "united by the strongest bonds of friendship," but their reunion blunts their predictable, heteronormative modes of expression, even within the confines of their own storytelling. Re-inforced by gales of stormy weather, Herrman and Hellfried "come out" of their mental and emotional closets to reveal to one another (and to us) their unspeakable secrets, which until the moment of rev-elation, they have kept well hidden. Much like Catherine and Isabella, whose social views are shaped by their readings of terrifying gothic encounters, Herrman and Hellfried are likewise motivated first by their desire to amuse one another with "their stock of entertaining narratives [that] seemed to be inexhaustible (8) and second to ratio-nalize their experiences of the unexplainable and the unspeakable, buttressing their mutual beliefs in the supernatural, even as they at-tempt to "unriddle" it (9).

The theoretical work of Eve Kosofsky Sedgwick extends the im-plicit significance of homosocial relations in English literature from the Renaissance through the nineteenth century, attaching special significance to the figure of the unspeakable within the narrative frames of Gothic works, arguing that the "Gothic unspeakable was a near-impenetrable shibboleth for a particular conjunction of class and male sexuality" (95). Austen succeeds in homogenizing same-sex female friendship in *Northanger Abbey*, transforming the sexual frisson that underlies the "Gothic unspeakable" in novels from which she drew inspiration (such as *The Necromancer*) into hetero-normative and unerotic female friendships. Austen's decoupling of the homosocial from the homosexual is consistent with the lack of homosocial female communities throughout literature. Lesbianism, to quote Nina Auerbach, "is a silent possibility," but there is certainly no "extrinsic" validation of sororal friendship or queer desire (7). Of course, covert lesbianism is often a prurient given, a grinning lurid-ness over which heterosexual men chuckle within their many ho-mosocial, clubby environments. But sodomy within fraternities pro-duces Gothic horror. It is the love that publicly dare not speak its name—where homosexual desire may at any moment (unspeakably) burst through the boundaries of acceptable homosocial contact and lapse into horrifying sexual otherness. Homophobia thus undergirds (homosocial) male bonding, while homosexual panic gives rise to Gothic terror.[1] And this panic is often class driven. As Sedgwick suc-

---

[1] See especially Sedgwick's essay, "Toward the Gothic: Terrorism and Homo-sexual Panic" in *Between Men: English Literature and Male Homosocial Desire*. For

cinctly argues in *The Coherence of Gothic Conventions*, "Throughout the Age of Frankenstein the relative impermeability, between classes, of any sense of homosexual possibilities and meanings allowed a single central homophobic/paranoid image of male threat and male solipsism to become accepted as the primal image of human nature" (x). The shock of recognition—"It takes one to know one" (xi)—is *a fortiori* the panicked moment in which men perceive read their own submerged homoerotic desire.

Like Sedgwick, George Haggerty puts forth a "queering" of the gothic that targets several versions of sexuality and interrogates the transgressiveness of same-sex friendship and not just same-sex desire. For Haggerty, "queer" becomes a "trope" that consistently "challenges" and "undermines" the dominant paradigm of heteronormative "configurations of human interaction" (3). This is not to suggest that for readers of gothic fiction heteronormative relations are not at some point restored; in fact, the cases of Herrman and Hellfried in *The Necromancer* point to just such a restoration. But in the end, such restoration remains superficial, falsely resolving the constructed appearances of apparitions and the fabrication of raised dead spirits. Still, restoration would seem to presuppose true confession, and from the heart, but Hellfried fails to tell his story to Herrman verbally. Instead, he writes out the rest of the story, accumulating documentation and evidence that support his version of events, and he oddly gives permission for Herrman to publish the documents that he has long hoarded, appearing to rationalize his life decisions and familial choices. For both Herrman and Hellfried, the only characters in the novel that readers actually meet, private experience of the Gothic Unspeakable has led them to believe in the supernatural. The actual telling of their stories to one another intends a short-circuiting of the Gothic content by rendering the mysterious and the exotic mundane and transparent and, thus, undesirable. Moreover, the personal histories that Herrman and Hellfried reveal, both to each other and through proxy storytellers, are aligned with the tradition of the rational Gothic that Radcliffe inaugurates in works such as

---

a powerful essay connecting Jane Austen's *Sense and Sensibility* to the forbidden pleasures of onanism and the historical discussions of masturbation that contextualize *Sense and Sensibility*, see "Jane Austen and the Masturbating Girl," *Tendencies*, 109-29.

The Mysteries of Udolpho and *The Italian*, and which Jane Austen drolly satirizes in *Northanger Abbey*.

On the other hand, Kahlert's work radically differs from Radcliffe's (and from Austen's). As Lucien Jenkins writes in his introduction to the Skoob edition: "In stark contrast to the methods of Ann Radcliffe, the centre of interest in *The Necromancer* is exclusively masculine and the relationships that matter are those between men" (iv). The disconnect between Herrman and Hellfried's beliefs about (and in) their stories hints, therefore, at a forbidden desire that is, to use Haggerty's phrase, embedded within their "psychological states and internal processes" (51). Looming within these "internal processes" is the specter of sodomy, which, in Kahlert's text(s), tropes queer male desire through its representation of both licit and illicit male groups—homosocieties that actively recruit men for membership. For example, the Lieutenant and other soldiers in the novel engage in the legal conscription of male bystanders into their respective armies. These recruiters regard these activities as employment merely, providing bodies for their employers but not believers in a military adventure or an ideological crusade. Their mutual need for men interestingly provides the initial impetus for their banding together to protect each other from the supernatural forces they wish to experience, a jolting contrast to their otherwise drab existences. Similarly, the robbers (*banditti*) literally form homosocial bands, criminal armies whose intentions find expression in the kidnapping (read recruitment) of men into their ranks. On such example is the Lieutenant's servant who disappears for much of the novel. When the Lieutenant finally meets John, his kidnapped former servant, the latter tells the chilling tale of being given the option of joining the gang or dying. Though he resists, he ultimately joins, marking him in such a way that he cannot become what he once was. And though later the Lieutenant is willing to have him again in his service; he refuses, irremediably altered by his homosocial contact and conduct.

The novel's stories of the legal and illegal dragooning of men into homosocial bands and thence into the bands' activities suggest, rather ironically, that queer male desire—reified by the image of the sodomite—figuratively governs the narrative frame and plot movement of *The Necromancer*. Despite all the heteronormative appearances that Herrman and Hellfried contrive, in old age, to convince one another of their lifelong mutual normalcy, their gothic storytelling inevitably functions to disinter queer desire from their memories of the homosocial tribes to which they were allied, however briefly, in order to banish the figure of sodomy in their imaginations, to expunge its existence and its after-effects. Indeed, it is significant that despite the relative brevity of their personal experience with the supernatural (and the homosocial), they are haunted years later by its images and psychological effects. The documents within the novel serve to make public the inversions of sodomy—to make its otherness visible, as is the case with Volkert, the necromancer himself. His magical conjurings, his raising of the dead for both licit and illicit homosocieties, though illusory, are nonetheless sodomy's objective correlative.

The Gothic nature of sodomy persists, even after Herrman and Hellfried's "confessions," precisely because sodomy can remain terrifyingly invisible. Haggerty writes: "No matter how vividly or how vilely some sodomites are identified...others are lurking in the guise of friends, merchants, or even members of the clergy to threaten and undermine the bonds by which hegemonic culture is structured" (49). Herrman and Hellfried's anxiety at the possibility of retributive ghosts becomes the textual double for queer fear, for the Gothic Unspeakable. The unmasking of necromantic rites, coupled with the dismantling of their power via narrative storytelling, function as a rationalization of Herrman and Hellfried's experiences. Their intense interest in viewing their own fear arises from their wish to establish that necromancy has no rational basis and that banishing it from view is the appropriate response to their initial intimidation by the necromancer. Once they succeed in banishing their fear, their friendship stands pure and intact. It survives their deaths, thereafter thrilling sympathetic readers with Gothic swagger, but from the perspective of heteronormative complacency and control. That their stories and their collected documents illustrate the worst of human nature—thuggery, theft, fraud, impersonation, kidnapping, conspiracy, betrayal, abandonment, gang violence, and murder—only serves as yet another iteration of their purging, their published expiation. Likewise, the rooting out and punishing of Volkert and other robbers at the end of The Necromancer reinforces the public desire to banish dangerous otherness in its midst. And while Minerva Press readers may indeed have been titillated by the mythical Gothicism of the Black Forest in The Necromancer, the setting for what Douglass

Thomson and Frederick Frank refer to as "primal Gothic territory," which "abound[s] in midnight rides and riders, demons' dens, warlocks' conclaves, blood-trailing shadows, driverless carriages speeding through the night, spook-crowded cottages, silhouetted ruins, and horizons studded with gibbets" (40), the real horror lies elsewhere, notably in the administration of justice thinly disguised as public bloodsport. "Haunted by secret awe did I arrive at the place of execution," writes the Lieutenant of Volkert's execution towards the end of the novel, "and horror made my blood run chill as I beheld the dreadful pile, which soon was to reduce to ashes the preserver of my life" (165). Far from embodying a deterrence effect, Volkert's death reifies public execution as the real Gothic terror in the enlightened world of 18th-century men and not in the ultimately campy and fictive creations of Volkert's overheated imagination, and certainly not in his banal larcenies. Kahlert's representation of Volkert's dignified death, despite the bloodthirsty circumstances ("[I] beheld Volkert undressing himself, and approaching with firmness the stool stained with the smoking blood of his friend…I shut my eyes involuntarily—a sudden hollow humming told me that Volkert had conquered," (166) reverses the trajectory that leads toward criminality and social ostracism. Now it is the condemning public that is guilty—of scapegoating, of hypocrisy—even as it wallows in gothic mystery and excess while ignoring its own complicity in the creation of criminal elements and bloodlust in seeing them destroyed.[1]

Volkert's death not only contributes to the Gothic spectacles of the novel, it becomes the moment of supreme punishment, in which the community asserts its moral authority and heteronormativity by eliminating social (and sexual) otherness. It is no coincidence that the novel's confusing and disconnected flurry of testimonies culminates

---

[1] Despite the rough treatment of "sodomites" by the law through the eighteenth century ("homosexual" does not come into common parlance until the nineteenth century), there was bustling subculture of "molly houses," establishments in which men cross dressed, sometimes "elaborately" both from the "world of the pastoral and high fashion" (Goldsmith 7). See Netta Murray Goldsmith, *The Worst of Crimes: Homosexuality and the Law* for a historical description of sodomy and its disposition in 18th-century British law. For interesting discussions regarding the figure(s) of sodomy in literature prior to the rise of Gothic fiction, see Gregory W. Bredbeck, *Sodomy and Interpretation: Marlow to Milton,* Jonathan Goldberg, *Sodometries: Renaissance Texts, Modern Sexualities,* and Cameron McFarlane, *The Sodomite in Fiction and Satire, 1660-1750.*

in a juridical process, in which Volkert confesses, is found guilty, and is executed. Through the eyes of the Lieutenant, shocked as he is by his friend's violent death, we see Kahlert's indictment of a social environment in which justice appears to be little more than a legal process, rather than a desired outcome. Indeed, the case of Volkert illustrates what Foucault postulates as the necessary mythologizing of the "living spectacle" entailed by punishing the criminal body. "From where the public is sitting," Foucault writes, "It is possible to believe in the existence of certain cruelties which, in fact, do not take place. But the essential point, in all these real or magnified severities, is that they should all, according to a strict economy, teach a lesson: that each punishment should be a fable" (113). Volkert's public execution is his culture's "fable," becoming, as Foucault also describes, "the major sign of punishment: the keystone of the penal edifice" (113). The public execution in *The Necromancer* justifies its "strict economy" of crime and punishment within all the communities of the Black Forest, and so it is no coincidence that Kahlert likens the city that executes Volkert to a Gothic Sodom. Escaping the aftermath of Volkert's execution, the Lieutenant unexpectedly turns around:

> At the city gate I looked back and beheld with horror a black column of smoke ascending aloft and darkening the pure serene air; I could not stand the horrible sight, and hastened to my apartments, determining to leave a place immediately, in which my peace of mind had been so much disturbed. (166).

Intentionally or not, Kahlert evokes the biblical Sodom in this passage, for like Lot's wife, the narrator beholds with horror the plumes of smoke that signal the city's destruction. The pastoral idyll, which Herrman and Hellfried's intense friendship attempts to preserve and their life stories evoke, is consumed by the necromantic rituals that both fascinate and repel them. As the queer sign for sodomy, Volkert's necromancy consistently draws men together within opposing homosocial networks. The bandits use necromancy both to profit from the use of Gothic terror, as well as a means to exert power over their social superiors. The soldiers defy necromancy to affirm rational discourse and to maintain their martial integrity and social status. Not surprisingly, then, Kahlert's novel unknowingly creates linkages between necromancy and sodomy. As they do in German legend, necromancy and sodomy are tropes that lurk within the "penal edifice" of execution.[1] Routinized within social and cultural rituals of inclusion and exclusion, necromancy and sodomy transgress the heteronormative foundations for right and wrong within the city. When George Haggerty asks rhetorically, "Why is gothic fiction always already queer?" (1), he is arguing, "Transgressive social-sexual relations are the most basic common denominator of gothic" (1), sometimes lying buried within the narrative, yet always pushing through the heteronormative repressions of the queer. And whether from characters such as Herrman and Hellfried or through public rituals that punish its enactment, as in the case of the executions of Volkert and his companions, the narrative reveals the constant struggle that desperately tries to prevent the Gothic Unspeakable from speaking.

Yet another sign of the buried trope of the sodomite at the heart of the necromantic ceremony lies in the theatrical production and reproduction of death through cross dressing. The "son of a neighbouring publican" (160) impersonates a dead female spirit several times and does so convincingly and effectively. A master of disguise himself, Volkert transforms himself into an old man who then performs magic and raises the spirit of a woman who has been "assassinated" by her husband and who wishes, in death, to be left alone by her now-dead husband (41). "She" does not call for justice, to which "she" is entitled; rather, "she" merely wishes for easeful death and obscurity. Later in the novel, during his confession, Volkert reveals the degree to which his chicanery had been responsible for the Gothic tricks that had assailed the Lieutenant, the Baron, and their companions and instilled in them a belief in ghosts, spirits, and apparitions. Volkert's magic show includes juggling tricks, smoke from the extinguished light of lamps, and a camera obscura that permits the apparition to rise from holes in the floor. In effect, Volkert con-

---

[1] See Theodore Ziolkowski's *The Sin of Knowledge: Ancient Themes and Modern Variations*. In his review of Ziolkowski's book, Robert Tobin recounts the "emergence of the printing press" as the prime mover for the accessibility of knowledge, out of which the Faust legend is born, "a shadowy figure accused of magic, sodomy, and necromancy" (349). It is likely that Kahlert had read the first part of Goethe's *Faust* and drew upon that legend in creating Volkert, a pathetic version of a would-be Faust, masquerading as a dangerous and powerful necromancer.

structs, with available technology, a Gothic theater for soldiers and aristocrats who crave evidence of existence beyond death. Following the work of Sedgwick, Helen Stoddart connects theatricality to the Gothic and set forth her views on its "will-to-spectacle." Quoting Dana Polan, Stoddart states: "The image shows everything, and because it shows everything it can *say* nothing; it frames a world and banishes into non-existence everything beyond that frame. The will-to-spectacle is the assertion that a world of foreground is the only world that matters or the only world that is" (5). Volkert's "world of foreground"—his unique version of the Female Gothic—conflates necromantic spectacle into the necromantic spectral, for the campy staging of ghostly female masquerade not only "banishes into non-existence everything beyond that frame," it also ironically insulates Volkert's spectators from both spectacle and specter. Part of Volkert's ritualistic pretense assumes that his spells prevent the spirits from attacking the spectators, that they are safe from the spirit world. Indeed, the German word for necromancer ("Geisterbanner") suggests a sorcerer who not only raises spirits, but also someone who "bans" them as well; this "Spectral Banner" (as one translation has it) raises ghosts and makes them vanish. The necromancer eerily resonates with the sodomite, for their power lies in negation. Both concretely theatricalize social, cultural, moral, and sexual inversion, and both oppose the conventionalities of heteronormative affirmations of life by reveling in the Romantic thrill of death. Queering Volkert's necromancy in Kahlert's novel just means to mark "the convergence of the spectacle with the spectral" (Stoddart 6), and, just as importantly, to discern that "the underside of [Gothic] spectacle is, potentially, always negation, death and disbelief" (6). In the end, therefore, even Volkert's beheading occurs on the stage; the scaffolding becomes a surreal proscenium wherein the theatricality of execution trumps the physical fact of death. Though thoroughly disproved and discredited, Volkert's necromantic powers linger in the spectral world and in the world of spectacle, the smoke of Sodom ever wafting in the eyes and minds of the audience, even as the cover stories of Herrman and Hellfried, as well as the concluding account of the bandit captain Wolf, desperately attempt to extinguish its fires.

With the introduction of Wolf, the novel lurches into corrections mode, leaving behind necromancy and the Gothic and, instead, embracing judicial rehabilitation, which pushes for the reintegration of the criminal back into mainstream life and culture. Critics remain befuddled by the novel's crazy quilt of narrators, leaving Thomson and Frank to question whether or not "the amorphousness of the novel may be the result of the translator's incompetent management of his Germans sources" (40). Particularly puzzling is the inclusion of the Wolf story following the demise of the necromancer. Lucien Jenkins properly describes the "horridness" of the novel as lying with Volkert, concluding, "The world of hauntings and conjurings, evil and doom, is no more than a veil behind which we find sad, disappointed and brutalized men" (13). Yet he also seems reticent at attributing significance to the inclusion of Wolf, except to note that "far from being born wicked, or being corrupted through demonic temptation, [people] drift into crime through a combination of circumstances and personal weakness" (13). Nonetheless, the confession of Wolf and the subsequent commutation of his death sentence tilt the narrative back to the heteronormative conventions and rules that the Gothic explodes and reintroduces. Moreover, the novel realigns desire with culture so that Wolf's absolution from his crimes represents a repudiation of the homosocial world over which he has ruled. What lies beyond the grave is not the necromantic world of shadows, the realm of sodomitical desires; rather, it is the sublime world of divine love and forgiveness.

> Wolf's life will be spared on account of his faithful confession, and the great assistance he has afforded his Judges in putting a final stop to the depredations which have been committee for a series of years in the environs of the Black Forest; he is to be committed for life to the house of correction where he will ample scope to reflect on his life past, and to prepare to meet that eternal Judge who sooner or later overtakes the wicked in his vile pursuits. (195)

In other words, Wolf's reconciliation to the social order tropes the Resurrection in much the same way as Volkert's execution by the social order tropes Sodom. Wolf's story must follow Volkert's, lest the world of shadows tempt its audience into "vile pursuits," into the mysterious "environs" of the Black Forest. His crimes ("depredations") far surpass Volkert's, yet they somehow fail to threaten (or to thrill) an audience in the way that Volkert's do. Moreover, despite the "spectacular" nature of Wolf's confession, it conforms to public ex-

pectations and the rules of the judicial system. Volkert tells only the
Lieutenant; thus, his "confession" lies outside the realm of judicial
review, not to mention the purview of religious authority and over-
sight. Moreover, unlike Volkert, Wolf notices women. When he joins
the gang over which he will eventually command, Wolf shows that
his heart belongs to women. He values the modest Maria rather than
the licentious Margaret. Even though his "imagination was fired with
wine and loose desires, [his] reason fettered, and [his] blood heated"
(228), Wolf never completely denies the attractions of virtue, nor is
he above asking for mercy. In modern parlance, he pleads special circumstances, that is, he would have acted differently, had he not been
rejected early on by the very society that now, through its represen-
tatives, judges him. He succeeds in blaming his criminal acts upon a
harsh environment, a sad tale worthy of the Victorian social realists
who follow in the next century. "I wish to live," he poignantly notes,
"in order to repair my crimes past, and to make my peace with human society" (183). In his case, reparations include snitching on his
gang of "fifty-three ruffians, who are dispersed all over the country,"
as well as "a great number of innkeepers and publicans, who were
leagues with that infernal set of ruffians" (195).

Finally, what makes Wolf's place in the novel so remarkable is
that it is he who contrives his gang of robbers to concoct the Gothic
scenes of midnight robbers and ghosts that terrorize the country-
side; it is he who creates the sinister myths surrounding the Haunted
Castle that scare the Lieutenant's friend, the Baron, nearly to death;
and it is he who uses Volkert in his schemes to defraud the public.
The restored and repaired mastermind (Wolf) is thus spared the axe,
while the outcast minion (Volkert) is ironically given the axe. At first
glance, it would appear, Kahlert balances justice (however harsh)
with mercy (however undeserved). In addition, because he concludes
the novel with mercy, he also restores the social and cultural balance
that the presence of the necromancer has unsettled. Upon closer in-
spection, however, the equilibrium that their respective fates evoke
is a false equivalence since Volkert's central acts of Gothic terror are
ultimately little more than the frauds of parlor tricks and the misde-
meanors of petty grifters. And while it is true that he is complicit with
his gang's more serious crimes, he is certainly no guiltier than Wolf,
who is permitted to live the remainder of his life in pursuit of self-

knowledge and atonement. Sedgwick's analysis of Gothic formats may provide some clues to unraveling this paradox. She writes:

> Of all the Gothic conventions dealing with the sudden, myste-
> rious, seemingly arbitrary, but massive inaccessibility of those
> things that should normally be most accessible, the difficulty the
> story has in getting itself told is of the most obvious structural
> significance...rarer still is the novel whose story is comprised by a
> single narrator, without the extensive irruption into the middle of
> the book of a new history with a new historian. (*Coherence* 13-14)

Even by these standards, the profusion of narrators in *The Necromancer* and the mounds of documentation that they introduce to ratio-
nalize the Gothic experiences of all the characters produces a delib-
erately confused narrative that "irrupts" in plain sight the actions of
the necromancer himself, Volkert, whose "magic" still persuades the
audience that his female ghosts were real and that they carried in-
disputable messages from beyond the grave. As Kelly Hurley attests,
any "deviance from sexual norms was identified as both a symptom
and a cause of social degeneration" (199). Volkert's necromancy is, to
use Hurley's words, a "challenge to traditional gender roles" and a
promotion of "social unrest and potential threats to national health"
(199). By queering Kahlert's text, we perceive, however unforeseen,
that Wolf may be the greater criminal, but Volkert is the greater
menace since his spectral spectacles target and frighten the very homosocial groups (such as soldiers) whose steely focus and martial
nerve (should) enable him to defend the city and the nation from all
kinds of intruders and forms of intrusion. While Kahlert submits to
the readerly expectations of social restoration within the communities of the Black Forest, he does permit necromancy (and its queer
double sodomy) to remain specters that frighteningly erupt in the
memories of his readers long after they have closed the book and vo-
raciously moved on to the next. Homophobia and homosexual panic
still lurk in the narrative shadows. What happens in the Black Forest
doesn't necessarily stay in the Black Forest.

JEFFREY D. CASS
Laredo, Texas

September 28, 2006

Works Cited

Auerbach, Nina. *Communities of Women: An Idea in Fiction*. Cambridge, MA: Harvard University Press, 1978.

Austen, Jane. *Northanger Abbey*. Ed. Anne Ehrenpreis. Harmondsworth: Penguin Books, 1972.

Bredbeck, Gregory W. *Sodomy and Interpretation: Marlowe to Milton*. Ithaca, NY: Cornell University Press, 1991.

Brownstein, Rachel. "*Northanger Abbey, Sense and Sensibility, Pride and Prejudice*," in *The Cambridge Companion to Jane Austen*. Ed. Edward Copeland and Juliet McMaster. Cambridge: Cambridge University Press, 32-57.

Butler, Marilyn. *Romantics, Rebels, and Reactionaries: English Literature and Its Background, 1760-1830*. Oxford: Oxford University Press, 1985 (1981).

Conger, Syndy McMillen. "A German Ancestor for Mary Shelley's Monster: Kahlert, Schiller, and the Buried Treasure of *Northanger Abbey*." *Philological Quarterly* 59:2 (1980).

Foucault, Michel. *Discipline and Punish*. Trans. Alan Sheridan. New York: Vintage Books, 1995 (1977).

Gamer, Michael. *Romanticism and the Gothic: Genre, Reception, and Canon Formation*. Cambridge: Cambridge University Press, 2000.

Goldberg, Jonathan. *Sodometries: Renaissance Texts, Modern Sexualities*. Stanford: Stanford University Press, 1991.

Goldsmith, Netta Murray. *The Worst of Crimes: Homosexuality and the Law*. Aldershot: Ashgate, 1998.

Grundy, Isobel. "Jane Austen and Literary Traditions," in *The Cambridge Companion to Jane Austen*. Ed. Edward Copeland and Juliet McMaster. Cambridge: Cambridge University Press, 189-210.

Haggerty, George E. "The Horrors of Catholicism: Religion and Sexuality in Gothic Fiction." *Romanticism on the Net* 36-37 (2004-05). http://www.erudit.org/revue/ron/2004/v/n36-37/011133ar.html.

—. *Queer Gothic*. Urbana and Chicago: University of Illinois Press, 2006.

—. "Romantic Friendship in *Millennium Hall*," *Unnatural Affections: Women and Fiction in the Later* 18*th Century*." Bloomington: Indiana University Press, 1998: 88-102.

Hurley, Kelly. "British Gothic Fiction, *1885-1930*." *The Cambridge Companion to Gothic Fiction*. Ed. Jerold E. Hogle. Cambridge: Cambridge University Press, 2002: 189-207.

MacCarthy, B.G. *The Female Pen: Women Writers and Novelists, 1621-1818*. New York: NYU Press, 1994.

Sedgwick, Eve Kosofsky. *The Coherence of Gothic Conventions*. New York: Methuen, 1986 (1976).

—. "Jane Austen and the Masturbating Girl." *Tendencies*. Durham: Duke University Press, 1993: 109-129

—. "Toward the Gothic: Terrorism and Homosexual Panic." *Between Men: English Literature and Male Homosocial Desire*. New York: Columbia University Press, 1985: 83-96.

Stoddart, Helen. "Early Female Gothic: *Zofloya* and *Manfroné; Or, the One-Handed Monk*." *Glasgow Review* 2. http://www.arts.gla.ac.uk/sesll/STELLA/COMET/glasgrev/issue2/stoddard.htm.

Tanner, Tony. *Jane Austen*. Cambridge, MA: Harvard University Press, 1986.

Tave, Stuart. *Some Words of Jane Austen*. Chicago and London: University of Chicago Press, 1973.

Thomson, Douglass and Frederick Frank. "Jane Austen and the *Northanger* Novelists." in *Gothic Writers: A Critical and Bibliographical Guide*. Ed. Douglass H. Thomson, Jack Voller, and Frederick Frank. Westport, CT: Praeger, 2002: 35-48.

Tobin, Robert. Review of Theodore Ziolkowski's *The Sin of Knowledge*. *Philosophy and Literature* 25 (2001): 347-350.

Ziolkowski, Theodore. *The Sin of Knowledge: Ancient Themes and Modern Variations*. Princeton: Princeton University Press, 2001.

NOTE ON THE TEXT

This edition follows the text of the first edition, published at London by William Lane's Minerva Press in 1794. The novel was originally published in two volumes; the beginning and end of each volume is signaled in this edition.

The novel was reprinted three times in the twentieth century, in 1927, 1968, and 1989. The 1927 edition, edited by Montague Summers, takes a number of unwarrantable liberties with the text, "improving" the text to make it more "English", even going so far as to change the main characters' names from "Herrman" and "Hellfried" to "Herman" and "Elfrid". The 1968 edition, edited by Devendra Varma, follows for the most part the original text, while modernizing the punctuation. The 1989 edition, published by Skoob Books with an introduction by Lucien Jenkins, follows the original text nearly verbatim, although it, too, alters in some respects the punctuation.

For the Valancourt Books edition, spelling and punctuation have been retained nearly unchanged from the first edition. Common eighteenth century spellings, such as "critick", "antient", "atchievement", "smoaked", etc., are unlikely to give problems to modern readers and have been retained here to capture the flavor of the original text. A very small number of obvious typographical errors have been silently corrected.

One aspect of the punctuation should be noted here. The novel is told in a frame structure with nested stories, often recounted second- or thirdhand, and in order for the punctuation to be correct under modern standards, double and triple nested quotation marks would be necessary. However, because an overabundance of quotation marks makes the novel's already difficult plot even more difficult to follow, the first edition's use of only single and double quotation marks has been retained.

THE

NECROMANCER:

OR THE

TALE

OF THE

BLACK FOREST:

FOUNDED ON FACTS;

TRANSLATED FROM THE GERMAN OF

LAWRENCE FLAMMENBERG,

BY PETER TEUTHOLD.

IN TWO VOLUMES.

VOL. I.

LONDON:

PRINTED FOR WILLIAM LANE,

AT THE

Minerva-Press

LEADENHALL-STREET.

M DCC XCIV.

Facsimile of the title page of the first edition (1794).

THE NECROMANCER

VOLUME I

PREFACE OF THE TRANSLATOR

THE wonderful Incidents related in the following Sheets, not being made up of tiresome Love Intrigues, repeated again and again in almost every new Book of Amusement, will, as I flatter myself, not be quite displeasing to the reader, on account of the Novelty of the Subject. The strange mysterious Events which occur in this little Performance are founded on Facts, the authenticity of which can be warranted by the Translator, who has lived many Years not far from the principal Place of Action.

If the Subject of the following Tale should be thought interesting and amuseing, the Public may expect a speedy Publication of a still more intricate and wonderful one, exhibiting a long Series of similar Frauds, perpetrated under the mysterious Veil of pretended supernatural Aid.

The Publisher being sensible of the manifold Defects of his Translation, will acknowledge with Gratitude the gentle Corrections of the dread Arbiters of Literary Death and Life, and Promises carefully to avoid, in a future Publication, the repetition of any slips the Critick's Eagle Eye shall discover in the following Sheets.

THE NECROMANCER.

THE hurricane was howling, the hailstones beating against windows, the hoarse croaking of the raven bidding adieu to autumn, and the weather-cock's dismal creaking joined with the mournful dirge of the solitary owl, when Herrman and Hellfried, who had been united by the strongest bonds of friendship from their youthful days, were seated by the chearing fire side, hailing the approach of winter. Thirty long years were elapsed since they had been separated by different employments; Herrman having been called, by the decrees of heaven, to distant countries, whilst Hellfried, leaving the University where their mutual friendship had began, hastened to his hoary parents, to ease the burthen of their old age, and to cheer the tempestuous evening of his dear progenitor's life.

On his journey towards his wished-for home, he rambled over some of the most charming parts of Germany; yet he was hunting in vain after pleasure, being separated from the dear companion of his juvenile days, and could no where trace the blissful abode of tranquillity and peace of mind. At length he found, in the circle of his family, what he had been seeking in vain abroad. The pleasure which his venerable parents felt, in beholding the offspring of their mutual love, soothed the inquietude of his mind; the joy sparkling in their eyes at the sight of the supporter of their declining years, tinged his cheeks with the rosy hue of contentment, and filled his soul with inward bliss. Ten years of congenial happiness were now sunk down into the endless gulph of time, when his aged father died, closing a well-spent life in his seventy-second year: The guardian angel of virtue carried his unspotted soul to the cheerful mansion of everlasting peace; the gentle smile of a good conscience sat still on his wan lips, when his sainted spirit arrived in heaven, hailed by millions of holy angels.

Hellfried now enjoyed twelve years longer the bliss of soothing the sorrows of his mother, and of supporting her under the heavy load of ever increasing infirmities, before she went over to the sacred abode of peace, to be re-united to the dear companion of all her earthly joys and cares. He dropped a tear of filial affection on her tomb, where she rested by her departed husband's side, and directed now all his care and tenderness towards the promoting of his only sister's happiness. The apprehension of drawing a blank in the great lottery of matrimony, strengthened by some terrifying examples within the circle of his friends, made him hesitate so long to choose a partner in his joys and cares, 'till he felt himself too infirm for the toils inflicted on the beasts of burthen, yoked to the cart of matrimony.—But he became, alas! too late, sensible of the bad consequences of his cowardice, when he began to want a tender nurse, a soother in his gloomy hours, and a sweet comforter amidst the self-created cares of hoary age. In order to disperse the clouds of gloomy dismal fancies, the usual companions of solitary bachelors, he took the resolution of undertaking a journey as far as the duty incumbent on his office would allow him, and left the care of his house to his maiden sister.

He was so fortunate as to meet, on his journey, with many friends of his earlier days, the companions in his former studies, and the partners of his academical life: At length he also traced out his dear Herrman, the most beloved among his youthful friends. Though Hellfried was, at first, angry with him, for having neglected writing to him in the course of so many years; for having omitted to ascertain him of his still being alive; and for his not having answered the letter he had wrote to him many years ago, in order to enquire after his health and happiness; yet he forgot at once all his anger, anticipating the pleasure of pressing him once more to his bosom, and got into his carriage with cheerfulness to hasten to his embraces. After a short and pleasant ride, he hung on Herrman's neck, a gentle tear of joy sparkled in his eye, as he pressed him tenderly to his bosom.

He found his worthy friend a favorite of fortune, blest in the lap of sweet contentment and unadulterated happiness.—A loving wife, who was a tender guardian of his tranquillity, and a careful mother to the pledges of their mutual love, was crowning the favors which fortune so abundantly had blessed him with: Kind Providence had surrounded him with an hopeful circle of promising children, two of whom had happily been married, and blessed him with two grand-daughters and three grandsons—Heaven's greatest blessings smiled upon him wherever he went, contentment and joy sat upon his reverend brow, and peace of mind had taken her abode within his heart.

"Good God!" exclaimed he, as soon as he could find words to give vent to the rapture of his soul, "do I then behold, once more before I die, the dear companion of my youthful days? Heaven be praised for that unexpected happiness! Now all my wishes are fulfiled—Oh, Hellfried! Hellfried! The separation from thee, the apprehension of seeing thee no more, was the only bitterness mixed in the cup of bliss, which providence has kindly administered to thy friend. Thou art alive—thou art alive, now I have nothing else to wish, than that my end may be as happy as this hour of bliss."

Hellfried related now, after the first ecstacy of rapture was over, how anxiously he had ever been enquiring after his dear friend; told him how many letters he had written to get informed of his abode, and of his being well, and was going to chide his faithful Herrman for his negligence, when he fetched a letter from an old acquaintance of his, who had wrote to him, that

"Hellfried had left the service of the Muses, enlisted under the banners of Pallas during the war of seven years, and, very likely, had fallen a victim of his martial spirit."[1]

"Thy turn of mind—" thus Herrman proceeded, after his friend had read that letter, "seemed always to make such a manner of life far more eligible to thee, than the peace and homely pleasure of a private life, how could I then doubt the authenticity of the intelligence given me by honest Erich? I have bemoaned thy untimely fate, what more could I have done?"

Hellfried was satisfied with what his friend said in his defence, and found now an additional reason of being pleased with his having seen him once more.

"Brother!" exclaimed he, "let us forget our age and let us live together, as long as I can remain with thee, as if the thirty years since we have seen each other never had existed, and be as merry as we have been in our youthful days."

---

[1] The Seven Years War (1756-63) was a "worldwide war fought in Europe, North America, and India between France, Austria, Russia, Saxony, Sweden, and (after 1762) Spain on the one side and Prussia, Great Britain, and Hanover on the other" (*The Columbia Encyclopedia*, 6th ed.)

Herrman's cheek glowed with pleasure, he squeezed his Hell-fried's hand, and both of them were as happy as it is possible to be in this vain world.

Six days were now passed in mutual joy: Herrman resided at a country seat, situated on the banks of the Elbe, and enclosed with an antient forest, which made it the most pleasant abode to Hellfried, who was passionately fond of hunting. Every morning they were rambling through the woods, and the two robust aged friends pursued the fleet game with juvenile ardour, 'till the din-ner bell summoned them to a substantial meal, and a bottle of old Rhenish wine; when the cloth was removed the goblet went cheer-fully round, and the two happy friends were drinking and talking 'till night came on, and the chimney fire illuminated the dusky room; the pipes were filled with aromatic canaster, the chairs put nearer to the fire, blazing briskly aloft, and they began to relate the atchievements of their juvenile days, and whatever had hap-pened during their separation. Thus the days rolled on like hours, and Hellfried did not yet think of parting.

The hurricane was howling (as I said before) and the hail stones beating against the windows in so uncivil a manner, that the two friends could not think of going a hunting, but stuck close to the social fire side, spending thus the day amid amusing conver-sations; their stock of entertaining narratives seemed to be inex-haustible.

The gloominess of the weather gave their conversation a seri-ous turn: They began to discourse on the calamities of war, of the dangers they had formerly undergone, and of many distresses and sufferings they had experienced in the earlier part of their lives; as night advanced the tempest grew more furious, the flame in the chimney was wafted to and fro, and began to die away by degrees. Father Herrman fed it with dry wood, poked the cinders out, and it began again to blaze aloft.

"Brother," now said Hellfried, who, meanwhile had been fill-ing his pipe, "brother, dost thou believe in apparitions? Dost thou believe in spirits?"

Herrman smiling shook his head.

"I also," thus Hellfried went on, "do not believe in apparitions; yet, when travelling through Germany, I have met with adventures which I still am unable to unriddle."

Herrman pricked up his ears, awaiting in dumb expectation the narrative of his friend's wondrous adventures: Hellfried kept him not long in suspence, and began as follows:

"The great fair was just beginning, when I arrived at F—, the bustle of the buyers and venders, the meeting with a number of dear friends, and the many different amusements, promised to afford me a great deal of pleasure, and I resolved to stay a few weeks at that town.

"The inn where I had taken lodgings was crowded with travellers; an aged hoary man amongst them was particularly noticed by every one, on account of his remarkable appearance: His looks were reverend, his dress, though very plain, was costly; he appeared to be a rich nobleman, and occupied the best apartments: A coach and six, with four servants richly dressed, carried him frequently out; he was seen at all the public places, was present at all amusements, yet, what raised my curiosity, he was constantly alone, and in profound meditation. I often remarked, that wherever he was, he did not take the least notice of what was doing around him, and, as if a prey to grief and inward sufferings, seemed to be insensible of all the objects that surrounded him. He was also continually alone when in his apartment, the door of which appeared to me to be always bolted: He rode out as soon as dinner was over, and commonly returned very late at night.

"I questioned the landlord about that strange man, but he shrugged up his shoulders and could tell me nothing. The waiters did the same.

"But," exclaimed I peevishly, "you certainly must know where he comes from, could not you ask his servants?"

"The servants," answered the waiter, "are as mute as their master. He is supposed to be an English Lord, that is all what I know."

"I was of the same opinion, when I first saw him; having met, on my travels, with many Englishmen, who had behaved in the same sullen and reserved manner. His melancholy mood I fancied to be the effect of the spleen, and did not trouble myself any more about him.

"I had not been above three days at F— when I lost my purse: At first I fancied I had dropped it somewhere in a shop, or my pocket had been picked in the street, and determined to be more careful in future; but, in spite of all my precaution and carefulness, I suffered a second loss the next day, missing a diamond ring, with a miniature picture of my deceased mother: I was sure that I, the preceding night had pulled that ring from my finger, and put it on the table, when I went to bed; I questioned the waiters, but they appeared to be offended at my inquiries—in short, the ring was gone.

"A few days after I went to the play, I had a snuff box, of very little value, in the right pocket of my coat; a gentleman who was sitting by me, at the left, begged me to give him a pinch of snuff, but I could not find my box. That insignificant theft made me smile. I staid 'till the play was over with very little concern, and was glad that I had left my purse at home.

"The play was over, and a boy with a lighted torch went before me to an adjacent tavern, I wanted to see what hour it was, but my watch was also gone. "Cursed misfortune!" exclaimed I. The boy reminded me of his money, I gave it him, and entered the supper room. An acquaintance of mine took notice of the paleness of my countenance, inquiring whether I was ill, I denied it, and took my seat at the table: I hurried down my supper without noticing my neighbour, and was determined to depart the next morning, being persuaded that some cunning rogues had singled me out, to try their skill with me, at the expence of my property.—As I was pushing back my chair, somebody close by me, asked me what o'clock it was. I did not answer, because that question, by reminding me of my loss, had vexed me, and was going to leave the room.

"Sir, what o'clock is it?" exclaimed somebody once more, tapping me on the shoulder. "I do not know," replied I without looking back, and paid my bill. "Have you no watch with you?" exclaimed the same person again. Now I turned round in great vexation, and, guess my surprise, the troublesome inquirer was my neighbour at the inn, the very same gentleman who had excited so much my curiosity some days ago.

"He stared me in the face, as if expecting an answer. "Sir," said I now, "my watch—"

"Has been stolen," interrupted he quickly. "I have catched the thief, there it is:" So saying, he put my watch into my hand. I was stunned with amazement, and could not help wishing to know the thief, that I might recover the other things I had lost, for I was sure that the same person who had robbed me of my watch, had also pilfered what I had lost before: But, ere I could signify my wish, the mysterious gentleman was vanished.

"I went home, struck with astonishment, but the stranger was not yet arrived. At length he came, as usual, at midnight; I rushed out of the door when I heard him coming up stairs, made a respectful bow, and begged him to give me leave to ask a question; but he passed me hastily, without taking notice of me, absorbed in melancholy thoughts, took the candle from the servant, and bolted his room.

"All my attempts of speaking with him were fruitless, like the first. When at home, his door was bolted, in the hall he took no notice of me, and in public places he shunned me. Vexed by his rude behaviour, I would not make another attempt at getting acquainted with that queer fellow.

"Meanwhile three days more were elapsed, and that strange accident had made me forget my departure; but now I renewed my resolution of setting off as soon as possible, and was determined to leave F— the next day, though no farther disagreeable accident had happened to me. I put every thing in order, had my trunks packed, and was obliged to find out a banker, who would take a Bill for Leipzig, which I had brought with me to F—.

"I found it very difficult to meet with one who would not take too great an advantage of my present inconvenience; towards evening I was so fortunate to find out a reasonable man; joyfully did I now put my hand into my pocket to take the pocket book out of it, but I could not find it. "For God's sake," exclaimed the merchant, when he saw me pale and trembling, "what is the matter with you?" "Nothing, nothing at all," stammered I, rushing out of the house.

"A faint ray of hope was still glimmering within my soul; I fancied I had left all the remainder of my little fortune at the inn, though I was certain that I had taken the pocket book with me. I arrived, trembling, at my lodging, and was hardly able to unlock my door; I entered slowly, as if I wanted to avoid the terrible blow that threatened me: I searched the room with an anxious look, but, alas! all my little wealth was gone!

"I could not believe the reality of my misfortune: I emptied my trunk more than ten times, and more than an hundred times did I search every corner of the room, thinking it impossible that the bill and the pocket book should not be there, however I could find neither of them.

"It grew late, and I was still sitting on my trunk, half distracted, leaning on my trembling hand, at length I resolved to go next morning to some of my acquaintance, and endeavour to get some money advanced. That terrible evening was followed by a more terrible night; morning dawned and I still could not sleep—my pride revolted against the thought of borrowing money, but the idea of the unavoidable want staring me in the face, got the better of it, and I went. Every one whom I applied to was sorry for what had happened to me, railed against and cursed the villain who had robbed me, but nobody would lend me money—scarcity of cash, the backwardness of the debtors; alas! these and a thousand other obstacles prevented my friends from assisting me. I went home in a gloomy melancholy mood, and did not know what to do. It struck one, the dinner was on table, but I could not eat. I was standing in my room with a downcast look, and musing on my distress, a son of misery and a slave of cruel necessity. I cannot tell how long I had been in that desponding situation, when a gentle knocking at my door roused me suddenly from my reverie: I exclaimed in an agony, come in! The door opened, and I was thunderstruck when I beheld the unknown gentleman before me. My soul was filled with rapture, I ran almost frantic with joy towards the stranger, clasped him in my arms, and exclaimed, "Have you, have you found it?"

"I have not!" answered he.

"Methinks I see him still standing before me, a tall lean figure, his face pale, his looks staring and serious: I trembled as he spoke.

"Not! not!" groaned I, "gracious heaven! how unhappy am I."

"Patience, young man," replied he, "although the thief may have made his escape, yet I am here."

"I gazed at him with astonishment. He took his pocket book, opened it, and gave me two papers. "There, take it," said he, "it is as much as you may want at present, the mail will set off to-morrow for your native country, I wish you an happy journey."

"Then he laid the papers on my table, and hastened out of the room: A strange sensation had fixed me to the floor, had fettered my tongue, and I neither could thank my benefactor, nor inquire how I was to repay him. I felt veneration for this singular man, admired his humanity, and yet I could not help feeling some inward sensations of horror; I was for a considerable time as motionless as a statue. Having recovered from my amazement, I went to the table, took up the papers, which he had left behind, and saw, with astonishment, that each of them was a draft for a hundred dollars payable at F—: It grieved me to be obliged to accept a present from a strange unknown man. But what could I do? How could I get access to him? Perhaps (thought I) he will send his direction, but I waited in vain for it. He got into his carriage and drove away.

"I also left the house and returned late, the stranger was not yet come home: However, I was determined to await his return, and as soon as he should enter the house, to hasten to his apartment, and to insist upon his taking a bond for his money, and if he should happen to refuse it, to force him to take back his present. This resolution was good enough, however I could not execute it because he did not return.

"Night being far advanced, I laid myself down upon a couch, and the harbinger of sleep surprised me; I began to doze. At once I heard a noise before my door, I got up, and all was hushed in silence. I fancied the noise I had heard had been the effects of those early dreams which sometimes amuse our fancy when sleep is coming on; but soon after I heard the same noise again. I got once more up from my couch, and all was silent again. Listening attentively, I heard the same noise repeated; it grew now louder and louder, and resembled the tapping of somebody who could not find the latch. I was going to open the door, but before I came into the middle of the room, saw it move on its hinges. I stopped, the door opened slowly, and now I could distinguish my visitor. It was a strange figure, tall and emaciated, clad in a white garment. As it entered the room, it advanced towards me with slow and solemn steps; I staggered back, and a chilly terror trembled through my frame. The apparition moved towards the table in awful silence. It took up my watch, looked at it, gave a hollow groan, and then laid it down again. I was thunderstruck. The phantom now moved slowly back, and I looked at its face as it was passing the table where the candle stood—Merciful heaven! how was I chilled with horror, when I beheld the features of my deceased mother! My knees shook, a cold sweat bedewed my face, and my strength forsook me.

"Meanwhile the apparition was come to the door, without having turned its face; it opened the latch gently, and when on the threshold, turned round, staring me in the face, with a ghastly look, and lifting up its emaciated hand, threatning three times in a horrible manner, and disappeared.

"I fell senseless back upon my couch, and when I could recollect myself again, I fancied I had been haunted by a bad dream.— The clock struck one as I was going to look at my watch.

"Vexed that the stranger did not come home, I went to bed, and slept 'till it was broad day. When the waiter brought my breakfast, I asked whether my neighbour was come home. He denied it. Then I asked if he perhaps had left F— ? The waiter answered, it may be, he always pays his bill after dinner, he carries no trunks with him, and none of his servants lodge in our house.

"I went with the waiter to the apartment which the stranger had occupied: The key was in the lock, we walked in, all was empty.

"I went back to my room, took up the drafts he had given me, and would have destroyed them, if I thus could have disencumbered myself of the obligation which I owed him. It suddenly came in my mind that they perhaps might be fictitious, or the name of the merchant who was to pay the money not known.

This thought afforded me pleasure, though I could expect nothing but misery if it should prove true.

"I hastened to the host, shewing him my draughts, under the pretext as if I wanted to know the direction of a merchant. He described the house and the street where he lived. I was frightened and went that same morning to the merchant. He looked slightly at the paper, but very seriously at me, and his eyes seemed to denote astonishment and pity. I expected, joyfully, that the bills would be protested; however, I was mistaken. He opened, sighing, his drawers, and counted down two hundred dollars, still looking at me with astonishment. I put the money in my pocket, and, being convinced that he pitied me for being obliged to that stranger, I took the liberty of asking him, by whom he was to be repaid; upon which he appeared to be disconcerted, shrugged his shoulders, muttered some unintelligible words, and left me suddenly. I went away under the greatest apprehensions, and the weather being fine, was tempted to take a walk to a public garden.

"The beautiful morning had assembled there a great number of foreigners and of the inhabitants of F—, I went into a remote bower, and ordered some chocolate.

"Retired from the noisy bustle of company, I could now muse on the strange accidents which I had experienced during my short stay at F—: I also recollected my dream, and reflected on it more seriously than before. Though I was very much tempted to deem it something more than a delusion of fancy, yet I was still disinclined to ascribe that strange incident to a supernatural cause, being strongly prepossessed against the belief in apparitions, and found myself bewildered in a maze of irksome fancies. I struggled hard with my imagination, striving to forget what had made me so uneasy; however, all my struggles proved abortive; the dream, or rather the apparition, continued returning to my remembrance, in defiance of my reasoning, and the nocturnal horrid spectre hovered still before my eyes, haunting me with gloomy thoughts.

"Being tired and wearied by the uninterrupted struggle between reason and fancy, I endeavoured to ease my soul of her heavy load, by a loud exclamation, and, without recollecting where I was, I suddenly broke out in the words, "No, it was a deluding dream.""

"It was no dream!" exclaimed a well known voice on a sudden.

"I cast down my eyes filled with shame and terror, imagine how I was surprised to behold the mysterious stranger standing before me.

"Young man," said he, without giving me time to utter a single word, "young man, do you wish for an explanation of the apparition of last night?"

"I gazed at him in dumb silence.

"If you wish to have unfolded that incident," he resumed, after a short pause, "then await me this evening, by ten o'clock, at the town gate, next to the inn."

"The stranger pronounced these words with a friendly courteous mien, made me a bow, and left the bower, disappearing amid the crowd.

"The waiter brought the chocolate, but I could not swallow a single drop. In vain did I now roam all over the garden, in hopes of meeting the stranger; in vain ask all my acquaintances and the waiters, describing minutely the stranger to every one; nobody had seen him.

"I hastened home, awe and terror struck me as I entered my apartment; the door of my chamber seemed to be in constant motion, and the figure of my mother haunted me without intermission. I could not get rid of the gloomy reflection on her threatening looks, and left the house. I now rambled about, in great uneasiness, the fore and after-noon, went from the coffee-house to the promenade, from thence to the museum, from the museum to the tavern, from the tavern to the exhibition of wild beasts, and at last to the playhouse, but I could no where find tranquillity and ease of mind.

"It was growing dark when I left the playhouse, my soul was disturbed by strange sensations, and I was consulting with myself whether I should go or not. Doubt and apprehension suspended my resolution for a considerable time, and overwhelmed me with pungent agony.

"Shall I go or not? Prudence asked, What hast thou to apprehend? I could give no answer, and fears and doubts continued keeping up a most distressing conflict. Curiosity on a sudden raised her bewitching voice, driving away every doubt, and bidding defiance to the wise counsels of prudence. "Thy departure is fixed, to-morrow thou art going to leave this town," thus the charming seducer whispered in my ear, "and to-day thou canst get rid of every teazing doubt: Thou wilt repent it one time if thou refusest to go today. Take courage, man, take courage, don't be such a coward to fear an old man; and" thus my pride added, "thou canst inform thyself how to pay the notes."[1]

"At once I was determined to go. "I will repair to the place of rendezvous," said I, and was instantly disincumbered of a load of uneasiness. I returned to my apartment with composure, called for a light and began to write some letters. Having continued that occupation 'till eight o'clock, I went down stairs, to amuse myself a little, and spent two happy hours at the table d'hote. When supper was over the landlord desired to speak to me in private. As soon as we were retired to another room, he said, I bring you happy tidings. I listened attentively.

"You have lost several things during your residence in our town?"

"I have," replied I, with surprise.

"Your loss has given me great uneasiness, on account of the reputation of my house."

"Let us come to the point," exclaimed I with impatience.

"You have lost a purse, a snuff-box, a ring and a pocket book."

"You know exactly what I have lost," answered I, with amazement.

"You will find every article in your room." 'I staggered back.

---

[1] Hellfried's meeting with the mysterious stranger resonates with Satan's temptation of Eve in the Garden. This ear whispering reminds the reader of the passage in *Paradise Lost*, in which Satan is found "Squat like a toad, close at the ear of Eve, Assaying by his devilish art to reach/The organs of her fancy, and with them forge/Illusions as he list, phantasms and dreams..." (4.800-803). Milton's passage occurs during the famous separation scene when Eve is most vulnerable to the temptations of the Garden, inasmuch as she is separated from Adam and the protective armor of his reason. Satan is the original "charming seducer," Teuthold's epithet for the stranger, and the only time Teuthold uses this phrase in his "translation" of the German text. The quotation from Milton is from the Merritt Y. Hughes edition of Milton's collected poetry and major prose (Odyssey Press, 1957).

"An unknown person brought all your things an hour ago."

"An unknown person? Was it perhaps that strange gentleman? But it cannot be him you know."

"Whom do you mean?"

"My neighbour."

"The landlord shook his head smiling, he was called away, and hastening to my room, I found every thing as the landlord had told me. The bill of exchange was in the pocket book, and I was lost in dumb amazement, not doubting that this had been a new trick of my unknown benefactor. "But why did he not wait 'till ten o'clock?" said I to myself, "Why not return my things on our appointed meeting? Should he have doubted my coming, or perhaps, have been obliged to depart suddenly?" The last was the most likely, but, at the same time, the most disagreeable to me, depriving me of the means of returning him his money, and paying my debt after I had recovered my property. But how could I be certain that he really was departed, since all his doings had been so strange and eccentric. How could a gentleman like him, a pattern of honesty, a friend to human nature, how could *he* be guilty of transgressing the first duty of an honest man? How could it be possible, that he should be able to break his word? He had appointed me to meet him at ten o'clock, and the landlord had not said any thing to the contrary.

"I went down to the supper room, requesting a few minutes hearing of the landlord, and asked him, if the unknown person who had brought my lost property, had left no message for me.

"He denied it, adding, his own words were, "there are the things Mr. Hellfried has lost," and without giving me time to question him any farther, by whom he had been sent, he went away.

"Now I looked at my watch, it wanted fifteen minutes to ten, I fetched my hat and great coat, and walked slowly towards the town gate.

"The night was exceeding fine, the moon shone bright, and was surrounded with millions of sparkling stars. It struck ten when I was already standing on the appointed spot, I mistook every passenger for the stranger, ran towards several of them, and began to speak, but I was always disappointed. It was now forty-five minutes past ten, and I began to be tired, my apprehension that the stranger, had been obliged to depart suddenly appeared to prove true.

"I will wait 'till it strikes eleven!" said I to myself, "and then I will return home, if he should not be here." The bell of the adjacent steeple tolled eleven and the stranger was not yet come.

"I will stay fifteen minutes longer, and then return to the inn."

"These fifteen minutes expired likewise, without his making his appearance: The stillness of midnight surrounded me, and nobody appeared; I went back.

"I was not gone ten steps when my dear stranger came walking towards me with hasty paces; nobody could be more rejoiced than I was, and forgetting entirely that I had waited so long, I ran towards him. He shook me heartily by the hand, and said, "I am sorry that I have kept you waiting so long."

"I would have waited with pleasure still longer," replied I, "without the least token of diffidence, if I had been sure of seeing you at last. I willingly would have undergone every difficulty in order to obey your commands, and to get rid of my doubts."

"That you shall," said he; "follow me."

"Now he began to walk so fast that I hardly could keep up with him; he uttered not a word; we arrived at the gate and it was opened at his command; our way led straight through the suburbs, at the bottom of which a solitary house was standing: My conductor knocked at the door; we were let in: The house appeared to be empty, and deserted, and we saw no living soul except an old decripid man, who had opened the door. The stranger ordered a light; a lamp was brought, and now he walked, without stopping, thro' a dark passage 'till we came to a door, leading into a garden, in the back of which was a small pleasure-house; my conductor opened the door, and we entered a small damp room.

"Now we are on the spot," said he, after having carefully secured the door, "now tell me, what you want to know."

"First of all, I wanted to give him a brief account of the recovery of my effects, and then to ask him, if he had been my benefactor. However, he prevented me from doing it, exclaiming, "I know it all, I beg you will concentre all you want to know into one question."

"I mused awhile, but I was not able to bring all my wishes to one point, and it is very likely that the presence of that strange extraordinary man, had greatly contributed to my perplexity. I found it impossible to make the question he had ordered me to do.

"Seeing my distress, he said, "Well, then, enquire after the name of the friend who has taken so much care of you."

"That was the very question which I was most eager to do; I had been inclined to propose it ere now, but I would not venture to do it for fear of offending the stranger; with great joy did I therefore reply, "Yes, that I will, that I wish to know."

"Well then," replied he, "you shall get personally acquainted with that friend of yours."

"Then I do not know him yet personally?" resumed I, "I thought it was you, Sir."

"The stranger shook his head.

"I am only his deputy," was his answer; "and," added he, after a short pause, "only through the third hand."

"I gazed at him with amazement, but he seemed to take no notice of it, and began to make preparations for introducing my friend in a most mysterious manner. He strewed sand on the floor, and drew two direct circles with an ebony wand, placing me in one and himself in the other.

"How will this end," said I to myself.

"The stranger was now standing opposite to me, in an awful and solemn posture: He folded his hand upon his breast, his looks being lifted up to heaven. Silent and motionless like a statue was he standing there. A chilly sensation of horror penetrated me, I did not dare to fetch breath.

"The stranger remained in that posture for a quarter of an hour, my fear was swallowed up in dumb amazement, and my heart began soon to fail me for fear, and for a looking after those things which were to come: At length my conductor broke his mysterious silence; I heard his voice, but I could not understand what he was uttering; the words he was pronouncing seemed to belong to a foreign language. The lamp afforded but a faint light, and I could not well distinguish the objects around me. All was silent as the grave. My conductor whispered only now and then some mysterious words, drawing figures in the sand with his ebony wand.

"Now I heard the clock strike twelve, with the last stroke the stranger began to turn himself round about, within the circle, with an astonishing velocity, pronouncing the Christian and surname of my deceased mother. I staggered back thrilled with chilly horror. On a sudden I heard a noise under ground, like the distant rolling of thunder. The stranger pronounced the name of my mother a second time, with a more solemn and tremendous voice than at first. A flash of lightning hissed through the room, and the voice of thunder grew louder and louder beneath my feet. Now he pronounced the name of my mother a third time, still louder and more tremendous. At once the whole pleasure-house appeared to be surrounded with fire. The ground began to shake under me, and I sunk suddenly down. The ghost of my mother hovered before my eyes, with a grim ghastly look; a chilly sweat bedewed my face and my senses forsook me.

"A violent shaking roused me at length from my stupefaction.

"The shaking did not cease, and I felt as if I was tossed to and fro; at the same time I heard a terrible creeking and whizzing not far off. As soon as I had recovered my recollection, I perceived that I was sitting in a coach, driving onward with an incredible velocity, and found myself closely confined. Something was snoring by my side, but I could not distinguish what it was, being surrounded with impenetrable darkness.

"You cannot imagine what I suffered in that terrible situation: I was seized with anxiety and apprehension, creating the most tormenting sensations, which cannot be described.

"The road my human or supernatural coachman had taken seemed to be very uneven, or, perhaps, he did not know the road, for I felt every moment the most violent jolts which increased my anxiety still more, by the additional apprehension of being overturned. My bones, which already had been hurt very much by my falling down in the pleasure-house, seemed to be quite dislocated. I had been in that state of agony about half an hour, when a most violent jolt overturned the coach. A voice roared, "Jesu Maria!"

Methought I felt the freezing hand of death upon my heart, and lost the power of recollection.

"At length I was roused from that state of insensibility, by the most excruciating pains. I opened my eyes; two men, each of them holding a horse by the bridle, were standing by me; a countryman, with a lanthorn, was in their company, and the broken coach was lying on the ground at a small distance. They wanted to raise me up, but being pierced by terrible pains, I entreated them, for God's sake, not to touch me. My leg was fractured in two places: The horsemen promised to ride to a neighbouring town for assistance, and disappeared; the countryman remained with me and endeavoured to comfort me.

"I waited half an hour and nobody appeared; the night was cold: I waited an hour and no assistance came: One fainting fit followed the other, at length I heard the rolling of a coach, the countryman went with his lanthorn into the middle of the road, and saw a coach and four; the honest man begged the driver to stop and related my misfortune. An old reverend man got out of the vehicle, lifted me, with the assistance of the good peasant, into the coach, and ordered the coachman to drive slowly onward.

"With the dawn of morning we came to a village. My kind deliverer was the Lord of it. Having been carried to the castle, a surgeon was sent for, meanwhile the old nobleman endeavoured by his kind conversation, to make me forget part of my pains.

"The surgeon arrived a little while after, my wounds were dressed, and I was carried to bed. At first my deliverer would not leave me, and visited me afterwards three times a day. May heaven reward him for his generous and humane behaviour.

"As soon as I had related to him all that had happened to me, he sent some of his people to look after the coach; but it could be found no where.

"After nine weeks confinement I was recovered so far that I could return to F—, the benevolent nobleman accompanied me thither, and my landlord was rejoiced to see me. Inquiring after the mysterious stranger I was told, that he had been seen no more since I had left the inn. My deliverer staid three days with me, and then we parted in a most affectionate manner. The next day I set out for my own country, where I happily arrived without any far-ther accident."

Here Hellfried concluded his wonderful tale, which he, as he added, never had been able to unfold, though he had taken the greatest pains to come at the bottom of it. He looked at his friend, eager to hear what he would say to those extraordinary adven-tures; but Herrman was lost in profound meditation for many minutes, at length he began: "Brother, thy tale is very wonderful, so wonderful, that I should not have believed it, if I had not met, on my travels, with adventures, which seem to have some con-nexion with thine."

Hellfried had apprehended that Herrman would laugh at his story, as many of his friends had done; he was therefore very much astonished at Herrman's words, and besought him to give a short account of the adventures he had hinted at. Herrman promised to give a full account of whatever had happened to him, partly by way of narration and partly in writing; however, he begged him to wait 'till to-morrow, that he might be able to arrange the neces-sary papers: Hellfried very readily consented to it.

The next morning was uncommonly fine, yet Herrman's guest had no inclination for a hunting party; As soon as breakfast was over he reminded his friend of his promise, asking whether he had found the papers he had been mentioning. Herrman affirmed it, telling his friend at the same time, that he intended to relate only that part of those adventures in which he had been personally concerned, the remainder he would give him in writing, but not before his departure, lest ghosts and necromancers might deprive him of the pleasure of making his dear visitor as comfortable and happy as possible. Hellfried having consented to it, the two friends took their places by the fire-side, lighted their pipes, and Herrman began as follows:

"Thou knowest, brother, that I, having finished my studies, was appointed governor to the young Baron de R—, to conduct him on his travels. On our return from Italy we took our way through Switzerland and Germany, and met, on this last tour, with the most remarkable adventure of our whole journey.

"Being arrived at the skirts of the Black Forest, our postillion missed his way, as it began to grow dark, and, at length, did not know what direction he should take. Our fright was not little, when he apprised us of his distress, being desirous to get out of that dreadful forest as soon as possible, on account of the many instances of robberies and murders committed within its precincts, which the postillion had enlarged upon on the road; we therefore exhorted the fellow to go on, whatever might be the consequence. He did so, and after half an hour we came to an open spot.

"Now we are safe!" exclaimed the postillion, joyfully, "and, if I am not mistaken, not far from a village."

"He was right—We soon heard the welcome barking of dogs not far off, and a little while after we saw lights.

"We entered a large village, but the inn was very indifferent, and the landlord was amazed at the uncommon sight of gentlemen. His whole stock of eatables consisted in some smoaked puddings, and a coarse sort of bread; he told us that neither wine nor beer could be got within the distance of many leagues, and even our postillion could not drink his brandy. We asked him where the Lord of the village resided; he answered, that he never lived there, because the castle had not been habitable for many years. I enquired the reason of it.

"At present," replied the host, "I dare not give you an account of it, to-morrow you shall know every thing: But, very likely, this night will make you guess the reason."

"The Baron and I entreated him to satisfy our curiosity, but he shook his head and left the room.

"Pinched by hunger we took up with our scanty supper, and then asked the landlord to shew us to our beds, but, alas! there was not one bed unoccupied in the whole house, and we were obliged to rest our weary limbs upon a bed of clean straw in the middle of the room.

"The Baron soon began to snore, but I could not get a wink of sleep. Now the watchman announced the hour of midnight with a hoarse voice, and on a sudden I heard the trampling of horses and the sound of horns: The noise came nearer, and methought I heard a number of horsemen rushing by, and sounding their horns as if a large hunting party were passing through the village; the troop darted like lightning through the street close by the windows of the inn: the Baron started up, asking me with a fearful voice, "What is this?" "I don't know," replied I abruptly. I listened attentively, and the troop could not have been far from our inn, when, on a sudden, all was again as silent as the grave; the Baron began to snore as before, and I to muse on that strange incident.

"I could not think it possible that any body would go a hunting, in so large a company, at that unseasonable hour, and was much inclined to think all had been a deluding dream, when I suddenly recollected the mysterious words of our landlord, I cannot but confess that I was seized with horror. I was just falling asleep when the voice of the watchman, crying one o'clock, roused me from my slumber. No sooner had he finished his round than the former noise was heard again at a small distance. I started up and ran to the window, but before I could open it the whole troop was rushed by like a hurricane. A little while after all was silent again, yet I did in vain beseech the brown god of slumber to take me in his arms.

"The Baron had heard nothing the second time, snoring quietly by my side, whilst I was ardently wishing for the morning, in order to satisfy my curiosity. I was too impatient to await the landlord's account of the castle, and when the watchman was crying two o'clock I hastened to the window, and began to converse with him.

"Watchman," exclaimed I, "what did that noise at twelve and one o'clock mean?"

"Hum," replied he, "your honor is certainly a stranger, for there's not a child in our village that does not know what that noise means; it is sometimes heard every night for several weeks, afterwards every thing is quiet again for a considerable time."

"But," said I, "who is that person that goes a hunting at night?"

"That I can't tell you at present," answered the watchman, "ask your landlord, he will tell you all the particulars, I am here on my duty, and under the protection of providence, but I dare not speak of what I hear and see."

"With these words he went away:—I wrapped myself up in my cloak, and sitting down by the window on a chair, expected, with anxious impatience, the rising of the sun. At length the eastern sky began to be embroidered with purple streaks, the crowing of the cocks sounded through the village, and the watchman announced the approach of day: The Baron awoke.

"You are very early," said he, rubbing his eyes, "pray tell me, what noise was it I heard in the night?"

"I myself am impatient to know it," replied I, "I wish the landlord would rise and unfold that mystery; the troop has rushed by again at one o'clock with the same terrible noise."

"While I was talking thus, I heard the trampling of horses, and looking out of the window, saw an officer with a servant. They alighted at the inn, knocked at the door, and entered the room. The officer, a lively young man, wore a Danish uniform, and was on the recruiting business; he had missed his way like ourselves, and we soon got acquainted with him. When the Baron related the nightly adventure, the officer at first thought he was joking, but when I most seriously affirmed every circumstance, he shewed an ardent desire to get acquainted with those nocturnal sportsmen.

"That honor you can easily have," said the Baron, "if you will stay here the ensuing night, we will give you company."

"Bravo!" exclaimed the officer, "perhaps the gentlemen will be so polite to invite us to their sport, and then we may be so fortunate to get a good haunch of venison."

"Now the landlord entered the room, "Well," said he, bidding us a good morning, "have you heard any thing to night, gentlemen?"

"More than I liked," answered I; "who are those sportsmen that go a hunting at midnight?"

"Why," replied he, "we don't talk of it, I would not tell you any thing about it last night, for fear your curiosity might expose you to some misfortune; yet, having promised you yesterday, to tell you as much of it as I know, I will be as good as my word."

"After having paused awhile, he began thus in a confidential tone, "Close by our village is a very large building, where formerly the Lord of this village used to reside. One of the former masters of the castle, was a very wicked and irreligious man, who found great delight in tormenting the poor peasants; every body trembled when he appeared: He trampled with his feet upon his own children, confined them in dark dungeons, where they were often kept, for many days, without a morsel of bread. He used to call his tenants dogs, and to treat them as such—in short, he was cruelty itself.

"Hunting was his only amusement, and he always kept a vast number of deer, which were the ruin of the peasants' little property, and reduced them to the utmost poverty; no one dared to drive them from his fields, and if he did, he was confined in a damp dungeon, under ground, for many weeks. When that wicked man wanted to hunt, then the whole village was called together, to serve him instead of dogs; if any one was not alert enough then he would hunt him, instead of the deer, 'till he fell down expiring under the lashes of his whip.

"One time after he had roved about from morning 'till night, he fell from his horse and broke his wicked neck: He was buried in his garden: But now he was terribly punished for his wickedness, having had no rest in his grave to the present day. At certain times of the year he is doomed to appear in the village, at twelve o'clock at night, and to make his entry into the castle with his infernal crew, but as soon as the clock strikes one, he is plunged back again into the lake of fire burning with brimstone. Nobody can inhabit the castle!—Many who have been so fool-hardy to attempt it, have lost their lives; whoever ventures to look out of the window when the infernal hosts are passing by, gets a swollen face as a punishment for his curiosity: We are now used to that nocturnal sport, and do not care for those infernal spirits, but many strangers have fallen ill through fright."

"Here the landlord finished his tale, and seemed to be pleased with our astonishment; however his pleasure was soon damped when the Lieutenant broke out in a roaring laughter.

"Laugh as long as you please," said he, "stay here 'till night, if you have courage, and then we shall see if you will laugh."

"That I will," replied the officer, "I will not only stay in your house, but I will also spend the coming night at that dreadful castle: I dare say, gentlemen," added he, "you will keep me company."

"The Baron, being a man of honor, thought it a great disgrace to betray the least want of courage, in the presence of the soldier, he therefore promised to accompany him thither: I made several objections, representing to the officer the danger we would run, not knowing who those spirits might be; however, he silenced all my remonstrances: "I am a soldier," said he, "and all ghosts and hobgoblins have ever been kept at a respectful distance by a martial dress."

"At length I was obliged to take a part in the expedition, if I would not desert the Baron. The landlord, who had all that time been staring at us in dumb amazement, lifted up his hands when I had consented to go to the castle, and entreated us, for God's sake, to desist from our undertaking: "If you go," added he, "then all of you will be dead before to-morrow morning: For heaven's sake, dear gentlemen, do not run into the very mouth of the devil thus wantonly!"

"However, the railery of the Lieutenant put him soon so much out of temper, that he left us in great wrath, swearing in the height of his anger, that the devil would make us smart for our fool-hardiness and unbelief.

"Gentlemen," began now the officer, "pray let us take a walk to that terrible place, where we are going to spend the night, and reconnoitre it before dinner."—Approving of that proposal, we went all three to that residence of terror.

"We approached and beheld the gothic remains of a half-decayed castle, the gate was open and we entered the fabric. The arched walls, overgrown with moss and ivy, echoed to the sound of our footsteps; a long narrow passage led to a spacious courtyard, paved with stones; now we espied a spiral stair-case of stone, and ascended it in dumb silence. A second long and narrow passage, which received a faint glimmering of light through several small windows, strongly guarded by iron bars, led us to a black door; the chilly damps of the long confined air rushed from the aperture when the Lieutenant had pushed it open; the apartment to which it led bore the gloomy appearance of a prison—the remains of half-decayed tapestry, covered with cobwebs, gave the room a dark dreary appearance; pieces of broken furniture were scattered about on the floor, a lamp hung in the middle on an iron chain fastened to the arched ceiling.

"Just as we were going to leave this abode of gloominess and horror, I perceived a little door in the remotest corner of the room, it was likewise unbolted, and we entered a second room, which bore the same gloomy aspect with the former apartment, being covered with half-rotten remains of broken furniture; another door led us at length into a spacious hall, where the cheering light of the day hailed us at last, many of the arched windows being either open or broken to pieces; the fresh air, the beautiful view meeting our eye from every side, chased at once from our countenance the solemn awe.

"Here," exclaimed the Lieutenant, "here we will meet the airy Lords of this Manor: Let us try, gentlemen, whether we cannot fit a table and some seats, from the rotten relics of furniture."

"We succeeded in our attempt, dragged a round massy table in the middle of the hall, supported it by four worm-eaten poles, then we fetched some pieces of wood from the adjacent apartments, placing them upon large stones round the table, and thus secured a resting place for the night.

"Now we rambled through several apartments on the other side of the hall, and meeting with nothing worthy of our notice except the traces of desolation, we returned by the way we had entered that gloomy mansion.

"We descended into the court-yard and made there likewise our observations: Spurred on by curiosity, we entered, through a ruinous side building, a garden, which still bore some marks of former grandeur; statues of marble, half destroyed by the voracious tooth of time and the inclemency of the weather, were here and there lying on the ground. We cleared with our cutlasses a way, through brambles and nettles, to a grove of beech trees; it likewise was hardly penetrable.

"Having worked our way for more than half an hour, with much toil and difficulty through a thicket of thistles and brambles, we arrived at length wearied and fatigued at an open spot; in the middle of it we beheld a statue, bearing in one hand an urn of black marble—we approached by the help of our cutlasses, and read the following inscription on the pedestal.

HIC JACET,
GODOFREDUS HAUSSINGERUS,
PECCATOR.
(Here lieth Godfrey Haussinger the Sinner.)

"A little lower down we perceived a cross engraved in the stone, and under it,

A. D. 1603.

"We stared at each other in dumb amazement, and being already too much fatigued, we did not like to work our way farther into the garden and returned.

"Gentlemen," began the officer, as we were going back, "what do you think of the inscription on that tomb?"

"I think," replied I, "it strongly corroborates what the landlord has told us."

"My companions smiled, and we came again into the courtyard, looking around we observed an arched opening in the wall opposite the stair-case; as we came nearer we saw a flight of steps leading to a cellar, which was shut up by a massy iron door, strongly secured by an enormous padlock.

"Having now examined every corner we returned to our inn.

"The landlord, who was ignorant of what we had been about, was struck with horror and amazement when we related where we had been, and did his utmost to persuade us to desist from our design; however, when he saw that he was spending his breath in vain, he kept his peace, and mentioned not a single word more about it during the whole day—we did the same—for the Lieutenant's conversation amused us so well, that evening stole upon us unawares.

"Our dinner had been better than our scanty supper on the preceding day, because the Lieutenant had brought with him an ample provision of ham and cold beef; some bottles of excellent wine which he had been provided with, raised our spirits, and increased his and the Baron's courage, in such a manner, that they expected the approach of night with the greatest impatience— they were constantly looking at their watches, and as soon as the clock had struck nine, thought it high time to go to the castle.

"We called the landlord to pay our bill, and the poor fellow tried once more to persuade us not to go to the castle; he entreated us not to expose our lives thus daringly to certain danger, and at last fell on his knees;—But when we left the room, without taking notice of his entreaties and ardent prayers, he lamented before hand our untimely death, gave us a lamp, and bolted the door, fetching a deep sigh.

"The Lieutenant's servant walked before us, carrying the lighted lamp in his hand, and a portmanteau stocked with provisions under his arm, and we kept close to his heels, armed with cutlasses and pistols.

"It was autumn, and of course very dark. We arrived at the castle; the faint glimmering of the lamp spread a kind of awful twilight around us as we were walking through the lofty arches of the vaulted passage leading to the court-yard. Having fired our pistols and loaded them again with bullets, we ascended the staircase; the doors leading to the hall we left open, that we might have a view at the court-yard, and sat cheerfully down to supper; a bottle of wine we had taken with us to keep us alert, was handed round, however we missed our aim, for every one of us began to grow drowsy soon after we had finished our meal—we rose and walked about in order to avoid falling asleep, but we were soon tired of it, the ground being so very uneven, and returned to our seats. I recollected now, very fortunately, that I had put the fables of Gellert[1] in my pocket, I took the book out, and began to read to the company; then I gave it to the Baron, and he was relieved by the Lieutenant—thus we were enabled to resist the powerful charms of sleep.

"Now it struck eleven. All around us was buried in awful silence, which only now and then was interrupted by the creaking of our feeble chairs: The Lieutenant wound up his watch and put it before him on the table.

"One hour more," began now the officer, "and we shall be in the other world." Then he awoke his servant, who was fast asleep,

---

[1] Teuthold refers to C.F. Gellert's *Fabeln und Erzälungen* (1746-48), a very popular series of didactic fables and tales, written simply and in clear language. The collection would have been recognized by Hellfried's audience, as well as by the reading audience of *The Necromancer*.

and the Baron began again to read to us.—When the Lieutenant's turn came for the second time, he looked at his watch and exclaimed, "Three quarters past eleven, we must be on our guard."

"He got up and went to the window, I followed him, impenetrable darkness surrounded us, no star could be seen: Awful silence was still swaying around, interrupted only by the snoring John, and the creaking of the wood; the pale light of our lamp produced an horrid glimmering in the spacious dreary hall; the Baron leaning his head upon his arm, struggled to forget every object around him, and the officer uttered not a single word.

"Now we heard a clock toll twelve at a great distance, and I walked softly back to my seat, the Lieutenant did the same, taking up one of his pistols, and rubbing the lock with his handkerchief. We looked at each other, and every one of us strove in vain to hide the horror he was struggling against.—The watchman cried the hour, the crowing of the cocks told us midnight was set in, and still all around us was as silent as the grave. The Baron laid the book upon the table, and the Lieutenant was going to raise a loud laughter, asking us where the spirits might be, when suddenly the trampling of horses and the sound of horns was heard—we all were fixed to our seats, staring at each other with a ghastly look; now the noise seemed to be under our window; the Lieutenant ran towards it, with a cocked pistol in his hand, but he was too late.

"All was quiet again, and an awful stillness swayed around the castle; however a few seconds after we heard suddenly a most tremendous noise in the court-yard, which was soon followed by a terrible trampling and a gingling of spurs on the stair-case, as if a great number of people in boots was coming up. The noise came nearer and nearer, my feet began to fail, my teeth to chatter in my mouth, and my hair to rise like bristles, while every sense was lost in anxious bodings; at length the noise grew fainter and fainter, and soon we could hear it no more, and midnight stillness resumed her awful sway.

"A long pause of dumb astonishment ensued, 'till at last the Lieutenant, who had recovered his spirits first exclaimed, "Shall we go down." I shook my head without uttering a word, and the Baron was likewise silent. "Then I will go alone," said the Lieutenant, snatched up a brace of pistols, drew his hanger, and hurried down. He returned a few minutes after, exclaiming, "It is surprising I cannot see the least traces of either men or horses."

"Now he retook his seat, casting down his looks in a pensive manner—his servant was still snoring—the Baron began again to read, and I fell fast asleep. At once I was roused by the report of a pistol, I and honest John started up at the same moment, and we heard once more the trampling of horses and the sound of horns, but it soon died away at a distance, and the Lieutenant entered the hall with the Baron.

"They also had not been able to resist the leaden wand of sleep, but the same noise in the court-yard we had heard at twelve o'clock, had soon roused them from their slumber. "As soon as we heard the noise," said the Baron, "we hastened to the outer room, our pistols cocked, but before we could reach it the noise was under the window of the castle, the Lieutenant knocked through one of the windows in the room close to the hall, and sent a bullet after the troop, which was rushing by like an hurricane, however, he was prevented by the darkness of the night from distinguishing any thing except some white horses."

"The spirits are afraid of us," exclaimed the Lieutenant now, "but come, let us return to our inn, we shall rest more comfortable on a bed of clean straw than on this damp ground." We all consented to it, and left the gloomy abode of those nocturnal sportsmen: We knocked a good while at the door of the inn before it was opened; at last the landlord appeared, stammering, lost in wonder, "God be praised that you are still alive, how did you escape?"

"The Lieutenant silenced him by some hasty lies, and promised to give him a full account of the whole adventure after he should have rested a little.

"Gentlemen," said he, as soon as he got up in the morning, "next night I will go once more to the haunted castle, and spend the night in the court-yard, will you keep me company?"

"The Baron looked at me as if he wished not to accept the proposal: I did so. "We cannot," said I, "stay here a day longer, and such an undertaking would, besides, be too dangerous for only four people."

"O!" exclaimed the Lieutenant, "if that is all you have to say against it, then I will soon make you easy: We will take a dozen stout fellows from the village with us, they will not hesitate to accompany us if we give them a couple of dollars and a good dram; it will be devilish good fun, and to-morrow, with the first dawn of day, I will depart with you."

"The Baron consented to the proposal, and I myself did not dislike it; in short, we remained, and sent our postillion through the village to publish, "That all young fellows who would go with us to the castle next night, should have six-pence each, and as much brandy as they could drink."

"In less than half an hour the whole village was assembled round the door of the inn. We selected fifteen of the stoutest, ordered them to provide themselves with proper arms, and to appear by ten o'clock at night at the inn. Our landlord, who beheld these preparations in dumb amazement, believed firmly that we must be arch necromancers, and his fancy having been fired by the wonderful account of our nocturnal adventure, which the Lieutenant had given him, he was himself not unwilling to go with us to the castle and to bid defiance to the infernal hosts: However, as soon as it grew dark, his courage died away, and he wished success to our undertaking, telling us, he could not leave his house.

"Our little army was assembled before ten o'clock, armed with scythes, poles, hay forks, and flails. We ordered the landlord to give a dram to every one, took some tables, benches, lamps, and a small cask of brandy with us, and marched in triumph towards the Castle.

"We pitched our camp in the court-yard, not far from the entrance, the peasants placed themselves round the brandy cask, lighted their pipes, and expected with pleasure the appearance of the airy gentlemen.

"Another advantage we reaped from that honest company was, that we had no need to keep sleep at a distance by reading, for the merriment of our little army rose soon to the highest pitch, and these jovial fellows being heated by the contents of our little cask, challenged his Satanic majesty and all his infernal hosts amid peals of roaring laughter.

"It was now past eleven o'clock, and the noise began to abate, some of our gentlemen were nodding, and some snoring, we were therefore obliged to beg those who had not yet yielded to the powerful charms of sleep, to give us a song, which they instantly did in so vociferous a manner, that our hearing organs were most painfully affected—the sleepers started up when they heard that terrible noise, and joined the jovial songsters with all their might: Thus we chased away the sweet god of sleep, who seemed not in the least to relish the disharmonious notes of our jolly companions.

"Now the Lieutenant beckoned to the blithsome crew, and the clamorous noise was suddenly hushed in awful silence. It struck twelve o'clock, the sound of horns and the trampling of horses was heard at a distance. The peasants listened, their mouths wide open, and gazed at each other struck with chilly terror: No sound was heard, except the palpitating of their hearts, and here and there the chattering of teeth—all of them moved their lips as if praying ardently. The noise came nearer and nearer, and now it seemed to be in the castle. Again every thing was silent, but in an instant the former noise struck once more our listening ears, and the infernal hosts rushed by like lightning—the Lieutenant, the Baron, and I darted through the passage leading to the gate, but the airy gentlemen were already out of sight, and we could see nothing, save a faint glimmering of some white horses: The mingled noise of their horns and of the trampling of their horses soon died away, the stillness of midnight swayed all around, and we returned to the court-yard.

"Our valiant crew was still fixed to the ground, seized with horror and astonishment: None of them were able to distinguish whether we were ghosts or their fellow adventurers; however, they recovered their spirits by degrees, and prepared to leave the residence of the infernal sportsmen.

"We left the castle, fully convinced that these nocturnal ramblers must be beings who were afraid of us, discharged our courageous troops, and went to rest.

"I awoke with the first ray of the morning sun, and roused the Baron and the Lieutenant; the latter seemed not to be inclined to fulfil his promise, being desirous to try his fortune once more, and to hide himself either in the court-yard, or before the gate: When he saw that we would not stay any longer, he postponed the execution of his design to a future time, and followed our example.

"We left our inn at six o'clock, the morning was gloomy and rainy, the wind swept furiously over the heath, and drove the black clouds still closer and closer together; after a few minutes we entered the Black Forest.[1]—Looking out of the coach, I saw the Lieutenant and his servant turn to the left, towards a brook, where we beheld an odd phænomenon.—A reverend old man was sitting there, and reading in a large book; bewildered in profound meditation, he seemed to take no notice of the howling storm, and not to be sensible of the rain rushing down in large drops upon his uncovered head, the tempest was sporting with his reverend grey locks, and the rain beating in his face, yet he did not stir—His long brown robe seemed to denote a traveller from the East—a long staff and a black wallet were lying by his side.

"I got out of the coach to view that strange being a little closer, and to speak to him, but before I could accost him, the Lieutenant exclaimed, "Greybeard, what art thou reading?"

"The old man appeared to take no notice of his question, and went on reading as if nobody had been there.

"What art thou reading?" exclaimed the Lieutenant once more, alighting and looking over his shoulder at the book.

"The old man answered not a word, but still continued to read. I also was now standing behind him, and looking at the book, its leaves were of yellow parchment, the characters large and of different colours.

"The Baron was close at my heels, and the Lieutenant being provoked by the old man's obstinate silence, shook him now violently by the shoulder, thundering in his ears, "Greybeard, what art thou reading?"

---

[1] The Black Forest appears "black" because the shadows of the densely thicketed trees darken the surroundings. The gloominess of the forest contributes to the gothic themes and mood of the novel; it becomes a "supernatural" habitat for lurking ghosts and vengeful demons. It also houses spooky castles; damp, infectious dungeons; and dead spirits walking. The subtitle of *The Necromancer*, "The Tale of the Black Forest," reinforces the gothic setting of the narrative.

"Now the old man lifted his reverend head slowly up, stared at us with angry looks, and then said, with a solemn awful voice, "Wisdom!"

"What language is it?"

Old man. (Reading again) "The language of Wisdom."

"What dost thou call Wisdom?"

Old man. "All what thou dost not comprehend."

Lieut. "If thou knowest what other people cannot comprehend, then I should like to ask thee a question."

Old man. (Staring again at him) "What question?"

Lieut. "There is a castle not far from the next village, where every night a numerous troop of spirits make their entry; I and these two gentlemen have watched there these two nights."

Old man. (Interrupting him) "And art not a bit wiser for't, for thou seemest not to be fit to converse with spirits."

Lieut. "But thou—?"

Old man. "I understand the language of Wisdom."

"The Lieutenant bit his lips, shaking his head with a contemptuous smile. Now the Baron accosted the old man, who again was immersed in profound meditation.

Baron. "Well then, if thy book contains such a treasure of wisdom, then tell us why that castle is haunted by spirits, and for what reason they go their nightly rounds?"

Old man. "That the spirits must tell thee themselves."

Baron. "What does then thy book contain?"

Old man. "The ways and means of forcing them to a confession."

Baron. "But why hast thou not forced them long ago to confess every thing?"

Old man. "Because I never cared for it."

Baron. (Laughing) "But if we should entreat thee to do it, and pull our purses, wouldst thou not do us that favor?"

Old man. (Frowning) "Vile mortal! can Wisdom be bought with gold and silver?"

Baron. "How can one then purchase it?"

Old man. "With nothing—hast thou courage?"

Baron. "Else we would not have watched in the dreadful castle."

Old man. "Then spend another night in it, I will be there a quarter before twelve o'clock—now leave me."

"We gazed at each other with doubtful looks: The old man resumed his reading and seemed to take no farther notice of us who were still standing behind him lost in silent wonder. At length the Lieutenant mounted his horse, and we went back to our coach. "Well," said the officer, as we were getting in our carriage, "well, gentlemen, will you return with me?"

"In vain did I make objections, the expectation of the two hot-headed young men was strained too much; it was impossible to subdue the eager curiosity of the young Baron, and the presence of the Lieutenant made me apprehend that all reasoning would not only be spent in vain, but at the same time make me contemptible; I therefore was forced to go back with them, and to embark in an enterprize, which, being not only useless, but also very dangerous, would plunge me in great distress.

"Our host was highly rejoiced and struck with astonishment, when he saw us come back with the intention (as he believed) to engage once more with the nightly sportsmen: Our valiant companions of the preceding night, had given a wonderful account of our adventure, relating how horribly the ghosts had looked, how courageously they had encountered the infernal crew, and how the strange conjurors at last had banished the tremendous host from the castle for ever.

"The whole village assembled, therefore, as soon as our return was known, gazing at us as supernatural beings, and consulting us about several matters. The Lieutenant had his fun with the simplicity of those honest people and the day was spent merrily.

"It was already dark, and the villagers had not yet left the inn, they unanimously intreated us to take them along with us to the castle. We were obliged to disavow our design, to feign sleepiness, and to order a bed of straw to be got ready.

"At ten o'clock we stole silently to the castle without a light, the Lieutenant's servant lighted our lamp in the court-yard, and we went to the hall, where we had spent the first night, waiting with impatience for the last quarter before midnight. The Lieutenant did not believe the old man would be as good as his word, I joyfully seconded his opinion, and would have been glad if we had not waited for him; but the Baron, who, from his juvenile days, had been fond of every thing bearing the aspect of mysteriousness, was quite charmed with the reverend appearance of the old man, and maintained, upon his honor, that he certainly would stick to his appointment.

"The Lieutenant began to discourse with the Baron on apparitions and necromancers, maintaining by experience and reasoning, that all was either deceit or the effects of a deluded fancy; yet the Baron would not relinquish his opinion, adding, that one ought not to speak lightly of those matters, and that the old man certainly would prove the truth of his assertion: We were still conjecturing who that strange wanderer might be, when we saw by our watches, that there were but sixteen minutes wanting to twelve; as soon as it was three quarters after eleven, we heard the sound of gentle steps in the passage.

"Our greybeard," said the Lieutenant, "is a man of honor," and took up the lamp to meet the old man.

"Now he entered the hall, his black wallet on his back, and beckoned in a solemn manner to follow him. We did so, and he led us through the apartments and the vaulted passage down stairs: We followed him thro' the court-yard to the iron gate of the cellar, without uttering a word; there he stopped, turning towards us, and eyeing us awhile, with a ghastly look; after an awful pause of expectation, he said with a low trembling voice, "Don't utter a word as you value your lives." Then he went down the two first steps, taking from his bosom an enormous key, which had been suspended round his neck by an iron chain, and opened, without the least difficulty, the monstrous padlock, the door flew open, and the old man took the lamp from the Lieutenant, leading us down a large staircase of stone; we descended into a spacious cellar, vaulted with hewn stone, and beheld all around large iron doors, secured by strong padlocks; our hoary leader went slowly towards an iron folding door, opposite to the staircase, and opened it likewise with his key; it flew suddenly open, and we beheld with horror a black vault, which received a faint light from a lamp suspended to the ceiling by an iron chain.

"The old man entered, uncovering his reverend head, and we did the same, standing by his side in trembling expectation,

awed by the solemnity that reigned around us; a dreadful chill-
ness seized us, we felt the grasp of the icy fangs of horror, being in
a burying vault surrounded with rotten coffins: Skulls and mould-
ered bones rattled beneath our feet, the grisly phantom of death
stared in our faces from every side, with a grim ghastly aspect.
In the centre of the vault we beheld a black marble coffin, supported by a pedestal of stone, over it was suspended to the ceiling
a lamp spreading a dismal dying glimmering around. The air was
heavy and of a musty smell, we hardly could respire, the objects
around seemed to be wrapped in a bluish mist. The hollow sound
of our footsteps re-echoed through the dreary abode of horror as
we walked nigher.

"The old man stopped at a small distance from the marble
coffin, beckoning to us to come nigher; we moved slowly on, and
he made a sign not to advance farther than he could reach with
extended arms. The Lieutenant placed himself at his right, I took
my station at his left, and the Baron opposite to him.

"Now he put the lamp on the ground before him, taking his
book, an ebony wand, and a box of white plate, out of his wallet:—Out of the latter he strewed a reddish sand around him,
drew a circle with his wand, and folded his hands across his breast,
then he pronounced amid terrible convulsions, some mysterious
words, opened the book and began to read, whilst his face was
distorted in a grisly manner; his convulsions grew more horrible
as he went on reading; all his limbs seemed to be contracted by a
convulsive fit. His eyebrows shrunk up, his forehead was covered
with wrinkles, and large drops of sweat were running down his
cheeks—at once he threw down his book, gazing with a staring
look, and his hands lifted up at the marble coffin.

"We soon perceived that midnight had set in; the trampling of
horses and the sound of horns was heard; the Necromancer did not
move a limb, still staring at the coffin with a haggard look. Now
the noise was on the staircase of the cellar and still he was motionless, his eyes being immoveably directed towards the coffin: But
now the noise was in the cellar; he brandished his wand, and all
around was buried in awful silence. He pronounced again three
times an unintelligible word with a horrible thundering voice. A
flash of lightning hissed suddenly through the dreary vault, lick-

ing the damp walls, and a hollow clap of thunder roared through the subterranean abode of chilly horror. The light in the lamp was now extinguished, silence and darkness swayed all around; soon after we heard a gentle rustling just before us, and a faint glimmering was spreading through the gloomy vault. It grew lighter and lighter, and we soon perceived rays of dazzling light shooting from the marble coffin, the lid of which began to rise higher and higher—at once the whole vault was illuminated, and a grisly human figure rose slow and awful from the coffin. The phantom, which was wrapped up in a shroud, bore a dying aspect, it trembled violently as it rose, and emitted an hollow groan, looking around with chilly horror. Now the spectre descended from the pedestal, and moved with trembling steps and haggard looks towards the circle where we were standing.

"Who dares," groaned it, in a faltering hollow accent, "who dares to disturb the rest of the dead."

"And who art thou?" replied our leader, with a threatening frowning aspect, "who art thou, that thou darest to disturb the stillness of this castle, and the nocturnal slumber of those that inhabit its environs?"

"The phantom shuddered back, groaning in a most lamentable accent, "Not I, not I, my cursed husband disturbs the peace around and mine."

Old man. "For what reason?"

Ghost. "I have been assassinated, and he who judges men has thrown my sins upon the murderer."

Old man. "I comprehend thee, unhappy spirit, betake thyself again to rest; by my power, which every spirit dreads, he shall disturb thee no more—be gone."

"The phantom bowed respectfully, staggered towards the pedestal, climbed up, got into the coffin, and disappeared; the lid sunk slowly down, and the light which had illuminated the dismal mansion of mortality died away by degrees. A flash of lightning hissed again through the vault, licking the damp walls; the hollow sound of thunder roared through the subterranean abode of horror; the lamp began again to burn, and awful silence of the grave swayed all around.

"Now the old man took up his wallet, and his book, beckoning to us to follow him. We returned to the adjoining vault, through which we had entered that abode of awful dread; it was as lonesome as we had left it; our leader locked the iron folding door carefully, then he took out of his wallet a large piece of parchment, on which a number of strange characters were written, a piece of black sealing-wax, and a monstrous iron seal. Having made several crosses over those things with his ebony wand, he fixed the parchment above the lock, and sealed it hastily on the four corners.

"This done, he went into the middle of the cellar, assigning us our places; then he strewed sand on the ground, drew a circle with his wand, and began again to read in his book, amid horrible convulsions. Now he brandished his wand, pronouncing three times with a most tremendous voice, the same word he had made use of in the burying vault. A flash of lightning hissed through the cellar, a clap of thunder shook the subterraneous fabric, all the doors, save that which had been sealed up, were suddenly forced open, with a thundering noise, the lamp was extinguished, and a blue light reflected in a grisly manner, from the staircase against the damp wall; woful groans, lamentations, and the dismal clashing of chains, resounded through the spacious caverns. The noise seemed to come from the staircase, gentle steps were heard, a numerous troop seemed to be descending into the cellar; the lamentations and the woful groans advanced nearer, and louder resounded the clashing of chains.

"Horrid to behold did now a second phantom appear before our gazing looks, staggering slowly towards us, and leaving a numerous retinue on the staircase; the garment of the spectre was stained with blood, the skull fractured, the eyes like two portentous comets!

"Who art thou?" roared our leader, with a thundering voice, and the dreary cavern echoed to the sound.

"The phantom answered with a hollow dismal voice, "A damned soul!"

Old man. "What business hast thou in this castle?"

Ghost. "I want to be redeemed from hell."

Old man. "How canst thou be redeemed?"

Ghost. "By the forgiveness of my wife."

Old man. "How darest thou claim it, reprobate villain? Return to thy damned companions in hell. Respect this seal, respect these characters."

"Here the old man pointed at the door of the vault which had been sealed up: The phantom staggered towards it but suddenly shuddered back, and sunk groaning on the ground; a flash of lightning illuminated the cellar, and a tremendous peal of thunder resounded through the lofty vault; all the doors were shut again with a terrible noise, a frightful howling filled our ears, and horrid phantoms hovered before our eyes; flashes of lightning hissed through the vault, and roaring claps of thunder threatened to overturn the whole fabric.

"The lightning ceased by degrees, and the roaring of thunder died away, a blue flame was still glimmering on the staircase, but it soon died away, and we were surrounded with darkness; groans and dreadful lamentations resounded still through the winding caverns, but soon all around was hushed in profound silence. After a short pause of horrid stillness, the trampling of horses and the sound of horns was heard again; yet that noise died also away before we recovered our recollection.

"When our astonishment began to subside, we perceived that we were standing in a dark cellar, without knowing whether any one of us was missing. A disagreeable sulphurous odour affected our smelling organs, and bereft us almost of the power of respiration; not a whisper interrupted the dead midnight silence which surrounded us. At length somebody took me by the hand, I shuddered back, my imagination being still the wrestling place of horrid wild phantoms, and my soul divining a thousand dreadful thoughts.

"It is I," said the Lieutenant, and I felt at once as if an heavy load had been taken from my breast. Now the Baron began also to speak, "Where are you?" whispered he, "Are you still alive?"

"We groped about in the dark, and at last found him leaning against the wall.

"How shall we get out of this cursed residence of horror?" exclaimed the Lieutenant, "come, let us try whether we can find the staircase; it must be just opposite to us, if I am not mistaken."

Then he began to walk on, and we groped after him, tumbling now and then over loose stones.

"I have found the staircase," cried our fellow adventurer, "at last, after a long fruitless search, I feel the first step."

"A ray of joy beamed through our hearts as we were climbing up, but, alas! it was soon most cruelly damped; the cellar door was locked up, and the blood congealed in our veins when the Lieutenant told it us. We exerted all our strength to force it open, but in vain. It was bolted on the out side. The Lieutenant called as loud as he could for his servant, whom he had left snoring in the hall; we joined our voices with his, calling with all our might, "John! John!"

"The hollow echo repeated, in a tremendous awful accent, "John! John!" but no human footstep would gladden our desponding hearts. Frantic with black despair did we now begin to knock at the massy door 'till the blood was running down from our hands, and to cry, "John, John," 'till our voices grew hoarse—the hollow echo still repeated in an awful tremendous accent our knocking and crying, but no human footstep was heard. "The fellow sleeps and cannot hear us," said the Lieutenant, at length with a faint voice, "Let us sit down and watch him when he shall come down."

"We did so, but I had no hope that the servant would come, yet I concealed my apprehension within my breast. The Lieutenant dissembled to be easy, and began to converse on what we had seen and heard; however his broken accent, the faltering of his speech, and his low voice, betrayed the anxiety of his mind. The Baron and I spoke little, and when we had been sitting about an hour not one uttered a word more; all was silent around us. Nothing interrupted the deathlike stillness of the night, except the violent beating of our hearts.

"At length the Lieutenant asked, if we were asleep; however, the anxiety of our minds and the dreadful apprehensions which assailed us, drove far away even the idea of sleep. We sat some hours in that dreadful situation, and it was now about five o'clock in the morning, when the Lieutenant exclaimed, "I fear we wait in vain for my servant, he cannot sleep so fast that he should not hear us! But where can he be?" Then he began again to knock violently against the massy iron door, but all was in vain. No human footsteps was heard, we remained some hours on the staircase, but all our waiting and listening was fruitless, no cheering sound of human footsteps would gladden our desponding hearts.

"I will not torment you by vain apprehensions," began the Lieutenant, at length, "however we seem to be doomed to destruction, yet let us try if we cannot escape some way or other, come down with me into the cellar, there we will have a better chance to espy an outlet than here."

"We descended, with trembling knees, without saying a word, and groped along in the dark a good while, knocking our heads against the damp wall, and the iron doors: Alas! our search seemed to be in vain, and the grim spectre of a lingering death stared us grisly in the face, my feet could support me no longer, and I dropped down wearied with anxiety.

"Now I began to reproach myself for having plunged into the gulph of destruction not only myself, but also him who had been entrusted to my care. The apprehension of being famished in that infernal abode, thrilled my soul with horror, and black despair; at first I heard the Baron and the Lieutenant still groping about, neither of them uttered a word; the hollow sound of their footsteps re-echoed horribly through the vault—at length the sound of the Baron's footsteps died away at a distance, and only one of my companions in destruction remained with me.

"Where are you?" exclaimed the Lieutenant.

"Here I am," replied I, "but where is the Baron?"

"The Lieutenant called him, and I did the same, but we received no answer: At once a sudden hollow noise struck our ears, and at the same time a faint glimmering of light darted from a remote corner of our dungeon: I started up, half frantic with joy, and we pursued the gladdening ray of light; it seemed to come from an opening in the wall. No words can express the rapture we felt when we beheld one of the iron doors half open; we went through it with hasty steps and entered a long vaulted passage: A faint dawn of light hailed our joyful looks at a great distance, from below. We descended a declivity, the farther we went the more the light increased, at length we reached the end of the avenue, and perceived some steps leading into a spacious apartment, at the entrance of which some boards on the floor had given way: We descended the steps, and, who can paint the horror which rushed upon us, when we beheld the Baron lying lifeless in the deep vault, upon some mouldering straw? I leaped down without a moment's hesitation, the Lieutenant did the same, and now we began to shake the Baron 'till we at length perceived signs of returning life. We continued our endeavours to recall his senses, he breathed, gave a hollow groan, and opened his eyes: His fainting fit had been the effect of sudden terror, and he had not received the least hurt.

"He now told us that he had met in the dark with a long narrow passage which he had pursued, in a kind of insensibility, 'till he had staggered down from an elevated spot, when the boards suddenly giving way, dragged him along into the deep vault.

"Looking around we perceived that we were in a spacious cavern, which appeared to have been formerly a kind of stable. High over our heads were two large round holes, grated with strong iron bars, through which the day light was admitted, and after a closer examination we espied a gloomy outlet in a remote corner, shut up by a wooden door, which we forced open without difficulty: We now ascended, through a dark passage, higher and higher, 'till we at length with rapture beheld an outlet which opened into the garden; we were obliged to cut our way with our hangers, through the underwood and the entangled weeds, and soon came to the court-yard: Tears of joy sparkled in our eyes, rays of unspeakable rapture beamed through our hearts, and we praised God for our unexpected deliverance from the grisly jaws of a lingering death.

"The dreary desolated court-yard appeared to us a paradise, the dazzling splendor of the bright morning sun, and the pure air which we now inhaled, filled our hearts with the strongest sensations of bliss. We congratulated each other on our resurrection from the dreary abode of mortality, where we were doomed to be entombed alive, and shook each other by the hand half frantic with joy.

"We went now to the hall in search of the Lieutenant's servant; the table and every thing was in the same condition we had left them, but John was not there. We went through the whole gloomy fabric shouting and hollowing, discharging our pistols, but no sound was heard except the hollow echo repeating our shouts and the reports of our pistols, in a dismal accent, all over the dreary building.

"Very likely he is returned to the inn," said the Lieutenant, "and we shall find him there."

"We left that dangerous abode of black horror, praising God again and again for our deliverance.

"As we entered the inn we beheld the landlord surrounded by a number of villagers, who were come to inquire whether we were returned from the castle. They were very much surprised when we entered the room, and, respectfully taking off their hats, told us, that the uproar at the village last night had been more tremendous than ever.

Every one was impatient to know the particulars of our adventure, but the Lieutenant having then no inclination of amusing himself with their simplicity, gave them a short answer, and asked the landlord where his servant was.

"I have not seen him since yesterday," replied he.

"It is impossible," resumed the Lieutenant, "where are the horses?"

"They are in the stable," replied the landlord, "I have just been looking after them."

"The Lieutenant gave us an apprehensive look, and begged the gaping peasants to look after him, all over the village and the adjacent places; they all were very willing to do it, and left the inn.

"It was nine o'clock when we entered the inn, and it struck twelve when our honest villagers returned, with the disagreeable news that they could find poor John no where.

"The Lieutenant thought it not prudent to remain any longer at that fatal place; the Baron likewise wished to depart, and I too was impatient to be gone. As soon as we had finished our scanty dinner, we departed a second time; the tears started from our landlord's eyes, and from those of the good villagers, when we bade them farewell, after having made them a small present, and they saw us depart with regret.

"The Lieutenant knew the ways through the Black Forest pretty well, he rode by our chaise leading his servant's horse with one hand, and we reached without any farther accident the limits of that dreadful forest. We parted company at the close of the second day, bidding each other a tender adieu.

"I thank you, gentlemen," said the Lieutenant, as we were getting into our chaise at the door of the inn, "I thank you for your kind and faithful assistance in the most dreadful adventure of my life; if I should be so fortunate to get at the bottom of the mystery, which hangs over that castle, as I shall endeavour to do, I will take the first opportunity to apprise you of my success. Farewell, remember now and then the 20th of September, Anno 1750, and do not forget your humble friend."

"The postillion smacked his whip, and we went different roads. On the fifth day we arrived, without any further accident, at the castle of Baron R—, the father of my pupil.

"And here," added Herrman, "my narration is finished. A letter which the Baron wrote me, and a manuscript sent me by the Lieutenant, contains every thing that has happened afterwards. But these papers you shall not get before your departure."

Though Hellfried's curiosity had been spurred very much, yet he could not but consent to his friend's proposal, and spent a fortnight more with him in uninterrupted pleasure.

The days rolled swiftly on, shortened by the conversation of his friend, by hunting and other diversions, and he at length was obliged to bid his host adieu. Herrman thanked him once more for his friendly visit, shook him by the hand, gave him a parting kiss, dropped a gentle tear, and then bade him farewell.

Before he parted with his Hellfried he gave him the above mentioned manuscript, assuring him that he would have given it him sooner, if he had been able to find it amongst a great many papers: He added, that he had searched for it in vain several days, and would have given him the continuation and conclusion of those mysterious adventures, by way of narration, if he could not have found the manuscript, but he had fortunately traced it out the day before his departure, amongst a number of old musty papers—Herrman cleaned it from the dust and gave it to his friend, saying to him,

"Take, brother, take here the continuation of my tale, and if thou thinkest the publication of it will amuse and benefit the world, thou art welcome to publish it."

Then they parted, alas! for ever. Herrman's wish was accomplished; he had seen once more the faithful friend of his younger days, and soon after went over to that better world, where good men will meet again the friends of their bosom, never to part again. Hellfried too is awaiting the solemn morn of resurrection in his grave, and he, before he died, set down in writing, the foregoing narration:—Now let us see what the writings which his friend had given him contain.

END OF THE FIRST PART.

THE NECROMANCER.

PART II.

BARON R——, TO MR. HERRMAN.[1]

B——, Nov. 11, 1772.

DEAR FRIEND,

It is with the greatest pleasure I am going to communicate to you a remarkable accident I met with this summer, when at Pyrmont. I would have given you the following account some time ago, if it had not been for some papers which I was obliged to wait for; they are arrived at last, and here I send them, beseeching you to remit them to me as soon as you shall have perused them.

I had been three weeks at Pyrmont, when I one time went to the promenade, in a very beautiful evening, there I happened to meet a gentleman whose features interested me very much, though they were unknown to me:—Walking slowly on, I soon saw him come after me; he passed me with hasty steps, and turning suddenly, stared me in the face; I did the same, being surprised that I also had attracted the notice of the stranger: He went on, but soon after turned round once more, directing his steps towards me, and staring again at me. I stopped and did the same. He moved his lips as if he wanted to speak to me, just when I was going to ask him whether he wanted something; however, we both remained silent, pursuing our walk. That pantomime we repeated

---

[1] At this point in the novel, the narrative continues in epistolary fashion, with a series of letters from several narrators. The disjointed narrative that ensues is an attempt to create suspense, sowing confusion with regard to the "supernatural" events that occur, even as the narrative moves inexorably toward rationalizing them. In addition, the series of documents gives the narrative a journalistic feel by placing the narrative within the frame of legal fact and reportage.

several times neither of us uttering a word; at length it began to grow dark and I went to my lodgings.

The next morning I awoke with the first ray of the sun, and went again to the promenade, to inhale the salubrious breeze of the morning air, and to hail the rising king of the day, under the canopy of heaven: I was no sooner seated on a bench beneath a majestic beach-tree, admiring the greatness of the Creator, so striking in the beautiful scenes of a fine summer's morning, when I once more beheld the stranger who had interested me so much the preceding evening. He came nearer, saluted me, and took a seat on the bench where I was sitting. We both admired, in profound silence, the beautiful scene around for a quarter of an hour; every object which surrounded us pronounced the greatness of God! Numbers of feathered songsters hailed the rising sun; diamonds and rubies sparkled on the leaves of the trees, loaded with the pearly drops of dew. Now the sun darted his warming cheerful rays all around, and the stranger looked at me with an inquisitive eye, "Sir," he at length began, "you will excuse me if I should be mistaken, I think I have had, some years past, the pleasure of being in your company somewhere or other."

"It is possible," replied I, "that I have had that honor, will you favor me with your name?"

"My name is B—, and I am Major in the service of the King of Denmark."

"B—! I think I remember that name; yet I cannot recollect where I have had the honor of seeing you."

"Perhaps I may," replied he, "if you will be so kind to favor me with your name."

"My name is R—."

"Did not you return from your travels to Germany in the year 1750?"

I replied in the affirmative.

"Then I am not mistaken," said he smiling. "Don't you remember the adventure at the Haunted Castle, on the skirts of the Black Forest, and that villainous Necromancer?"

I was struck with amazement. "How," exclaimed I. "Is it you? Do I not dream?"

"Yes, dear friend, it is I," he replied, "you are not mistaken. How strangely and how unexpectedly do friends meet sometimes in this world! I am at present governor to a young prince who is on his travels: We are here incognito, yet I could not resist the ardent desire of making myself known to you. Did you never wish to get some further intelligence of the mystery of that terrible castle and its strange inhabitants? With the greatest pleasure would I have communicated to you, what came to my knowledge since we parted, had I but known the place of your residence; I travelled on purpose to your native town, as soon as I had finished my recruiting business, but I was told you had been sent by your prince to England on affairs of state."

"Your kindness deserves my warmest acknowledgment, and I am very sorry that I had the misfortune of being absent when you intended to do me the honor of seeing me."

"Your absence vexed me very much," he replied, "because it not only deprived me of the pleasure of seeing once more an old friend, but also prevented me from performing the promise I had given you when we parted: This happy meeting affords me, therefore, the greatest pleasure, and if you will favor me with your company, at my apartments, I can give you a satisfactory account of several accidents which happened before and after our adventure at the castle, and which are nearly connected with what we have encountered."

I accepted his kind invitation, and went with him to breakfast at his apartments. On the way he enquired after you, and was rejoiced to hear that you are well and happy, blessed with the love of a dear and virtuous wife. He particularly seemed to be pleased with my little narrative of your matrimonial bliss—I forbore to enquire after the reason of it, fearing to renew the pains, which perhaps the recent loss of a dear beloved object might have inflicted upon him, and gave our conversation another turn 'till we arrived at his apartments.

After we had breakfasted we seated ourselves by the window, and he began a tale which took an unexpected and a most wonderful turn, but the accidents were so various and many, that he only could give me a short sketch; which being interspersed with many episodes, was rather confused: He was himself sensible of the defects of his narrative, and promised to send me a written account of those wonderful accidents as soon as he should have finished his travels.

I spent five happy days in his company, and then we parted reluctantly. Two months after he sent me the enclosed continuation of his adventures, which will strike you with astonishment.

Major B— sends you his best wishes, he longs ardently to see you once more.

Farewell, and remember

Your faithful,

R—.

CONTINUATION OF THE ADVENTURES OF LIEUTENANT B—.

I was lost in profound meditation after I had parted with my companions; all the horrid scenes of the adventure at the castle hovered before my imagination; I fancied myself at the inn, in the ruinous hall, and then in the cellar, still beholding the Necromancer and the phantoms, seeing the flashes of lightning, and hearing the roaring of the thunder, and the hollow voices of the spectres. My fancy renewed all the horrors which had rushed upon me when shut up in the cellar, as well as the joy I felt, when we had the good fortune to find an outlet from our infernal dungeon; my restless fancy painted all these pictures with the strongest colours, painted them so grisly, that I sent up to heaven the most fervent thanksgiving for my delivery from that infernal abode.

These horrid dreams vanished at length, giving room to contemplations of a more serious cast. I was every moment reminded of the unhappy fate of my faithful John, and felt an ardent desire to get at the bottom of those mysterious events, that I might be enabled to deliver my poor servant from the clutches of the spirits, or, at least, avenge his death: I was however sensible, that I alone should not be equal to it; the peasants of the village I did not think fit for assisting me in my enterprise, and the whole undertaking too hazardous without the assistance and the counsel of an experienced and resolute man: I therefore was determined to search for such a man, and, aided by his counsel and assistance, once more to encounter those nocturnal sportsmen.

This resolution was the result of my meditations on the first morning after my separation from my companions, and I burned with impatient desire to rid myself of that load of incertitude which lay heavy upon my mind. At length I arrived at the place of my destination, and resumed my recruiting business, assisted by two old serjeants.

I hastened to return to the skirts of the Black Forest, and went to F—, where always a number of recruiting officers reside, on account of the great number of journeymen constantly travelling through that town; there I met with Prussian, Austrian, Hessian, and Swedish recruiting officers, and now and then with an old acquaintance of mine.

Amongst others I got acquainted with an old Austrian officer, who was highly respected by every one; when he said any thing, which happened not often, then every body listened with the greatest attention, and when, now and then a quarrel arose, every thing was soon settled by his interference.

A man who thus powerfully could influence a set of people, who admit no law but that of superiority, soon engaged my admiration in the highest degree, and I concluded he would be the fittest person to assist me in the execution of my design, to unfold the mystery of the Haunted Castle, if I could but gain his confidence; yet I was sensible that it would be no easy task to ingratiate myself so far with him, that he should not refuse believing a tale like mine, which bore such glaring marks of fiction: I apprehended an old veteran of so much experience, and so serious a turn of mind would laugh at my narrative, and treat it as a nursery tale.

I was the more inclined to fear this apprehension might prove true, when I learned by experience that his curiosity was always guided by cool and just reasoning: His cheerfulness never exceeded the limits of moderated seriousness, and his smile was nothing more than an almost imperceptible unfolding of the wrinkles, which contracted his reverend brow; his mirth bore the resemblance of his carriage, and whoever knew him, trembled at his anger, though none of his acquaintances had ever experienced the least mark of passion in his countenance, and much less had he ever betrayed a symptom of unbridled wrath.

I let slip no opportunity of doing him some little services, and thus endeavoured to gain his favor; however, he appeared to take no notice of my unremitted zeal to please him. I treated him with marks of the highest veneration, whenever I was in his company, but he seemed not to regard it. All my most anxious endeavours to win that strange man over to my interest, proved abortive, and, at last, I gave over every hope of engaging his attention.

Chance befriended me, at length, unexpectedly, and I got by accident what I already had despaired to attain by the most indefatigable endeavours.

The inn where one of the recruiting officers lodged was reported to be haunted; many strange stories circulated on account of that report, which the then owner of the house endeavoured to laugh off, because he had lived a fortnight in it without perceiving any thing uncommon.

This subject afforded one evening matter for a serious discourse among the officers. The Austrian veteran maintained, contrary to our expectation, that one ought not to treat with ridicule some events of supernatural appearance, and no argument could make him relinquish his opinion. My heart panted for joy, for now I could hope that he would not refuse to credit my wonderous tale.

I was already going to relate the strange events which I had witnessed at the Haunted Castle, when I suddenly was checked by the apprehension of drawing upon me the laugh of the company, or that some one or other would offer to encounter with me the nightly sportsmen, without being equal to that hazardous undertaking.

The Austrian spoke with uncommon warmth, his eyes sparkled, and the wrinkles on his brow were contracting closer and closer, and when the company persisted in contradicting his opinion, he offered to enforce his arguments by undeniable facts, which he himself had experienced, requesting to be heard in profound silence, which could not but be granted to a man like him. We expected to hear something very uncommon, and for some time gazed at him in dumb expectation, 'till he at length began as follows:

"If I maintain that apparitions of supernatural beings ought not wholly to be rejected, then I must tell you, gentlemen, that I do not only mean that it is merely possible that departed souls, or supernatural beings of another class, can appear when and wherever they please; but I also promise to convince you by my own experience, that there are people who can affect apparitions of that kind, at certain times and under certain conditions."

We stared at each other in silent wonder: The preamble of the Austrian gave us reason to expect some horrid tale, and the seriousness of his looks and the solemn accent of his words commanded general awe. After a short pause, our solemn narrator related the following tale.

In a regiment of the garrison in which I served as Lieutenant, about twenty years ago, was a man, who gave the most undeniable proofs of the truth of my assertion: He was a serjeant, about forty years old, and of a morose and gloomy appearance; he was respected by his superiors, prompt and exact in the service, and never would brook an affront. The unthinking called him a sorcerer, and people of a more serious cast of mind talked of his connexion with superior beings, taking great care not to offend that terrible man, whose name was Volkert. In the whole he was a very good sort of a man, never offended any body, if not provoked, was averse to company, and fond of solitude.

He was reported to have performed many strange and wonderful exploits; an ensign, who had severely chastised him for a slight neglect in his duty, was said to have been deprived ever since of the proper use of his right arm; and a captain, who once had scolded him without reason, to be afflicted with a deficiency in his speaking organs, since that accident had happened: In short, strange things were every where related of Volkert, and in so serious a manner, that no impartial man would laugh at those reports.

I had not, as yet, had an opportunity of getting more nearly acquainted with that wonderful man, and I must confess, I was not very desirous of being introduced to him, for I always treated with scorn such supernatural events, yet I never liked to make those matters a subject of ridicule.

Some of my comrades were frequently inclined to have a fun, as they used to call it, and to request the sorcerer, Volkert, to raise up the ghost of one of their companions, who had died suddenly, in order to ask his departed spirit, whether he had found pretty girls and good wine in the other world; but I always dissuaded them from it, endeavouring to direct them to some other amusement:—Meanwhile the rumour of Volkert's exploits increased from day to day, and some people would swear solemnly, that they had seen and conversed with their departed relations, through his assistance.

Amongst those who related such strange things of Volkert, was a woman, whose husband had died suddenly some months ago, and entreated her, before he expired, not to give her daughter in marriage to a certain tradesman who had courted her. The girl doated on the young man, and he likewise was exceeding fond of her; the distress this young couple felt, at that sad and cruel prohibition, cannot be expressed by words; their grief was unspeakable when they were thus unexpectedly removed for ever from the happiness of being united by the bonds of holy wedlock, just when they flattered themselves to have reached the aim of their fondest wishes.

Volkert was quartered in the same street, where the unhappy girl's mother lived. She requested him to find out, by means of his supernatural skill, what reason might have induced her departed husband to forbid his daughter, on his death-bed, to marry the man of her choice, though he had not only never had the least objection against that union, but also had always looked upon it with the greatest satisfaction. Volkert promised to take the matter into consideration, and answered, some days after, that the deceased himself must be applied to.

The poor girl was very much frightened at this declaration, however, the hope of being at last united to the darling of her love-sick heart, revived her spirits, and she consented at length to suffer the rest of her parent to be disturbed. The mother refused for a considerable time to consent to it, however, at last she agreed to Volkert's proposal, and the day, or rather the night, for the execution of the conjuration was fixed.—The mother, added the Austrian, has related to me the whole transaction, and I will let her speak herself.

"It was on a Saturday," said the good old woman, "when we were assembled in a back room, the same wherein my late husband had breathed his last, myself, my daughter, her lover, and two of my neighbours being present; at eleven o'clock we began to sing, as Volkert had ordered us, penetential hymns and psalms 'till the clock struck twelve, when we left off singing and Volkert entered the room, clad in a white garment, barefoot, and with a pale and disordered countenance; under his arm he carried a black carpet, a naked sword, and a crucifix, and in each hand a lighted taper. As soon as he entered the room, he beckoned us to rise, and made a sign not to utter a word; then he placed a table in the middle of the room, covered it with the black carpet, and put the crucifix and the tapers upon it, holding the sword in his hand: This done, he took out of his pocket a bottle with consecrated water, and sprinkled us and the floor with it.—After we had pulled off our shoes and stockings, he burned perfumes in a chaffing-dish, and began the conjuration, mumbling many mysterious words, and brandishing his sword as if fighting with an invisible enemy; at once the combat seemed to cease, he grew quiet, and turning towards us who had been standing round him, exclaimed, "I have succeeded, he is coming!"

"A thick smoke overdarkened suddenly the room, the lights were extinguished, and a shiny figure, resembling in a most striking manner my deceased husband, appeared.

"Ask him," said the Necromancer, "ask him before he vanishes."

"I shuddered, seized with horror, and was unable to utter a single word: My daughter was in the same situation: The phantom gave us a ghastly look, shaking his head, as if denying something. The Necromancer exhorted us once more to ask the spectre, and one of my neighbours took courage to question him. "Who art thou?" asked he with a faltering voice. "Godfried Burger," answered the phantom, in a hollow woeful accent.

"May thy daughter marry Anthony Smith?"

"No! no!" replied the apparition, gave a deep hollow groan, and shook his head in a ghastly manner.

"Why not?" resumed my neighbour.

The phantom shuddered, lifting up his hands in a menacing manner, staggered back, and, when disappearing, added in a most rueful accent,

"He is her brother!"[1]

"Night surrounded us, the Necromancer pushed the window open, and the tapers began again to burn. Now I could breathe again, and looking anxiously around, beheld my poor child stretched on the floor in a fainting fit: The unhappy girl recovered soon, but, alas! her reason was gone. We were seized by the chilly hand of horror when we beheld her roving like a frantic person, wringing her hands, in a grisly manner, tearing her dishevelled hair, and beating her breast in an agony of despair. A burning fever had disordered her mind, and, alas! after three days she was no more! Wild despair drove her lover into the wide world, and heaven knows whether he is still alive, or has fallen a victim of his wretched fate. I am a poor disconsolate mother, and haunted by the agonizing pangs of a tormenting conscience, can find neither rest nor comfort here below; the spirit of my poor child, murdered, by my consent to that wicked infernal transaction, hovers constantly before my bewildered fancy; my peace is gone for ever; I dare not to pray to the supreme ruler of the world, for comfort and mercy, though he who dwelleth in heaven knows that I reluctantly consented to that wicked transaction, for no other reason but to promote the happiness of my murdered child, murdered by her own mother, who ought to have been her guardian angel! O! God of mercy, what! what will become of me, when I shall be called to the tribunal of the All-seeing! when I shall behold her standing before the Supreme Judge, and hear her accuse me in the face of heaven as her murderer? How shall I, how can I answer the stern questions of him, who has entrusted her to my care, to

---

[1] In his recent book *Queer Gothic*, George Haggerty refers to "erotic fear" as being one of the hallmarks of gothic fiction (22), which in this case plays upon the terror associated with incest. Horace Walpole's *The Castle of Otranto*, Ann Radcliffe's *The Italian*, and Matthew Lewis's *The Monk* capitalize on this erotic fear for their work, from which gothic imitators like Kahlert borrow and exploit.

watch with a mother's tenderness, over her life and happiness? I tremble, seized with chilly horror, when my frantic mind anticipates that awful moment, when he who sitteth on the throne of majesty shall, with the voice of thunder, say unto me, wretch! who hast cruelly murdered thy child, depart from me into everlasting fire, prepared for the devil and his angels!—Alas! I feel already within my breast, the worm that shall never die, and the fire that shall not be quenched."

Having thus given vent to her grief, she tore her hair in wild agony, beating her breast, and the tears of sorrow trickled down her cheeks—she appeared a grisly ghastly figure.

Her narrative, though incredible in the highest degree, made an unspeakable impression on me. I beheld the poor disconsolate mother, standing before me in an agony of unutterable grief; saw the briny tears of her who had with her own eyes witnessed the apparition, and heard her bemoan her unhappy child.

Having mused awhile on these dreadful events, I felt an ardent desire to unfold the mystery hanging over that wonderful transaction; or, if I should not succeed, to convince myself, by my own experience, of Volkert's supernatural skill.

I interrogated the woman about several circumstances, which had appeared to me rather suspicious; and asking her, at last, whether she had any reason to think that the lover of her daughter had really been a son of her deceased husband, she was prevented, by her tears and sobs from answering that question, I therefore dismissed her, with the firm resolution to make the strictest inquiries at her neighbours, which I did the same day, but all my endeavours to unfold that mysterious transaction proved abortive; they could tell me no more than what I had known already, repeating the unhappy widow's tale without any material alterations; I was left in the dark and found myself necessitated to check my ardent curiosity.

I now waited with impatience for an opportunity of witnessing Volkert's skill, being determined to be present if he should perform another transaction of that kind.

I went to him, requesting him to give me notice if he should happen to make a new experiment, and to admit me as a spectator: He hesitated not to give me his word, but seemed very little inclined to perform his promise, being terrified by the last transaction and its fatal consequences; the whole town talked of it, and the widow was sued at law on account of the death of her daughter. Volkert was prohibited by his general from making any farther experiments of that kind. He had not mentioned to me that interdiction of his commanding officer, yet I perceived that my request gave him some uneasiness, which I took for mistrust when I afterwards came to know that circumstance.

A few months after my application to him, a new accident happened, which gave him an opportunity to exhibit an astonishing proof of his supernatural skill, and tempted him forcibly to disregard the earnest prohibition of his general.

A friend of mine happened to fall out with a foreign officer, who had been visiting his parents, the foreigner challenged my friend, who most readily consented to decide the quarrel by the sword. Business of the greatest consequence obliged the foreigner to depart in the night preceding the morning on which the duel was to be fought—he wrote a note to my friend, promising upon his honor to appear at the appointed place on the ninth day, and my brother officer consented to the delay.

I and a few more officers of our regiment paid a visit to my friend who had been challenged, two days before the duel was to be fought; we were in high spirits, played, eat and drank amid the cheerful laughter of merriment, not recollecting, that after three days our host, perhaps, might be no more: He himself appeared to have entirely forgotten the quarrel, 'till he at last, at the close of our merriment, recollected the duel he was going to fight, telling me who was to be his second, to remind him the following day of his killing business, lest his valiant adversary, Captain T—, might wait in vain for him.

"Upon my soul," added he, heated with wine, "I wish he was here now, d—m me if I would not send him to Paradise, to rest in Abraham's bosom."

"Why, brother," exclaimed one of the visitors, "could you not have him summoned hither by Volkert?"

"That would indeed be excellent fun!" resumed my friend, "but you know Volkert dare not do it, we must of course let him alone; yet, if the rascal does not come the day after to-morrow, Volkert must be applied to, and, even if I should be obliged to ask the general's permission, he shall conjure him hither, that I may pierce his cowardly soul."

An unanimous bravo rewarded this unripe joke of our jovial host, we separated, and I went home, lost in profound meditation.—Having some reason to suspect that Baron T— would let us wait in vain, his departure having been so abrupt, I thought this would prove a fair opportunity of putting Volkert's supernatural power to the test. At last I resolved to wait quietly the issue of that affair, and if T— should give us the slip, to try whether I could be able to persuade Volkert to give us a sample of his skill.

Though I had unjustly doubted Baron T—'s courage, as it will appear in the sequel of my narrative, yet what we had suspected happened afterwards.

The day fixed for the duel came, but no Baron T— appeared: We waited for him six hours, and still he did not come. Now I hastened to Volkert without telling a syllable of my design to my friends: The mysterious man smiled as I entered the room, and appeared to have a little more confidence in my honesty than when I paid him my first visit. I broke the business to him without circumlocution, and he seemed not unwilling to chastise the foreign officer for his want of courage, yet he endeavoured to make me sensible of the disagreeable consequences which likely would arise, if the transaction should transpire. I summoned up all my little rhetoric, and refuted his objections, by assuring him, that my friends would give him their word of honor never to betray him, and thus screen him from every disagreeable consequence; and that, if an unforeseen accident should unhappily make the transaction known, our joint interference should save him from punishment.

These arguments, accompanied by golden encouragements, conquered at last all his remaining fear; he promised to serve me at any time, however he entreated me not to invite too great a number of friends, that the danger of detection might not be increased without need. Having promised to act according to his desire, I left him with the greatest satisfaction, and went directly to my disappointed friend, who was railing with much asperity against the cowardice of his adversary.

"What, brother," exclaimed I, "what will all this anger boot thee? It certainly will not give courage to Baron T—, and thou canst not be blamed on account of his ungentleman-like behaviour, having not challenged him. There are a great many who would be glad to sneak off so cheaply and yet so gloriously; you rather ought to pity the white-livered fellow, than to be angry with him, yet, if you like, we may hit him a blow when he least suspects it."

Not knowing whether my friend would approve my plan or not, I pronounced the last words in a jocose tone, to secure a fair retreat, in case he should not relish my proposal.

"How else," resumed I, "could one get at him, than by *forcing* him to wait on us? Didst thou not lately swear to have him conjured hither by Volkert, if he should give us the slip?"

My friend seemed at first to be offended, looking upon my proposal as an unseasonable joke; but when I went on talking of Volkert, and his occult arts, he asked me at last, "Seriously, friend, dost thou believe in the secret arts of that fellow?"

"I believe nothing," replied I, "what I have not seen; let us make a trial how far the common talk of his supernatural arts deserves being credited."

He stared at me with astonishment, asking me, after a short pause,

"Dost thou expect to prevail on that Necromancer to agree with our wishes?"

"What wouldst thou say," replied I, "if he had already consented to give us his assistance?"

My friend stared again at me, and exclaimed at last, with visible satisfaction,

"Well then, let us see what honest Volkert can do."

Every thing requisite for the accomplishment of our design was now talked over and settled. Two of our brother officers, whose discretion we could rely upon, were chosen to be of the party, and my friend agreed to win them over to our purpose.

I returned to Volkert, and was not a little surprised when I found him less willing than ever to assist us in our undertaking: He pretended to have pondered my proposal, but thought it too dangerous to exert his supernatural knowledge in the present case, because the conjuring of a living person could have the most dreadful consequences, which very likely might happen on the present occasion, because the Baron seemed not at all to be over-stocked with courage. Though I could not contradict him, yet I endeavoured once more to dispel his apprehensions, by the re-peated assurance to screen him, with the assistance of my friends, against every disagreeable consequence. At length he appeared to be easy in respect to that point; yet he did not think it convenient to execute our design in the apartment of my friend, but when I proposed my room, he consented, after many persuasions, to look at it. Having gained his consent, I left him with rapturous joy.

Volkert came the next day to my lodgings, faithful to his promise, but having looked over my apartments, he raised new objections, telling me that none of my rooms were fit for the un-dertaking. I could not conceal my displeasure, which he, however, did not seem to notice.

At last he made me another proposal before he left me, offer-ing to speak to an honest tradesman, who had an empty room, which would exactly fit his purpose, and, as he hoped, be at our service, if we would but make a reasonable acknowledgment to its owner. I consented to that proposal, Volkert went away, and returned after half an hour with the joyful tidings that he had pre-vailed on the man to let us have the room, fixing, at the same time, the ensuing night, for the execution of our design. He re-quested me to repair to the place of rendezvous after nine o'clock, describing the street and the house so minutely that I could not miss it. Having reminded me once more of my promise, he left my room, and I went out to tell my friend and our two associates to resort in good time, to the place of appointment. At eight o'clock they came to my apartment, burning with impatience to witness the mysterious transaction, and we hastened a quarter before nine o'clock, to the house where our curiosity was to be satisfied.

"I knew the owner of the room which Volkert had chosen, as a worthy, honest man: When we entered his house he accosted us with much good nature, requesting leave to be admitted to the experiment, which we the more readily consented to when he cautioned us to be on our guard against the cunning of Volkert, whom he very much suspected to be an artful impostor.

"I, for my part," added he, "have taken all possible care to prevent the Necromancer from imposing upon us, and I would lay any thing that we shall catch him in some foul play or other."

When we told him, that imposition would be impossible, because the gentleman who was to be summoned was still alive, he burst out into a loud laughter, requesting us to wait in his parlour 'till Volkert should call us up stairs.

"He will not be disturbed in his toilsome labour," added he, smiling, "and has made the whole evening such a tremendous noise, that one should think he had been hunting up and down the whole infernal crew of his satanic Majesty."

Time passed quickly on in the company of that queer good-natured man, who fetched two bottles of excellent old wine, bidding us to be of good cheer. The clock struck ten before we were aware of it, and as soon as the last stroke was heard, Volkert entered the parlour, holding a lighted taper in his hand, his looks were wild and ghastly, his face pale, and every muscle of his countenance distorted, as if some horrid accident had filled him with terror. Every smile of merriment took its flight as he entered the room, our jovial mood was checked at once, and our faces grew deadly wan, like his, bearing all the marks of secret awe. He beckoned us to follow him, and we obeyed his solemn command like machines, forgetting where we were.

He led the way, with tottering knees, in awful solemn silence, and we followed him with beating hearts, expecting to behold unheard and wondrous things. We stepped into a spacious room, in the back part of which we saw a little door, Volkert opened it, leading us through an empty narrow anti-chamber to a folding door; there he stopped, looking back with a ghastly boding aspect, and put the key in the lock—now he turned it slowly and carefully, the folding door flew suddenly open, a thick smoke broke from it, as we entered, and darkened at first all the objects around.

'Ere long, I observed in the back part of the spacious apartment a human figure clad in a white garment. The smoke evaporated by degrees through the open door, and the figure grew brighter and brighter, and, advancing a few steps towards it, I fancied to discern

some known lineaments. The smoke was now entirely evaporated, and the vision hovered clear and discernable before our gazing
looks; I shuddered back when I beheld the exact image of Baron
T— before me. His tall slender figure, clad in a white night gown,
struck our senses with awe, as he stood motionless before us—his
looks denoted a man in the agony of death, his long black hair covered partly his pallid woe-worn cheeks, floating in a grisly manner
down his shoulders.

The vision stared at me and my companions with a ghastly
rueful aspect, it made my blood congeal, thrilling my soul with
deadly horror; my hair rose up like bristles, and I staggered back
towards my friends, who were standing by the door like lifeless
statues, their faces wan, their looks bewildered—they resembled
midnight spectres, just risen from the yawning grave. I collected
all the small relics of courage, advancing again some paces towards the dreadful phantom, and saw the vision hovering nearer,
making some feeble signs with his left hand. I made an attempt to
speak, but what I said I do not know.—The phantom uttered not
a word, but was still making anxious signs with his left arm. Now
I understood what he meaned—the right arm hung in a sling as if
fractured.

As soon as I comprehended this pantomime, the phantom
staggered back, a dark mist arose from under his feet and surrounded the vision by degrees 'till we at last could see him no
more. I panted for breath, my senses forsook me, an horrid humming noise filled my ears, my eyes grew dim, I staggered to the
wall and was nearly fainting. At once I felt my senses returning,
and, opening my eyes, beheld myself in a spacious empty room,
my companions around me, panting for breath like myself—Volkert was no where to be seen.

It lasted a good while before we could entirely recover the
proper use of our benumbed senses. My comrades were chilled
with horror, and every one seemed to ask his neighbour, by his inquisitive looks, whether what our senses had witnessed had been
a deluding dream or reality.

The landlord was standing behind me, trembling like my
companions, with crossed arms and downcast looks, buried in
profound meditation, and exhibiting a woful picture of pallid

fright; at length he begged us to follow him down stairs, and we went into the parlour with dejected spirits, he offered us a dish of tea, but we refused staying any longer, gave him two louis d'ors, and left his house.

The next morning I awoke, wearied and dispirited, having had only a few moments of restless sleep. I expected Volkert would come to fetch his stipulated reward, but I was disappointed, and esteemed him higher for his seeming disinterestedness. At noon my friend who had been challenged paid me a visit.

"Brother," exclaimed he, as he entered the room, "tell me, what did the vision of last night mean by the anxious motion of his arm?"

"That his right arm was fractured," replied I hastily.

"There, read that letter," resumed he, throwing an open letter on the table; I took it up and read as follows:

"Sir,
        "An unhappy accident prevents me from fulfilling my promise, the day after to-morrow, having been thrown from my horse and fractured my right arm. However, as soon as I shall have sufficient strength to make a journey of twenty leagues, I shall insist upon your giving me satisfaction. I am fully persuaded that you would not suspect me of foul play, though I should not have sent you the inclosed certificate; yet, not to give you the least room to suspect my honor, and to screen yourself by mean sub-terfuges, I send you the inclosed certificate of our Surgeon-Major. Within six weeks at farthest I hope to recover the use of my right arm, by the skill of that honest man, 'till then I remain, without either spite or enmity,

Baron T—.
Signed with my left hand.

I gazed in dumb amazement at my friend, who was walking up and down the room with hasty steps, and in a pensive atti-tude.

"Well," exclaimed he at length, "what dost thou think of that letter? It was, as I suppose, only owing to the carelessness of the postman, that I received it so late. The certificate cannot be suspected, and I would have believed the Baron though he should not have sent it."

I remained silent, reading over again and again the letter of the unfortunate T—. The preceding night and the whole morning I had been wavering between doubt and belief, but now I was convinced of the Necromancer's skill, as I am still, and dreaded to see his face. At length I suffered myself to be persuaded by my friend to pay him a visit; he was not at home, and we went several times to his lodgings without seeing him, 'till we at last, on the third day, met him on the parade. I approached him, and my three fellow adventurers did the same, Volkert wanted to give us the slip, when he saw us coming towards him, however we came up with him, and with great difficulty persuaded him to come to my lodgings in the afternoon—having promised to meet us, he went instantly away with hasty steps.

At three o'clock he made his appearance. We shewed him the Baron's letter—having read it with apparent unconcern, he said, that he as well as ourselves had known the contents of it three days ago. We persuaded him with great difficulty to accept four louis d'ors for his trouble, and he promised to see us now and then, and to convince us of his warmest gratitude by every service in his power, if we would but promise him, on our word of honor, never to desire him any more to raise up ghosts.

"I have suffered very much," added he, "and I am determined to expose myself no more to like dangers: I am afraid some additional disaster awaits me. Baron T— is no poltroon, which I am glad of, but I fear, I fear lest—"

Here he stopped, taking up his hat; we asked for the reason of his apprehensions, entreating him to speak without reserve, but all was in vain, and he left the room with these words, "I wish all may end well."

We could not comprehend the meaning of these words, and did indeed not much mind them, my friend being quite unconcerned about the duel, which we thought Volkert had been hinting at.

Eight days were now elapsed without any disagreeable accident. None of us had spoken a word, as well of our adventure as of the duel, but on the ninth day we were reminded of it in a most terrible manner: My friend entered my apartment at a very early hour, with a pallid disordered countenance, flinging a folded letter on the table. I took it up, seized with terrible apprehensions, and saw that it was a second letter from Baron T—. "If you will give me leave, gentlemen, I will read it to you"—we all consented to it, and he read as follows.

"Sir,

"Having recovered my strength a little, I hasten to request you to acquaint me with the particulars of a dreadful accident, which you, without doubt, will be able to unfold.

"In the night succeeding the day which was fixed for our meeting, an accident happened to me which I cannot unriddle, and most willingly would suppose to have been nothing but the delusion of a disordered imagination; if not, many of my friends had witnessed the unspeakable sufferings I have endured. I was seized after eight o'clock in the evening, with an agony more terrible and excruciating than that of a dying person, expiring amid the most pungent horrors and torments of a violent death. Drops of cold sweat bedewed my face, a chilly trembling shook my limbs violently, and the leaden hue of death rendered my countenance wan. I hoped to find relief if I was to walk up and down the room; however I was seized by the burning fangs of still greater, still more agonizing pains, and the despondency preying on my bewildered fancy increased every minute. I shivered and trembled in such a manner that the chattering of my teeth could be heard at a great distance; all my muscles were contracted, by horrid convulsions; the pangs of excruciating agony increased for two hours of infernal torture, 'till at last, my friends despairing of my life, carried me to bed, there I lay for half an hour as if my spirit had been separated from my body, which really has been the case. I can give no better description of the last degree of my agonizing pains, than by comparing my feelings with the torments of one, whose whole frame suddenly is pierced with a red hot iron.

"After that terrible shock I was in a state of lethargy, but I dreamed an horrid frightful dream. Methought I was violently dragged away from my weeping friends, and, on a sudden beheld myself in the company of some known persons, who seemed to be highly delighted with my torments, and inflicted still greater pangs, on my woe-worn frame.

"Suddenly I recovered my recollection, to the utter astonishment of my afflicted friends, but I awoke in such a pitiful state of weakness, that every one present, and even the physician who attended me despaired of my recovery. They all are of opinion that my enemies must have effected those infernal torments by supernatural means, and I myself cannot think otherwise. You certainly must have some knowledge of that shameless horrid transaction, and it is you to whom I ought to apply for an explanation. I expect your answer by the returning mail. I repeat it once more, you must know the particulars of that infernal transaction, &c. &c."

"The impression this letter made on us," resumed the Austrian, "cannot be described. I read in the countenance of my friend the bitterest reproaches, for having seduced him to employ the infernal arts of Volkert to so shameless a purport."

The serious unhappy turn which this dark transaction began to take, made us apprehend that it would end with a most melancholy catastrophe, yet all our apprehensions were trifles light as air in comparison to the dreadful anxiety which poor Volkert was overwhelmed with, when these said tidings were reported to him. We now plainly comprehended the tendency of the mysterious words he had uttered, when we had seen him last—I never saw a man in a more distressing situation than he was as he perused the Baron's letter. His agony rendered him almost distracted, when he came to the conclusion of that melancholy epistle. He wrung his hands in wild despair, was beating his breast, and tearing his hair, exclaiming in an accent of unspeakable agony, "I am undone! I am undone!"

Then he fell on his knees, imploring us for God's sake to spare him, and to save him from ignominy and ruin. "I have foreseen it," groaned he, "I have foreseen it; O had I but that time not suffered myself to be deluded to lend an helping hand to that wicked infernal transaction!"

We did all that lay in our power to make him easy, and promised him to take all disagreeable consequences upon ourselves;

however, he would not listen to the comfort we administered to him.

"I am too much known," exclaimed he, and left us in wild despair.

I now consulted with my friend what was to be done, and we agreed at last that it would be best not to answer the Baron's letter, but quietly to await his arrival. Volkert, who was now more submissive and humble than ever, came frequently to see us, and approved our resolution; but he was always in the greatest anxiety when the idea of the Baron's arrival crossed his mind. Mean while the time when we were to expect the Baron drew nearer and nearer.

Six weeks were now nearly elapsed since we had received his last letter. One morning as I was reading, and smoking my pipe, with much tranquillity, my servant entered my room, telling me, a foreign officer desired to see me. Not suspecting that I should be the first person to whom the Baron would give notice of his being arrived, I was struck with surprise when I beheld Baron T— before me, and I cannot but confess that I was seized with horror, when I saw him. The marks of a recent dangerous illness were still visible on his pale countenance; his gloomy melancholy aspect strongly denoted the sufferings of a deeply afflicted mind, and his whole carriage horribly reminded me of the detestable dark transaction of that unhappy fatal night. He entered my room bowing silently, and began, after a portentous pause, to address me thus:

"Sir, you are the second of Mr C—, who has injured me in a most glaring and disgraceful manner; first, by having insulted me in public, and then by having employed infernal arts to torment me; I dare say you are no stranger to the horrid means your friend has made use of in order to let me feel his wrath: I will not publicly accuse your friend of that black shameless transaction, the dreadful effects of which you can still read in my countenance; however, he shall answer me with his heart's blood, for that ignominious transaction, and for the sufferings he has made me undergo. I have written to him, but he has not thought it proper to answer my letter, which is a certain proof of his having been concerned in that horrid deed, the reality of which I am now fully convinced of; I know every thing, even the wretch who has assisted in the per-

formance of that diabolical business. Do not ask me how I came to
know it."

He spoke this with such an emphasis, that I was unable to utter a single word in defence of my friend, and he appearing not to
expect any thing of that kind, added, after a short pause,

"My arm is not yet fit to manage the sword, for which reason I
request, he may bring with him two brace of pistols. You may tell
this your friend, I hope he will not oblige me to *force* him to accept
my terms. At seven o'clock next morning I shall be at the spot we
have appointed long ago, 'till then farewell, and tell your friend
that I have not waited on him, because he prefers to converse with
unbodied beings, and that I have written to him no more because
he has not thought proper to answer my last letter."

So saying, the Baron rose and left me in such perplexity, that I
was not able to utter a word in reply. My friend was not less frightened than myself, when I told him, his antagonist pretended to
know the whole of our secret transaction. The remainder of the
day was spent in preparations for the duel, and in settling all the
affairs of my friend, in case he should be killed.

Volkert came in the evening as usual, being afraid of being
known to have any connexion with us: He trembled violently
when we told him that the Baron was arrived, but understanding
that he would not make public the dreadful wrongs which he had
suffered, the poor fellow recovered from his fright, and offered to
assist the Lieutenant's servant who was scowering his master's pistols. This task was soon finished, the two braces of pistols cleaned
and charged with bullets.

We sat down conversing and drinking punch 'till midnight,
when Volkert left us with the promise to see my friend once more
next morning. He seemed little inclined to give us his opinion, on
the means by which the Baron could have got intelligence of the
conjuration, and the man who had performed it; yet he promised
to tell us next morning all he knew about it. I remained with my
friend the whole night, and began to sleep a little towards morning. At six o'clock Volkert interrupted our slumber, telling us that
he came to take leave of us.

We gazed at him with astonishment and surprise.

"Yes, gentlemen," exclaimed he, "I am going to leave this town, and I am very fortunate that I can do it in an honorable manner. I promised you last night, to tell you how Baron T— has traced out his tormentor; know then, that he has written to his family the same what he wrote to you in his second letter; his relations soon suspected me, being known here as a Necromancer these many years, they gave notice to the governor of the supposed transaction, and he bearing me a great regard, would not meddle with this affair; he has however requested my general to remove me to some other place, as soon as possible, which my commanding officer was very willing to grant. He sent for me the day before yesterday, and when I appeared before him accosted me thus:"

"Volkert, I have warned thee several times to practise no more thine infernal tricks, I expected thou wouldst shew some regard for thy General, but seeing that all my endeavours to recall thee to thy duty are fruitless, I must send thee away, yet do not fear that I shall be unkind to thee, I know thou art a clever fellow, and I will give thee a commission as recruiting officer, which employment, I suppose, will not be disagreeable to thee, because it will afford thee an opportunity to make a proper use of thy talents."

"My heart was ready to leap into my mouth for joy," added Volkert, "when I heard these welcome tidings, for this is the very situation I had been hankering after. Yesterday I received my instructions, my commission, and plenty of money, and I shall set off as soon as I shall have seen the decision of Mr C—'s affair, and begin my new employment with pleasure and vigour."

We were surprised to see the gloomy melancholic Volkert on a sudden so cheerful and merry, but he did not give us time to disclose our astonishment, taking an hasty leave:—Having wished success to my friend, he shook us heartily by the hand, and told us, that if Mr. C— should kill the Baron he expected him to join him on the road, adding,

"Perhaps I may then have a better opportunity to convince you of the love and high esteem I bear you." Having promised to see me once more after the duel, if possible, he left us; however I saw him no more. The hour fixed for the fight drew nearer and nearer. We now took an hasty breakfast and went to the appointed place where we found the Baron awaiting our arrival in company with a foreign officer his second. He was impatient to begin the combat directly, but I begged him to have patience, and to remove a little farther from the town, into the field, lest the report of their pistols might be heard by the sentinels on the ramparts. Though the young spark thought it needless to be over cautious, as he scornfully called it, he consented at last to my proposal, riding a good distance farther. We thanked him for his readiness to oblige us, and alighted.

The combatants were placed opposite each other, within the short distance of four paces. My friend fired first, but missed his antagonist; the Baron doing the same was not more successful; my friend fired a second time, but he missed his aim once more; Baron T—'s second ball grazed his antagonist's cheek; Lieutenant C— was vexed, and, seeing him take up the third pistol, with a trembling hand, I asked the foreigner whether he was satisfied; he shook silently his head, and my friend missed him again; the Baron returned the shot, and his ball entered the shoulder of C—: I entreated the foreigner to desist from farther animosities, however he would not listen to me, and turning with a malicious grin towards his second, he took the fourth pistol from his hand; my friend discharged his into the air, but the Baron, less generous, took his aim, and his ball whizzed through his antagonist's hat; then shaking my friend smiling by the hand, he mounted his horse, and rode in full speed to the town, accompanied by his second.

The Lieutenant grew fainter and fainter from the loss of blood, and all my endeavours to stop it were fruitless. At length my servant, whom I had sent to town, arrived with a coach and a surgeon, who declared that the wound was of no consequence, and, having dressed it, we conducted my friend to his apartments.

On our arrival we were told that the Baron with his second had been arrested as they had entered the town gate, but nobody could tell us who had been the informer. The auditor of the regiment made his appearance soon after, and examined me strictly, yet he assured me that we had nothing to fear, "It is known," added he, "that your friend has not been the aggressor."

When I begged him to tell me the name of that informer, he paused awhile and then replied,

"Well! I will tell you to whom you owe that kind service, he is no more here, it was Volkert, the noted Serjeant of Colonel R—'s regiment."

"Volkert?" exclaimed I, the words dying on my lips.

The auditor affirmed it and left me. I followed him to the door, inquiring whether Volkert had said any thing else.

"I don't think he has," replied he, "he departed this morning on the recruiting business, and before he left the town has told the governor, that a foreign officer, a notorious wrangler, had challenged Lieutenant C—, and that they were going to fight a duel this morning. The governor ordered a file of soldiers to arrest you, but they were too late. When Baron T— returned to town, he was arrested along with his second. That is all that I know of the matter."

I returned to my wounded friend in a pensive mood, not knowing what to think of Volkert's strange proceedings. I was inclined to look upon this step as a proof of his concern for my friend's safety, yet I could not conceive why he had not given earlier notice to the governor, having known the hour when the duel was to be fought.

The wound of my friend was not dangerous, and he was able to go abroad after the tenth day, when he went to the governor to make his submission. Having expected to be condemned at least to four weeks confinement, he was surprised when that gentleman, who was known to be very rigorous, dismissed him with a slight reprimand. Our general took not the least notice of the whole transaction, and Baron T— returned to his garrison after having been arrested four weeks. All our brother officers spoke highly of his noble behaviour, telling us, that he had rejected all the proposals of his relations to interfere in his behalf.

"However," added the Austrian, "I will not abuse your patience any longer, and here conclude my wonderful tale, thinking to have fully proved my paradoxical opinions, by the account I have given you of Volkert's experiment, and I thank you cordially for your kind attention to my long mysterious narrative; you will excuse my prolixity, having been desirous to give you a faithful account of that strange man. Although I am not able to clear up his character in a more satisfactory manner, yet I am convinced that you now will believe that spirits can appear to the eye of mortals."

Here he ended, seeming to care little what sensations his odd tale might have produced in the mind of his hearers. The serious tone in which he had been speaking, and the high respect we bore him, prevented us from making our observations on his tale; I, for my part, could not help thinking it very extraordinary and fabulous, yet I could not harbour the least mistrust in the narrator's veracity, in despite of the struggles of reason, being fully convinced of his honesty. My design of relating to him our adventures at the Haunted Castle began now to ripen, and I was determined to catch the first opportunity that should offer to impart to him my secret.

The other officers sat in dumb silence, seeming to ponder how to abide by their first opinion without opposing their reverend antagonist: "It is pity," one of them exclaimed at last, after a long solemn silence, "it is pity that Volkert is not present, for I am sure he would convince us also, by occular proofs, of a matter which bears such evident marks of impossibility, in the eye of the impartial friend of truth. I do not in the least suspect your veracity, being fully persuaded that you are convinced by your own experience of the reality of the strange incident you have related; yet you will not take it unkind if I assure you, that my reason will prevent me from becoming a convert to your opinions, until I shall have been an occular witness of an experiment of that kind."

The Austrian replied not a word to that speech, but rose and took up his hat in dumb silence.

"But, pray Sir," resumed another, "have you had no farther account of Volkert? Did he never return from his recruiting business."

"He is dead," replied the Austrian.

"Dead!" we repeated with one voice.

"He is," repeated the old veteran, coolly, "he met with a sad misfortune in the second year of his employment; ten of his best recruits gave him the slip, and, being called to an account for his negligence, he fell a victim of wild despair, blowing his brains out."

"A sad exit for a Necromancer," resumed he who had put the question to the Austrian.

"But a common one with gentlemen of that line," added another, rather forward.

The Austrian gave him a stern scornful look.

"I wish Volkert was still alive," said he who lodged at the haunted inn, "I wish he was still alive, he soon would restore tranquillity to the house of my landlord, and put a stop to the disagreeable talk that is rumoured about, and so hurtful to the poor man."

The Austrian made a silent bow to the company, and left the room. I followed him with hasty steps, and, coming up with him, accosted him respectfully. "You will excuse the liberty I am going to take, to request of you a private hearing, wishing to impart to you something."

"That I will hear to-morrow," interrupted he drily, and went away.

The night being far advanced I went to my lodging. I awoke with the first dawn of day, arose, and, having put on my cloaths, waited with impatience 'till it should strike eight o'clock, at which hour I intended to pay a visit to the Austrian. It was about five o'clock when I got up, and the seeming slow progress of time was very painful to me. At length the wished for hour arrived, and I went with hasty steps to the veteran's lodging. He received me as he was wont to do, with great kindness, giving me a pipe, and after I had lighted it he asked me, what my pleasure was: "Speak freely," added he kindly, "I am an honest man."

After some circumlocution I broke the matter to him, giving him a full account of our adventures at the Haunted Castle. He listened with great attention to my tale, and hinting, at the conclusion of it, that I wished he would assist me in unfolding that mysterious matter, he looked seriously at me without uttering a word. Having waited some time for his answer with anxious impatience, he rose, and walked up and down the room in profound meditation.

"Friend," said he at last, after a long and painful silence, "what reason have you to engage in that dangerous undertaking?"

"I have no other motive," replied I, "than to chastise the impostors, and to deliver my servant from their clutches."

He shook his head: "Are you certain," resumed he at length, after a short pause, "that your servant has not been associated with those nightly sportsmen."

I stared at him and replied, after having meditated awhile, "No, it is impossible, the fellow was too honest; and what motive—"

"You are right," interrupted he, "it cannot have been a preconcerted plan, for you have delivered yourself to the power of the spirits."

He walked again up and down the room in a pensive mood, and then exclaimed suddenly in a determined tone, "Well, I will be one of the party, and, if you like, we will set off instantly."

I eagerly accepted his proposal, and having put in readiness every thing necessary, we agreed to depart in the evening. He proposed to take one of his serjeants with him, and I resolved to do the same. I returned to my lodging against noon, highly pleased with my success, in order to prepare myself for a speedy departure.

We left F— at eight o'clock in the evening, nobody was privy to our design, and our serjeants fancied we were going on official business, wondering very much how recruiting officers in the service of two different princes, could act thus in concord: But on the road we undeceived them, and were much rejoiced that our hoary veterans did not dislike our enterprize.

Three days after our departure from F— we arrived within a small distance from the place of our destination, without having met with any sinister accident.

We were now on the skirts of the Black Forest but could see no village; the spot where the houses leading to the castle had began was deeply impressed on my memory: I shewed to my fellow traveller the rivulet, on the borders of which the old man had been sitting when we first had met him,—We looked about for the houses but we could find none. I did not know what to think of the matter.

Pursuing our route, we ascended a rising ground, gracious heaven! how was I shocked when I at once beheld an heap of ruins on the spot where the village had stood! We could still trace the marks of conflagration. In the back ground we saw only a few miserable huts left, and a little farther distant the castle presented itself to our view. We gazed at each other in dumb astonishment, and the Austrian alighted; I and our two hoary veterans did the same, and we climbed, after much difficulty, over the heap of ruins. As we approached the few remaining houses, the inhabitants came running towards us covered with rags, and exhibiting pale woe-worn countenances. I never beheld such an horrid picture of wretchedness and misery;—they wrung their hands, crying for alms, and wept bitterly.

Having distributed money amongst them, I inquired when that misfortune had happened. "Alas!" groaned they, "who should have thought, when your honor left us, that you ever would see us in such a miserable state? We all are ruined; all our little property has been consumed by the flames. Good heaven! how shall we keep our little helpless babes from starving."

Repeating my question, when that terrible accident had happened, the poor unfortunate people told me, their village had been set on fire the day after we had left them.

Dreadful apprehensions filled my soul, and the Austrian's looks seemed to confirm them.

When I inquired after my former host, I was told that he had lost his life in the flames. The fire, said the poor people, broke out suddenly, in different places, in the dead of night, they had not been able to save their property, and a great number of the inhabitants, with their cattle, had perished in the flames. This horrid tale made my blood run chill, being convinced that I had been the primary cause of that dreadful event.

As we entered one of the miserable huts, we were met by the lamentations of people half naked; they all recollected me, receiving me with hideous groans. All my money was not sufficient to comfort the unhappy sufferers, but I divided it willingly amongst them, feeling an inward pleasure in being able to ease at least their sufferings a little. The Austrian smiling at me, followed my example as far as the expences of our journey would admit.

At last I ventured to inquire after the Haunted Castle; the poor sufferers shuddered at the question, telling me, without reserve, that they did not doubt that the last visit we had paid to that abode of horror, had drawn upon them the dreadful ire of the revengeful spirits, which I in vain wished to be able to contradict. Unwilling to behold any longer the marks of sorrow and distress so deeply imprinted on the faces around me, and stung to the heart by the tormenting thought to have partly contributed, by my idle curiosity, to provoke the lurking tempest of woe, that had thus cruelly crushed the earthly happiness of the wretched villagers, I hastily inquired for the next village, they shewed us the way, and we bade them farewell with a bleeding heart, riding away in full speed.

But, alas! I could not escape the hideous spectre of self reproach, pursuing me with icy fangs: The scene of misery which my eyes had witnessed hovered constantly before my gloomy fancy, the groans of woe which I had heard still vibrated in my ears, the haggard looks of these unhappy people, undone by my heedlessness, stared me in the face ever and anon, and I struggled in vain to shake off the grisly spectre pursuing me with unrelenting resentment. "How comfortless and miserable is the man," said I to myself, "whom conscience accuses of having plunged into the gaping gulph of misery a fellow creature!"

The Austrian saw the painful workings of my soul, kindly striving to dispel the gloomy clouds hovering over my brow. "How can you accuse yourself," spoke the reverend veteran, "of having been, though involuntarily, accessary to the fatal blow that has thus cruelly destroyed the happiness of these people, whose fate you are bemoaning? It was the high decree of a superior power, that rules the fate of man. The ways of the all-wise are ever good and just, though surrounded sometimes with impenetrable darkness. Men are but tools in the hand of providence, and never ought to murmur against the father of the universe. It is not you who have destroyed the happiness of these poor sufferers; your heart is good, and you could not foresee the dreadful consequences of your juvenile rashness; cheer up, young man, and trust to the supreme ruler of all things, that he knows best what is good and fit, he produces light from the womb of darkness, and leads sometimes his children to greater bliss over the thorny path of misery and woe."

I listened with eager attention to the soothing speech of comfort flowing from the reverend lips of my sage companion, and an
heavy load was taken from my heart, when he had finished, the
clouds of gloominess dispersed by degrees, and a ray of cheerfulness darted through my mind. After half an hour's ride we beheld
a large village before us; we agreed to wait there the setting in of
night, and then to visit the Haunted Castle secretly.

Our host could not, or perhaps would not answer our inquiries concerning the desolated castle, and we endeavoured in vain
to know whether the nightly sportsmen were still housing there
or not; my serjeant went abroad to get some information, and was
so fortunate to draw from the schoolmaster of the village as much
as we wanted to know; returning after an hour with the corrobo-
ration of our suspicion, that the spirits residing at the castle had
set fire to the desolated village, and that they since that time had
forsaken their former abode.

Although the latter part of his intelligence gave us but little
hope that we should succeed in our design to unfold the mystery
of the ruinous castle, yet we determined to make at least a trial, the Austrian being very desirous to explore the noted building, and we went all four to the Haunted Castle as soon as it was
dark.

We arrived at the gloomy fabric after a short walk, lighted
some torches we had brought with us from F—, entered the court
yard, and ascended the spiral staircase; the Austrian searched every corner, and I found all the rooms in their former condition,
the seats and the table we had constructed were still as we had left
them, unmoved, untouched.

When the Austrian had carefully searched every thing, we
descended the stairs leading to the cellar, but found the iron door
strongly fastened as before. We entered the garden, searching and
prying around, 'till we at length espied the aperture of the cavern
through which we had effected our escape from the grisly jaws of
a lingering death. The hollow sound of our footsteps re-echoed
horribly through the dreary subterraneous abode as we entered,
and the light of our torches reflected grisly from the damp mossy
walls of the deep and narrow passage.

Stepping into the ruinous stable, we espied with pleasure the hole in the boards through which the Baron had fallen down, and detected in one of the corners a ladder, and above the place where it was standing, a trap-door. Having ascended the ladder I opened the half-decayed door, with one violent push, and entered with my fellow adventurers the well-known spacious apartment, leaping over the gaping opening where the boards had given way. Looking around we beheld several small iron doors, one of which flew open at the first push of the Austrian, and presented to our eyes the avenue of a damp arched vault, from which a stone staircase led to that part of the fabric which faced the cellar door.

Without stopping there, we pursued our way to the large folding door leading to the great hall under ground, but found it strongly bolted on the inside, and all our hopes of farther discovery were blasted at once. We made the utmost efforts to disengage the massy door from its rusty hinges, but all our labour was lost, its strength proved superior to our united endeavours of forcing it.

While we were standing before that door, consulting whether we should go back or not, we heard suddenly a distant noise, as if a lock was opening, and soon after a folding door seemed to fly open, with an hideous creaking, which instantly was followed by a terrible noise of numerous steps, as if people in boots were descending: When the noise drew nearer we could distinguish the clattering of many spurs, and the harsh voices of men; the whole subterraneous cavern was at length filled with a most tremendous noise, and we gazed at each other rather pleased than frightened, being four vigorous men, used to danger, provided with four cutlasses and as many brace of double barrelled pistols. The Austrian standing nearest to the door, retained his equanimity unimpaired, and, ere long, an hollow voice like the distant rolling of thunder, exclaimed, "Come hither with the booty." A confused bustle ensued, the tinkling of money was heard, some quarrelled and some cursed and scolded, but were soon reconciled. At length the bustle ceased, a door was opened close by us, and money locked up in a chest. Mean while the following discourse took place in the unknown assembly.

First Voice. "To-morrow we will way-lay the gentlemen of Norrinberg, and ease them of their golden burthen. I trust you will behave like men, my jolly boys! It would be pity if they should give us the slip once more."

Second Voice. "By holy Peter! they shall not escape."

Many voices. "They shall not, they shall not."

Third Voice. "I wonder where our grey-beard may stay so long, I have not seen his holy face since our last fun."

Fourth Voice. "Take my word, brother, he sits by the fire side and chaunts penitential hymns. The fellow is of no farther use to our community, we must send him to the devil."

First Voice. "Let him alone, my boys, he has rendered us many good services, has saved many of our brave companions from the hangman's ruthless fangs; don't grudge him a little rest, he will soon return and bring us joyful tidings."

Second Voice. "He has procured us many a golden booty; has, by his cunning, extricated us from many neck-breaking difficulties; it would be ungrateful to be angry with him. What would become of our noble band if he did not guide our arm by his sage counsels?"

Third Voice. "Bravely spoken, my lad, he is a good sort of a fellow, it is a thousand pities that he begins to grow old and infirm."

First Voice. "Let him grow old and infirm, if he but escapes the gallows."

Here somebody was locking the door of an adjoining room, an hollow bustle and humming ensued, and the robbers (for such they must have been) were going to withdraw.

"Shall we break in upon the scoundrels?" whispered the Austrian to me.

"By what means?" replied I, shrugging up my shoulders.

"Through the garden, or the adjoining wing of the castle," resumed he.

"But the danger," said I.

"Is not so great as you fancy," interrupted the Austrian, "yet it will be better to force the gentlemen to open the door; if they should refuse to do it, then it will be time enough to surprise them in the court-yard, for I do not think it prudent to venture on the staircase, because they would then have too much advantage over us."

Now all was silent in the cellar, 'till after a short pause a new conversation began.

First Voice. "I say, brother, what shall we do with the officer's servant we have entrapt? The dog is good for nothing, and we are in danger that he will betray us one time or other."

Second Voice. "Let us knock his brains out."

Third Voice. "Let us give him his liberty."

Fourth Voice. "Or sell him to a recruiting officer."

First Voice. "We will take thy advice, brother Rasch, and set him at liberty. If his master has saved his life, the servant may share the same fortune with him; but first the blockhead shall swear a terrible oath never to betray us, else I will break his rascally neck."

Many Voices. "Well spoken, Captain, let us break the scoundrel's neck, if he refuses to swear."

Now we heard them ascend the staircase with a terrible noise, and instantly the Austrian knocked with his hands and feet against the door; a momentary silence ensued.

"Open the door ye miscreants!" roared my friend with a thundering voice. "Open the door, ye rascals," exclaimed I and my fellow adventurers, but before the hollow sound of our voices had ceased re-echoing through the vaulted passage where we were standing, the whole crew was running up stairs with a tremendous noise, and we hurried with all possible speed through the long winding passage, our pistols cocked, but before we could reach the end of the subterraneous avenue, we heard the trampling of horses, which soon was dying away at a distance. A gust of wind had extinguished our torches, but the light of the moon was shining so clear that we soon beheld an opening in the garden wall leading to the field, where we could see at a small distance, a numerous troop of horsemen galloping away at a furious rate. On our return we observed that the horsemen had taken their flight through the garden, which appeared to have been their common in and out-let since the burning down of the village.

I left the residence of these robbers very much dissatisfied; the Austrian, on the contrary, was highly pleased, representing to me that we should not know much more of the matter than we had heard, even if we had surprised them; that I did wrong if I complained of having been disappointed, being now informed of my servant's fate, and the mystery of the castle; and that every wish of taking personal vengeance on these miscreants was not becoming men like ourselves, because the hangman would have been defrauded of his perquisites if we had killed some of them.

"All what we could do," added he, "would be to give notice of what we have seen and heard to the magistrates of the next town; but I fear the gang is too numerous than that they could be taken prisoners besides, they will take care not to suffer themselves to be entraped; and if the magistrates were to take cognizance of our denunciation, and should fail in their attempt to destroy the whole crew, they perhaps would be made a second example of the revengeful daring spirit of these lawless wretches, and pay dearly for having enacted the laws against them. Remember the agony of grief you felt when you beheld the horrid consequences of opposition against these outlaws, in viewing the ruins of the village which but lately has fallen a victim to their cruel resentment, and then tell me whether it is advisable to inform against them? We had better leave their punishment to that supreme Judge who certainly will overtake them with his vengeance when their measure shall be full."

I returned to our inn at the next village, comforted by the seasonable reasoning of my worthy friend, and I never shall forget the wise instructions he gave me on the way; I never shall forget his tender exhortations to take care not to follow the first impulse of the moment, but always to listen attentively to the voice of reason before I should engage in any undertaking, and to bridle the youthful ardour of heedlessness by prudence and cool reflection.

We entered our inn at two o'clock in the morning, and we were met by the landlord, who had been very uneasy at our staying away so long, because many murders had been committed lately within the environs of the village. We told him we had taken a walk, but having missed our way, had strayed about 'till the dawn of day had assisted us in finding our way back. He appeared to believe our words and we went to rest.

We awoke at eight o'clock, and departed at nine for F—, where our absence had not been much taken notice of, those secret journeys being very common among recruiting officers; yet some of my friends puzzled themselves very much, by various conjectures, about the reasons of my connexion with the Austrian; but neither we nor our trusty serjeants communicated our adventures to any one of our acquaintance.

During our absence a strange accident had happened to one of our comrades, which had made every one wish for the return of the Austrian, and no sooner were we arrived, before all the officers repaired to my room to inform us of it.

The officer who lodged at the haunted inn, coming home against midnight three days ago, sat down to finish a letter to his colonel. As soon as it had struck twelve o'clock he heard a tremendous rap at the door, which he did not mind at first, but continued writing. A second rap, more violent than the first, disturbed him soon after, but he still took little notice of it. A third, not unlike a clap of thunder, ensued, after a short pause, the door of his apartment flew open, and a white figure was going to enter the room.

"Fearless," these are his own words, "did I start up, unsheath my sword and run towards the phantom; it retreated, but I pursued, and pierced it with my sword, it gave an hollow scream, but what further happened I cannot tell; I awoke as if from a deluding dream, and was lying stretched on the floor at the bottom of the stairs, surrounded by a great number of people with lighted candles; terrible pains had seized me, and my sword was still in my hand."

When the narrator had finished his wonderful tale, I perceived visible marks of its authenticity on his face, and inquired whether he had been hurt by the fall. He told me he had suffered no material injury except a few bruises.

The Austrian began now to question him.

"Have you perceived any thing uncommon before that strange accident happened?"

Officer. "Nothing at all except an insignificant noise, after twelve o'clock."

Austrian. "Have you, perhaps, before you met with that misfortune, been thinking on my tale of Volkert's exploits?"

Officer. (Vexed.) "I was writing to my Colonel, how could I therefore think on that fellow? Or do you think it impossible that any one besides you can experience things, the possibility of which you have proved by facts."

The Austrian, apparently lost in profound meditation, gave him no answer, but was walking up and down in solemn silence.

Our companions acquainted us now with the purport of their visit, signifying a desire to encounter the kingdom of spirits and hobgoblins in pleno corpore, under the command of my serious friend. Thinking the old veteran would relish their proposal as little as myself, I thought it would be agreeable to him, if I could prevail on the spirited sons of Mars not to urge the matter farther; addressing them in a jocose manner.

"Gentlemen, it seems you do not consider that these airy disturbers of nocturnal rest are not fond of large companies; or do you suppose the apparition, which I suspect to be a female one, a second Semiramis."[1]

However, it was in vain to attempt persuading them to drop the adventure, their imagination having been heated too much by the Austrian's tale, as that they would give up their design: Turning their backs against me, highly displeased with my harangue, they solicited my friend with the greatest impetuosity to comply with their request. He inquired whether Lieutenant N— was still an inhabitant of the haunted inn, and being told that the valiant son of Mars had removed to another lodging the next morning after the nocturnal rencounter, he refused flatly to yield to their entreaties, telling them, he was sure the apparition would give them the slip.

"Well, well," exclaimed the undaunted warriors, "we will run the risk and watch the ghost, though we should sit up ten nights for it; we are determined to unfold that mystery."

So saying they left the room in great hurry.

"What do you think of the matter?" said I, when the visitors had left us.

"Nothing," replied he, with much sang froid, shrugging up his shoulders.

---

[1] Semiramis is the legendary queen of Assyria, who reportedly created the Hanging Gardens of Babylon.

"But the ghost," said I.

"Is an offspring of their childish fancy," replied the Austrian.

"The fall of Lieutenant N—," asked I.

"Is very natural," replied the Austrian, "I could cite you more than hundred incidents corroborating the truth, that people have a very confused idea when their senses are tied up by fear and anxiety.—As soon as cool reflection gives way to the horrors of a disordered fancy, we are but too apt to create phantoms and spectres around us, we do not see what really exists, but what we fear to behold."

I could oppose nothing to this reasoning of his, founded so strongly on experience, and suspected the courage of our valiant Lieutenant very much, having no doubt but his fear had made him miss the staircase; I therefore took no farther notice of our bravado and his companions, not caring what would be the finale of their trifling adventure. My friend was likewise quite unconcerned about the matter, and, without mentioning it any farther, we went about our business.

When night invited us to rest from the toils of the day, we dedicated the remaining hours to the mutual enjoyment of hallowed friendship's cheerful bliss.

Eight days of peaceful happiness were now elapsed, when Lieutenant N— entered my apartment one morning, with a countenance exhibiting the strongest marks of horror.

"I come to you," said he, "because I apprehend a second refusal from your friend, if you do not support my request."

Asking him whether he intended to apply once more to my friend to encounter the ghost, he replied, it was his intention to try his fortune once more with my obstinate friend.

"Then you must excuse me," exclaimed I, peevishly.

Having stared at me awhile in profound silence, he began walking up and down the room, and at last seated himself by my side, resuming, in a cool and tranquil tone, "Hear what I am going to say, before you refuse to intercede with your friend, and I will acknowledge myself to be unworthy of your confidence if you persist any longer in your resolution, not to speak in my behalf to your worthy friend."

The solemn awful manner in which he pronounced the last words engaged my attention, and made me apprehend to hear a tale of horror. Having moved my chair closer to his he went on.

"You know what I and my friends intended to do, we have executed our design: All our efforts to make the ghost appear proved abortive at first; in vain did we watch, make a noise, search every corner of the house, and try to provoke the spirit for three nights, we could neither hear nor see any thing uncommon."

I was going to interrupt him, and to argue the imprudence of their proceedings, but he squeezed my hand gently, and begged me not to interrupt his narrative.

"The fourth night appeared," thus he continued after an awful pause, "it still makes my blood freeze when I recollect the horrible scene of terror my eye beheld in that night of dreadful note. We all repaired to the abode of that airy disturber of the stillness of night, taking our residence in a lonely hall, in the second story, within a small distance from my former apartment. We sat down to the inviting punch bowl after eleven o'clock, as we had done the preceding nights, filling our pipes and cursing the cowardice of the spectre, seemingly afraid of meeting an assembly of hardy soldiers; but it took ample vengeance on our forwardness, in so horrid a manner, that one must have been an eyewitness of its ire, if one will form a just idea of our situation.

"Our impatience increased as the punch began to heat our blood, we took the candles from the table, unsheathed our swords, and began to search every corner of the house and the cellar without success. My friends looked gloomy, the clouds of dissatisfaction were hovering over their brows, and a storm was gathering, which perhaps would have ended in a serious quarrel, if it had not been for the Austrian's tale, which, as yet, had sheltered me against their boiling anger, and from the suspicion of being an impostor or a coward. They began ridiculing the landlord and myself on account of our self-created fright, as they called it, declaring, all we had heard and seen to be a mere phantom, the offspring of a deluded fancy; however they were soon convinced of the truth of our narration, in a most shocking manner.

"We were ascending the staircase, and the foremost had not yet reached the last step, when a sudden hollow noise arose. It was not unlike the howling of the tempest rushing through the chinks of an old ruinous building. The noise carried something frightful with it, which cannot be expressed by words. My hair rose up like bristles, an irresistible horror made my blood run chill, and my ridiculing friends became as serious as if a magic wand had touched them, gazing at each other in dumb astonishment. The dismal noise continued a few seconds, and then every thing was as silent as the grave.

"We pursued our way to the hall, and retook our seats, wondering what could have caused that dreadful howling, and one of the company opened the window to see whether a tempest had gathered in the air, but the sky was clear, and not the least wind blowing. Sensations of unspeakable awe thrilled our souls, the fumes of punch evaporated, and solemn stillness swayed all around; nothing was heard save the violent palpitations of the heart, the chattering of our poor landlord's teeth, and the knocking together of his trembling knees.

"A few moments more of profound silence, and then the dismal howling arose again with redoubled force; a sudden violent gust of wind threw the windows open, and the door from its hinges, extinguishing all the candles; a tremendous clap of thunder shook the house, a terrible flash of lightning hissed through the room, and prostrated us to the ground; an hideous lamenting noise assailed our ears, and lifting up my head I beheld the phantom that once had frightened me, advancing with a threatening grin; grisly was its shape, and its eyes rolling like two flaming comets.

"I was the first who recovered the use of his senses, and, calling in vain for the landlord, my companions started up, and we found the poor fellow prostrated on the floor, half frantic with terror. At length he also recovered a little from his fright, and after many persuasions, ventured down stairs, accompanied by me, to strike a light. Every body in the house was snoring, except our crest-fallen fellow adventurers, who exhibited a rueful ghastly group, being all as pale as ashes. Looking at our watches, we saw it was past two o'clock, sat an hour longer without perceiving any thing farther, and returned against morning to our respective lodgings."

Here he stopped, but as it seemed only to draw breath for a longer narrative, I omitted giving any opinion, expecting that he was going to unfold the mystery, but his tale took such an unexpected turn, that I felt myself soon warmly interested.

"I would not," resumed he, "have troubled you with an account of this strange incident, if not, an accident was connected with it, which has happened last night.

"My recruiting business having called me abroad yesterday, I returned in the afternoon; in the dusk of evening I entered a thicket, in a gloomy pensive mood, all around was lonely, and buried in profound silence; no sound was heard except the dismal dirge of the screech-owl, and the shrill chirping of the amorous cricket.[1] At length I heard a whispering within a small distance, and cocking one of my pistols, I rode on with the greatest circumspection. At once I saw a manly figure coming out of the thicket, but could not distinguish his dress; advancing a little farther, I beheld somebody in a peasant's garb, walking on briskly and talking to himself. As I came up with him I observed a black wallet on his back, and a thick branch of a tree in his hand, serving him instead of a walking cane. He seemed to take no notice of me, pursuing his way with hasty steps, and still muttering between his teeth. I saluted him but he gave me no answer.

"Whither art thou going, good friend," exclaimed I.

"To men!" replied he, to my utter astonishment.

"Very likely to F—," resumed I.

"Yes," said he, "there are men."

"Supposing him to be a lunatic, I passed him, pursuing my way in a brisk trot; when I came out of the thicket I saw that I was nearer the town than I thought, and made my horse quicken his pace; but how was I astonished, when I beheld again the same figure walking before me.

"Old gentleman," exclaimed I, "it seems thou knowest the road better than I do."

"I think so myself," answered he dryly, "and I believe I know many things better than you do."

"Strange being," resumed I, "who art thou?"

"A friend of wisdom!" was his answer.

---

[1] The *chirping of the cricket* is a noise which the male one makes with his wings, in order to attract the attention of the female. *Vide* Goetze Ueber Natur Menschenleben und Vorsehung. [Author's note.]

"Thy wisdom," replied I, "must be as odd as thyself! But pray what dost thou call wisdom?"

"What you do not understand," was his reply.

Hearing the words friend of wisdom, I was suddenly struck with a suspicion which my readers will easily be able to guess, and that suspicion was strengthened when the narrator informed me of his definition of wisdom. I strongly suspected that he was the same person I had met in the Black Forest, under the garb of a pilgrim, and I hardly could refrain from exclaiming, art thou here, impostor?

Every one may guess the conclusion of the Lieutenant's wonderful tale, I scarcely had patience to await it: The narrator being highly charmed with the hoary juggler, could not find words to express the sensations his reverend aspect had raised within his breast. He had fancied to be in company with a robust countryman, but when he entered his house in the suburbs, to which he kindly had invited him, he beheld the countenance of an old man with silver hair, and a mien exciting awful respect. He offered him a glass of excellent wine, and began by degrees to become more cheerful and communicative.

The old man's conversation on the road having betrayed a high degree of occult knowledge, had very nearly tempted the Lieutenant to communicate to him his adventure at the haunted inn; that temptation returning now with redoubled force, he could no longer resist, and told him every thing that had happened. The result of the ensuing conversation was, that he entreated the old man to come and conjure up the apparition, to which he, after many seeming struggles at last consented, under the condition that no more than six persons should be present, and the landlord's leave could be obtained. The Lieutenant left him in high spirits, after having promised to fulfil strictly these two conditions.

I could not bridle any longer my ardent desire to hasten to the Austrian and to get rid of my visitor, who now became exceeding troublesome to me, being tired of his overstrained encomiums on the old deceiver, I therefore, anticipating the renewal of his request to speak to my friend, promised that I not only would engage to persuade him to assist at the conjuration, which was to be performed the ensuing night, but I also assured him, that I myself would be present.

The Lieutenant's raptures exceeded all bounds, he almost stifled me by his embraces, and called me more than hundred times his kind benefactor, and his dear obliging friend. I was however entirely indifferent to his raptures and endearments, pondering how I might best confound the vile dissembler, and put a final stop to his enormous cheats. I begged the poor hood-winked Lieutenant to give me leave to go directly to my friend, and to win him over to our party, which he instantly did, after having fixed an hour in the afternoon, when he would wait on me to hear how far I should have succeeded with the Austrian.

"Mean while," added he, "I will go to the owner of the haunted inn, in order to talk the business over with him, and to engage three able assistants more from among our friends."

Not finding the old veteran at home I was vexed very much, but when dinner time came, I had the pleasure of meeting him. The recapitulation of Lieutenant N—'s account of his late adventure at the inn, and his conversation with the hoary juggler, produced the desired effect. Though a man like him, who was of a cool temper, and never suffered his passion to get the better of his reason, could not be seized with a fit of amazement, yet I never saw him so violently agitated.

Having with apparent emotion awaited the conclusion of my tale, he exclaimed at last, after a short pause, during which his desire for vengeance and punishment seemed to struggle with his reflection and prudence,

"Friend, what do you intend to do?"

"To seize the Necromancer."

"Before or after the conjuration?" asked the Austrian.

"After it," replied I.

Now the dinner bell rang, and he left me, with the promise to repair at night to the place of action.

Having accustomed myself by degrees to examine minutely what likeliest might be the result of my noble friend's almost unfathomable considerations, before I determined on any thing he was concerned in; I succeeded sometimes in my anxious endeavours to act in unison with his principles, and to coincide with his ideas, but in the present case I was quite at a loss how to proceed conformable to his wish, having not the least clue by which I could expect to extricate myself out of the labyrinths into which he had led me, leaving every thing to myself.

However, after much reflection, I was at last so fortunate to hit upon a plan which he fully approved, proposing to conceal myself 'till the whole transaction should be finished, and then to rush like lightning upon the hoary deceiver, to upbraid him with his glaring cheats, to force him to a confession of the dark fraudulent means he had employed to play that infernal trick upon us, when he left us in the lurch in the cellar of the Haunted Castle, and then to make him a prisoner without farther ceremony.

We both agreed to deliver him up to the civil power, after having convicted him of his roguery, and to order four stout corporals to rush into the room at the first signal, in order to arrest the shameless cunning deceiver. Flattering ourselves with hopes of good success, we parted, after a mutual promise to repair to the place of action at eleven o'clock.

Lieutenant N— came to my lodging at three o'clock in the afternoon, to inform me that everything was ready for the performance of our nocturnal adventure. The landlord had made no difficulty to give his consent to the conjuration, and was desirous to be admitted one of the spectators, being elated with the hope that his house soon would be cleared of that troublesome being which had, 'till now, banished all his customers, and very much impaired his circumstances. He knew the reverend Necromancer, as the Lieutenant was pleased to call him, and was in raptures that the honest old man was returned to F—, and had consented to restore the tranquillity of his house, exclaiming,

"Now I am easy; Father Francis is the very man! It is a thousand pities that he visits these parts so seldom, and that he, if present, buries himself in solitude."

"He could not tell me precisely," added the Lieutenant, "how the old man employs his time, because nobody was on an intimate footing with him, nor could any one tell where he came from, or whither he was travelling so often, but that it was universally known that he possessed houses in most of the adjacent towns,

where he was living in the same retired and harmless manner as
here."

The Lieutenant, highly pleased when I told him, that the Austrian had consented to be present at our nocturnal meeting, went
now to the other associates, in order to settle every thing, and
invited myself and my friend to supper, which I readily consented
to.

END OF VOLUME ONE.

THE NECROMANCER

VOLUME II

THE NECROMANCER.

PART III.

Having shifted my clothes, that the old deceiver might not know me so easily, I went to the Austrian, whom I, without difficulty, persuaded to sup with me at Lieutenant N——'s. We repeated our orders to our trusty corporals and left the house.

Strange sensations occupied my mind, spreading a gloom over my countenance:—The expectation of seeing something extraordinary and wonderful thrilled my soul with awe, and an unaccountable chill trembled through my limbs; perhaps it was the effect of a foreboding of my approaching separation from my ever beloved friend, who appeared as cool and unconcerned as ever. When he saw me so silent and gloomy, he said, "So solemn, my friend, it seems you wish very little for your old acquaintance."

"It is no pleasant task to unmask an impostor," said I.

"But an useful one," answered he, taking me under the arm, and relating to me his transactions of the day.

This being quite out of his usual way, I could not mistake his intention, and endeavoured to appear cheerful, in which painful task I succeeded at length; however there was still lurking in my soul an awful strange sensation, quite foreign to my character, tho' the latter had been tinged with a sullen hue since I had frequented the company of my new friend.

When we came to Lieutenant N——'s apartment, we met two of his most intimate friends, who had been present at the late alarming apparition of the ghost, and were determined to engage the spectre once more.

They all were rejoiced at the Austrian's coming, and soon began to recount the terrible visitation of the ghost, and the anxiety they had suffered, which they did in a most prolix and tedious manner. The Austrian begged to talk of something else, and not to deprive themselves of the necessary firmness of mind by the recollection of what was past; he at the same time endeavoured to give the conversation a more cheerful turn, and I cannot but confess, that he never had been so amusing and pleasing since I had known him.

The cloth being laid we sat down to supper, but none of us did honor to the meal except the Austrian; the wine promised to dispel the clouds of gloominess from our circle; however our host plied us in vain with bumpers, the heart-elevating juice of the grape could not raise our crest-fallen spirits, and the Austrian was the only one who relished it, and experienced "its powers divine".

The farther the night advanced the lower our spirits sunk, in despite of my friend's endeavours to spread the glow of merriment around and to encourage us to join him heartily in his libations. Though he sounded the praise of the wine's excellence, by words and deeds, yet he kept within the bounds of soberness, and when it struck eleven o'clock, bade us drink a final bumper to good success, and then took up his hat and sword.

I did the same, and our companions followed our example with fear and trembling. We went down stairs in solemn taciturnity, and groped our way through midnight darkness to the Haunted Inn.

The master of the house welcomed us most cordially, thanking us beforehand for the expected tranquillity of his house and the return of his prosperity—he led us to the hall where the above mentioned dreadful apparition had appeared, enlarging with indefatigable garrulity, on many horrible incidents which had taken place, within the space of a twelvemonth, in that disastrous apartment.

The Austrian uttered not a word, but searched closely every corner of the spacious lonely room, and then took up a candle and went out. Having been absent a good while, he returned at length, pulled his great coat off, and entered into a long conversation with the master of the house, asking him many different questions, which betrayed his diffidence in the poor fellow's honesty. I was not much pleased with his unequivocal marks of suspicion, knowing the inn-keeper as an upright honest man, void of disguise and art, and that he himself had suffered the most glaring damages by those nocturnal apparitions: His inn had been unfrequented by travellers these many months, on account of that sleep-disturbing phantom, which haunted the weary wanderer in the dead of night, and he swore, by every thing holy and sacred, that he had never seen Father Francis, (so he called the hoary deceiver) though he had heard of many marvellous deeds perpetrated by that wonderful man.

"It is now," added he, "a good while since I have heard of that sagacious old man, they say he is gone to a distant place, offended at the ingratitude of the people of our country: Formerly he has told the people's fortunes, but without fee. My father, the late possessor of this house, has told me many marvellous instances of his astonishing skill in detecting thefts, and recovering stolen goods; as how he has been possessed of a wonderful sagacity to read in people's looks, at first sight, whatever they had done all their life long; discovered and solved the spell of witchcraft, and horribly punished the old hags that dared to bewitch the countrymen's cattle. In short, said my father, God rest his honest soul, Father Francis has indeed been a father and a friend to every one in distress, and a baneful foe to the Black Spirit and his infernal hosts."

The Austrian appearing still to harbour thoughts of suspicion against the simple inn-keeper, watched closely all his motions, was always at his heels when he left the room, and ever busy to ply him with various questions. I and my companions kept close together, myself burning with desire for the beginning of the drama, and my fellow adventurers awaiting it with fear and trembling.

It struck twelve when the innkeeper was still in close conversation with the circumspect Austrian. The door opened, and father Francis entered the room; the sight of the hoary deceiver made my blood boil in my veins, and I clapt my hand involuntarily to my sword; the Austrian, who was standing at a small distance from me, hiding a part of his face under his hat, and holding a brace of pistols in his hands, seemed to ask me by a side glance, whether Father Francis and my old acquaintance in the Black Forest was one and the same person. I affirmed it by a quick motion of my eyelids, and the Austrian turned his back to the Necromancer; I removed behind Lieutenant N—, and peeping over his shoulders, watched the proceedings of the juggler, who advanced with solemn steps into the middle of the apartment, where he stopped, resting his inquisitive looks on the countenances of the company.

Profound silence swayed all around, and we were fixed to the ground like so many statues, thrilled with anxious expectation, and scarce ventured to breathe.

The old man was clad in a long robe of black silk, his snow-white head uncovered, a white silken sash, marked with strange characters, was tied round his waist, and the well known black wallet hung on his back; having taken it down he untied it, and exhibited the mysterious instruments of conjuration: at his mute command the host carried a table in the centre of the room, put two lighted torches upon it and bolted the door.

Now he gave us a signal to form a circle round him; the Austrian placed himself to his left side, turning his face towards the door, Lieutenant N—, by the conjuror's own desire, to his right; the inn-keeper stood close by the Austrian, one of Lieutenant N—'s friends took his station by the landlord, and I placed myself close to the latter. The Necromancer appeared to care little for the right wing, and I could clearly observe that his left neighbour raised his suspicion.

However, he began his conjuration with apparent firmness, after he had strewed a reddish sand on the floor, and delineated a treble circle with his ebony wand. The particulars of the act of conjuring were nearly the same as in the cellar of the Haunted Castle, except his reading aloud the greatest part of the form of the conjuration, and his face being not so horribly distorted by convulsions as in the subterraneous rooms of that terrible haunt of robbers.

Now the ceremony was finished, he cast his book on the table, and pronounced thrice the well-known mysterious word: Suddenly a howling blast of wind rushed against our faces, a thick column of smoke ascended from the floor, overcasting the whole apartment, and extinguishing the torches. Darkness and horror surrounded us.

'Ere long a faint gleam was breaking from the floor, sparingly illuminating the objects around, and rising higher and higher on the opposite wall 'till it reached the ceiling. At once the floor seemed to shake beneath our feet, and we beheld with chilly horror an human figure hovering on the wall; its garments and face, bearing the grisly marks of corruption, appeared to have suffered by the flames. It shook its head and fiery sparks flew around. A sudden smell of brimstone almost suffocated us.

After we had gazed at the phantom some time, with secret horror, the Necromancer exclaimed with a thundering voice, "Who art thou?"

Phantom. (Staggering back) "A soul from purgatory."

Old man. "What is thy desire?"

Phantom. "To be redeemed from the flames."

Old man. "By what means?"

Phantom. "By the sale of this house."

Old man. "For what reason?"

Phantom. "Because I have got it by fraudulent means."

Old man. "How can the sale of this house expiate thy crime?"

Phantom. "It can, because my children will be saved."

The Necromancer was silent and the phantom disappeared.

A violent gust of wind rushed again in our faces, the smoke evaporated, and the torches began to burn. Lieutenant N— with his friends and the landlord were struck with amazement, and unable to stir; the Austrian lifted his hat, which had hidden part of his face, staring wildly at the hoary cheat, and I expected with impatience the signal for seizing the rascal, who, with great tranquillity and unconcern, was busied with putting his gewgaws again into his wallet.

Now the Austrian came forth, and I clapped my hand to my sword: Awful silence reigned around, and our companions were still fixed to their places, whilst the Austrian's sparkling looks rested on the Necromancer, who now had packed up the instruments of fraud, and thrown the wallet over his shoulders. Just when he was going to leave the room, his eye caught the glowing face of my friend, and he seemed thunderstruck. Their looks evinced a mutual emotion of an uncommon nature; my friend's stern looks grew more and more terrible, and the old man was apparently grasped by horror's icy fangs: Our expectation rose to the highest pitch, and we were standing around them in a grisly attitude, most of us thrilled with secret awe, and I not without chill.

"Yes," began now the Austrian with a trembling voice, "yes, it is thou, Volkert! it is thou!"

The old deceiver shivered violently, his face was distorted by terrible convulsions, he gave a hollow groan, and fell lifeless on the floor.

We all seemed to be touched by a magic wand, and the Austrian was standing a good while in our middle, in a state of wild stupefaction; at length he recovered his recollection, drew with his wonted firmness nearer to the lifeless Necromancer, raised him up, shook him with all his might, and exclaimed,

"Volkert, Volkert, return to life once more."

But all was in vain, the old man gave no sign of life.

"Volkert, Volkert," exclaimed my friend once more, but he did not hear him.

The inn-keeper ran down stairs fetching a glass of water and some drops, but all our endeavours to restore the hoary villain to the use of his senses proved abortive and he remained senseless in our arms.

"Well then," resumed the Austrian, his eyes flashing with anger, "if amicable means will not do, then I must have recourse to violence." So saying, he discharged a pistol, the door flew open, and four corporals rushed in with their swords unsheathed.

"Tie the rascal's arms and legs," roared the Austrian, "away with the villain, he is our prisoner."

"Your prisoner!" replied the grey deceiver, who had recovered at last, "your prisoner," roared he with a ghastly grin, disengaging himself from our grasp.

The corporals rushed upon him.

"I am a citizen of F—, of a free imperial town, who dares to touch me?"

The corporals retired hastily, and the Austrian's brow was covered with terrible wrinkles, his eyes flashed anger, his mouth foamed, and his whole frame trembled in an agony of furious rage. I never beheld a more terrible aspect.

"Infernal spirit! hell-born villain!" roared he, gnashing his teeth, "I am deceived!—deceived by thee, Volkert!—Volkert!"

At once the thunder of his voice lowered to an entreating accent.

"Volkert, Volkert, for God's sake have mercy on me; save me from an ocean of doubts; spare me, O spare me; save me from the disgrace to appear to myself and my friends a fool and a superstitious fanatic! Tell me, O tell me, am I indeed deceived? O, I will forgive thee, I will pronounce thee my benefactor, my saviour, only speak—tell me I am not deceived!"

The tears ran down his cheeks, as he pronounced these words, spoken in the most violent passion.

It is a terrible awful sight to see a *man* weep. I turned my eye away from that affecting scene, not being able to behold it any longer. The rest of my companions were seized anew with dumb stupefaction, when they saw the violent emotions of my venerable friend, and a pause of unutterable horror ensued, after the Austrian's speech. The old man either would or could not speak, and the Austrian began once more to address the hoary deceiver in an accent of utter insensibility, and with a sternness of look not to be described.

"Volkert, thou wilt not know me. I will spare thee the disgrace of confessing thine own guilt, but if thou wert in my power—"

His eyes darted flashes of lightning, and his voice was like the roaring of thunder.

"If thou wert in my power, I would make thee confess thy cheats, and if I should be forced to beat thy old rascally limbs to atoms, and to draw thy black blood from thy diabolical heart by single drops, I would make thee confess: But," added he in a more gentle accent, "thou art not within the reach of my power, and it is well that it is so. Volkert, here is my hand, I forgive thee. Thou not only deservest my forgiveness, but also my sincere gratitude, because thou hast given me a wholesome lesson, hast taught me, that every body, though ever so wise, may be deceived; and I think I have not paid too dear for it."

Volkert wanted to speak, but he could not, being overcome by a sudden emotion, and hid his face with his hands.

"Well, Volkert," resumed the Austrian, "I see thou art not quite so bad as I thought, I will not compel thee to a confession, though I am wishing most ardently to have my doubts cleared up, and trust that thou wouldst tell me more than I want to know. I will not distress thee any longer by my presence; I am going to leave this house and this town for ever.

"Gentlemen," added he, addressing us, "I have deceived you, by supporting the reality of things which have been nothing but illusion; from this moment I have forfeited your good opinion, and the honor of being admitted any longer to a circle where I have been respected. You may call my resolution pride, caprice, or what ever you please, I cannot remain here any longer, and I am determined to depart this instant, farewell, live happy."

Having addressed us in so unexpected a manner, he hurried out of the room, taking no particular leave of me. Sympathizing with his feelings, I thought it proper not to pay him a parting visit, because I knew it would recall disagreeable recollections, and give him pain.

A parting look which he gave me, when he was leaving the room, told me more than words could have done. Mine eyes were bathed in tears. I have seen him no more, and shall never forget that unhappy night which has robbed me of such a valuable friend, and deprived me of the darling of my soul.

When the Austrian and the corporals had left us, the Necromancer was likewise going to leave the room: His appearance was sullen and gloomy, his looks cast down: My friends were also stirring and stopped him, forming a circle round him.

The landlord was still in a maze of silent wonder, not knowing what to think of what had happened. I was dejected and melancholy, and had banished from my soul every idea of vengeance; my companions, however, seemed not inclined to let him get off so cheaply, and insisted on his explaining how he had contrived to cheat us; but the inn-keeper interfered, imploring them not to ruin him entirely, by quarrelling in his house.

Lieutenant N— threatened at last to give him up to the civil power, if he would not confess, which I at first likewise had determined to do, how he had deceived us; however, his stubborness could not be shaken, and he remained as silent as the grave.

Seeing that every farther means to break his obstinacy would prove fruitless, I interfered, advising my fellow adventurers to let him depart in peace.

"Upon the whole," added I, "it matters not how we have been deceived, our friend, the Austrian has set us an example, how one ought to behave on such an occasion: Let us, like him, forgive the wretch, he is below our resentment."

These words produced the desired effect on the minds of my fellow adventurers, who were stung with shame and remorse, but none of them more than Lieutenant N——: He blushed at his idle fears and his credulity, leaving the room abruptly, accompanied by his friends and the landlord.

Being now left alone with the Necromancer, I flattered myself to succeed better than my companions, and to get informed of what I so eagerly wanted to know; but I was mistaken, his stubborn reserve baffled all my solicitations.

"Farewell, Lieutenant," said he, as he was going to leave the room, "I did not know you at first, and I am rejoiced that you have escaped your doom: I do not deserve your noble generous treatment: Farewell, and remember sometimes Volkert the Necromancer: If you could see my heart, you rather would pity than despise me; I may perhaps one time find an opportunity of being serviceable to you, and of proving my gratitude by deeds."

I went down stairs with him, and having seen him to the door he squeezed my hand and hurried away. I left the fatal house in a strange situation of mind, and it struck one o'clock when I came home. I went to bed, but not to rest, my fancy being haunted by gloomy ideas, which kept sleep and repose at a distance. Early in the morning my fellow adventurers came to see me, requesting me to unfold the mysteries of the preceding night.

"We know," began Lieutenant N——, their spokesman, "we know that you are, or at least have been, very intimate with the Austrian, and you will, of course, be able to inform us, how your friend came to be acquainted with the cheats of the Necromancer. We have reason to think that he would have acted with more circumspection, if he had known that the Necromancer was no other person than Volkert, his former intimate favorite: We hope you will be so kind to clear up the matter: The Austrian's firmness of mind, his solid character, and his unshaken belief in the possibility of apparitions, give us strong reasons to think that he cannot have acted thus without mature deliberation."

Being but ill-disposed to enter into a circumstantial narrative, and not at all inclined to inform the intruding gentlemen of our adventures at the Haunted Castle, I called one of my corporals, who had been on the watch in the fatal inn the preceding night. "This man," said I, "will tell you more of the matter than I know, having watched every motion of the Necromancer, and discovered all his secret machinations."

The old veteran was very willing to satisfy their curiosity, and began a prolix narration of every proceeding in the lower apartment of the inn. The inn-keeper was, as he related, deceived like ourselves, but his servants had acted in concert with Volkert, and enabled him by their assistance, to impose upon us.

Not being disposed to listen to his tale, I did not mind what he related, but my visitors, more attentive than myself, appeared at least to be fully satisfied and left me, after a profusion of thanks for having freed them of their doubts and errors.

The separation from my venerable friend had spread a melancholy gloom over my mind, which nothing could dispel: His conversations had been so instructing, his principles so noble, his heart so sensible and good, that I should have been unworthy of his friendship if I had not severely felt his loss: Wherever I went, the image of the darling of my heart was hovering before me, and I was haunted every where by the distressing painful thought that I should see him no more. His wise counsels, his sage instructions, still vibrated in my ear, and nature had lost all her charms, since I could no more admire the greatness of her Creator, wandering by his side, and hear him enlarge on the praises of him who showers down his blessings on man, and on the worm that is creeping beneath our feet; how my heart was thrilled with unutterable bliss, when he was pointing out to me the wisdom and power of God, who is as great in the meanest reptile, as in the structure of the majestic king of day; how my bosom panted with rapture, when, in the evening of a toilsome day, I could rest on his heart, and listening to the effusions of his noble mind, could sympathize with him in his virtuous feelings.

The third day after his departure, I could no longer stay in a place where every object reminded me of so many hours of bliss, and of the man, whose friendship had made me so truly happy; I bade my servant pack my trunks, ordered my corporals to keep themselves ready, and left F— after a few days; however I cannot deny that I left with regret a town where I had found, and, alas! lost so soon, so valuable a treasure.

My journey afforded me but little amusement, being not able to wean my gloomy mind from the painful recollection of the time past, the image of my friend rushing ever and anon on my soul, and I could not resist the ardent desire of being re-united to him: In vain did I consider the bad consequences a longer connexion with him perhaps would have produced; in vain did I struggle to convince myself, that the gloominess of his mind would have, sooner or later, infected the peace of my heart, and poisoned my tranquillity, though he had been ever so brave and good. I could not but be sensible how beneficial this sudden separation would prove to me, and that I certainly should have been infected with very dangerous opinions, if the Austrian's pride had not been wounded so deeply by the detection of Volkert's frauds, and if he had not been prompted thus to confess that he had been deceived.

The high opinion I entertained of his rectitude, the superiority of his understanding, and his infallibility, would, without doubt, have converted me entirely to his belief in supernatural apparitions, and that certain people had the power to effect phenomenons of that kind, a doctrine which exposes us to the artful wiles of every cunning cheat, darkens our understanding, stains our reason with superstition, and poisons our happiness: He was, nevertheless, still dear to my heart, and the idol of my soul, and even now I would willingly sacrifice any thing if I could be united again to that extraordinary man, who, by his reverend appearance, his exemplary manners, his equanimity, and his firmness of mind, won the hearts of the virtuous and the wicked without intending it.

But let us return to the continuation of my adventures.

I sat in the stage musing on what was past, revolving in my mind the strange events of the Haunted Castle, and the Inn, and examining minutely all the particulars, but I grew not a bit wiser: That Volkert was an impostor could not be doubted, but how he had managed his artful cheats and what his views had been in deceiving us, I could not unravel in a satisfactory manner; I examined singly all his transactions I knew, pondered with the greatest accuracy what the Austrian had related of his earlier exploits, but I was not able to dispel the impenetrable darkness which I was bewildered in.

The final result of my meditations was, that every body, though ever so circumspect and wise, would, like my worthy friend, have been deceived by his intricate machinations, and tempted to adopt the opinion that enlightened officer had once defended so stoutly.

I was almost angry with myself for having let slip the opportunity of forcing that dangerous man to a confession of his dark and diabolical transgressions. It is true, I myself knew him as an hardened impostor, but could he not drag into the gulph of perdition many of my fellow creatures, who, like myself, would fall an easy victim to his deceitful hypocrisy?

This thought overwhelmed me with a load of uneasiness, and I reproached myself severely for having imitated the over generous example of the Austrian, and suffered the accomplished villain to decamp, without punishment. I had, indeed, reason to apprehend that the magistrate of F— would not have regarded much the information of a recruiting officer, against a citizen, and that the inn-keeper would have been induced, by fear or bribe, to contradict our denounciation; nevertheless, I should have had the satisfaction of having performed my duty, and cautioned the inhabitants of F— against that dangerous villain.

Tormented with this and similar thoughts did I finish my first day's journey, struggling in vain to recover my wonted cheerfulness, my mind being then too much occupied by gloominess, and an entire stranger to joyful feelings. My travelling companions prefered sleep to an amusing conversation, and I wished ardently for my corporals to chat with them, and thus to chase away the cheerless thoughts crowding upon my mind; but I had most unfortunately ordered them, along with my servant, to meet me at N—, by a different route.

Not being able to get a wink of sleep all night long, I was haunted without rest, by the gloomy offsprings of my fancy, distressed by the appearing slowness of time, and entirely cut off from every comfort by the snoring disposition of my fellow travellers, which made me resolve to leave the stage next morning, and to continue my journey on horseback. I left, therefore, my cheerless and sullen companions, with the first dawn of day, bought a horse in the first village where we stopped, and trotted briskly onward.

I was not in the least acquainted with the roads in those parts, a circumstance which ought to have come sooner in my mind: I was obliged to ride back several times, and when it began to grow dark, found myself bewildered in a dreary forest, without knowing which way to turn. My jaded horse being hardly able to stir, I alighted, leading the poor beast by the bridle, in order to advance with more expedition.

It was now so dark that I could hardly distinguish the objects before my eyes, when a sudden rustling in the thicket made me start: I listened, but all was silent again, and I pursued my way without any apprehension, thinking it might have been a deer; but I was not gone far when I heard the rustling again much louder than at first, and close by me: I now beheld, on a sudden, a man with a sack on his back, and a staff in his hand, coming out of the thicket, within the short distance of two or three paces. This unexpected sight gladdened my heart, flattering me with the sweet hope of getting a friendly conductor out of that dreary wilderness, who would direct my weary steps to a place of rest.

"Whither art thou going, good friend?" exclaimed I.

"To the mill," answered he, groaning under his burthen.

"Is the mill far from hence?" said I.

"No farther than half a league," he replied.

"May I find a shelter there for myself and horse?"

"No," replied he.

"Why not?" asked I.

"Because," replied he, "the miller does not admit strangers."

"I am sorry for it; but is there no house hereabouts where one could get a night's lodging?"

"O yes," answered he, "not far from hence, if you turn to the right lives a wood-cutter, who lodges travellers."

"But do you think I shall be safe there?" asked I.

"What do you mean by that?" said he.

"Don't you know, good friend," replied I, "that this part of the country is the constant haunt of robbers?"

"Would to God I could stay this night with good Master Max, I would not be uneasy on that score; but I must go on, and alas my burthen is heavy."

"If my poor beast was not so jaded, and so much tired, I would be glad to lend it you," said I.

"Thank you, Master," returned he, "I am used to hardships, and have laid in a good stock of patience."

Discoursing thus we went slowly on together, 'till we came to a foot-path, where the wanderer stopped to direct me to the wood-cutter's cottage: "You cannot miss your way," said he; "if you pursue this path you will soon see a light."

I hesitated a little while, whether I should follow the advice of the honest man, or not, but the increasing darkness, and a rising tempest, which shook the oaks around, fixed soon my wavering resolution, and I pursued the path, bidding the honest wanderer good night.

I soon found myself on an unbeaten foot-way, obstructed by brambles and underwood; my poor horse threatened, every moment to sink down, and I could not resist the apprehension of having been sent on a fool's errand by the unknown man, and misled into an unfrequented lonesome part of the forest. This made me look about with more circumspection, 'till I had ascended a rising ground with great difficulty, my horse fell frequently on his knees, and it would have been impossible to proceed a mile farther; you may therefore easily think how rejoiced I was when the glimmering of a light apparently at a small distance, bade me hope a speedy end of my distress.

Quickening my steps I soon perceived a small cottage, the owner of which made his appearance as soon as I had knocked at his humble door, hailed me with a hearty welcome, and bade me, with much good nature, enter his hospitable abode.

Not expecting much conveniency, I was struck with wonder when he shewed me into a neat little room, not in the least corresponding with the poor appearance of his hut: I had expected to be introduced to the residence of poverty, and found an habitation that bore evident marks of prosperity, and seemed rather to be the abode of a gentleman than that of a poor wood-cutter.

Mr. Max, this he told me was his name. Mr. Max took no notice of my astonishment, but prepared, with much alacrity, to provide me and my weary horse with food and drink.

While he was busy to prove his hospitality I had full leisure to satisfy my curiosity, and to take a view of the objects around me, assisted by the faint glimmering of a lamp.

The first object that struck my fancy was an enormous sword, hanging by his bedside, which, as I thought at first, was rather an improper furniture for a wood-cutter's dwelling; but I soon made myself easy when I recollected, that he, living in an unfrequented part of the forest, might want sometimes an instrument of that kind to defend himself against unwelcome visitors, but my apprehension returned when I beheld a brace of pistols hanging on the wall, which I found were charged with balls.

I went farther in my search, and saw a great number of guns, pistols, and swords, in a recess close by the fire side; I was chilled with terror, and just as I had taken the lamp in my hand to have a closer view at this alarming furniture, Mr. Max entered the room, with a large plate of greens, a piece of ham, and a bottle of wine.

"Well," exclaimed he merrily, as he entered the room, "there, I have brought you something to silence your grumbling stomach with, sit down, good Sir, and take up with my frugal fare."

Alas! my appetite was gone, but he fetched knives and forks, and a large loaf of bread, and began to eat with great avidity, taking at first no notice of my backwardness to follow his example; perceiving at length that I did not eat, he exclaimed, "Well, Sir, why don't you eat? I think one must be hungry, if one has travelled far and missed one's way."

His joviality revived a little my spirits, but his country-like simplicity, and his seeming honesty appeared to me very little corresponding with the great number of fire arms and swords which I had seen, yet I joined him at last in eating and drinking.

When supper was over I could no longer suppress my curiosity, and asked him why he kept so many guns and swords in his house.

"What," replied he rather angry, "what is this to you? I get sometimes visitors for whom I must keep them."

"But why," resumed I, "so great a number as I have seen in the recess by the fire-side?"

"These are fine doings," said he angrily, "who bade you to search my room? Is this becoming a guest?"

I arose and asked him how much I had to pay for my supper? He fell a laughing, and exclaimed, with marks of astonishment,

"You don't intend to depart in this dark and tempestuous night? Don't you hear how the tempest roars, and how the rain beats against the windows? I hope you don't think you will be shot or stabbed because there are so many fire-arms and swords in that recess? No, no, good friend, you need not be afraid, all these things are not mine, they belong to sportsmen who have laid them up here, that they may have them when they are a hunting in this part of the forest; perhaps you may see them yourself to-morrow morning; the sword by my bed-side I bought some years ago from an Austrian deserter."

Though I was not inclined to stay for the sportsmen, I did not know whither I should go with my jaded horse in that dark tempestuous night, and dreaded to run the risk of escaping from an imaginary danger, only to fly in the face of a real one, which, at last, determined me to stay. I begged Mr. Max to shew me the place where I was to sleep, intending to charge my pistols with balls before I should go to bed in case of accident.

My host opened a side door leading to a small chamber, where a bed was.

"Here," said he, "you may sleep 'till it is broad day, and rest your weary limbs at your ease; I keep this chamber on purpose for travellers; take this lamp, I will fetch it when you shall be asleep."

So saying, he left me, shutting the door after him.

Taking a nearer view of my bed chamber, I observed that it had no windows, and, in order to be prepared for the worst, I charged my pistols, which I had put in my pockets before I had entered the cottage:—This done, I considered whether I should go to bed, and thus deceive my host, which, on mature deliberation, I thought would be the best.

With that intention I took my lamp to see whether the bed was fastened, lest I might sink down with it into the cellar. Though this apprehension was groundless, I made another discovery which thrilled my soul with horror: Perceiving traces of blood on the pillow, I was seized with a sudden terror, my hands trembled violently, the lamp fell on the floor, and I was in the dark.

As soon as I had recovered a little from my fright, I searched for my pistols, groping about a good while before I could find them in the dark. My fear abated a little when I found them at last, after a long and fruitless search, and I sat myself down on a little stool by the bed-side, listening whether any body was coming. All was quiet at first, but after a quarter of an hour I heard somebody entering the adjacent room, and approaching the door of my chamber, which was gently opened, and the voice of my host called, "Are you asleep?" I uttered not a word, and after a short pause the same voice resounded once more, "Have you extinguished the lamp?" I still gave no answer and the host retired.

All was hushed again in profound silence, but it lasted not long, my ears being suddenly assailed by the sound of many voices, the tinkling of spurs, and a humming noise, as if a number of people were discoursing; I could understand nothing, the discourse being held in so low an accent, that I was unable to distinguish the sound of their words. At once I saw, through the crevices in the door, somebody striking a light, which gave me some comfort. The discourse was still carried on in that secret mysterious manner: At last it seemed as if the company were sitting down, and I could now better distinguish the different sounds. The voices of those that spoke were rough and the words seemed to belong to a foreign language.

I sat near an hour on my stool, like a poor culprit who awaits his doom, but was determined to defend myself to the last drop of blood: I intended several times to rush into the room, and to force my escape through the company with cocked pistols, but something within my breast admonished me to stay where I was, and patiently to wait 'till they should think it proper to pay *me* a visit.

My situation was exceeding painful, and at the least noise which seemed to approach my chamber I started up, putting myself in a posture of defence. My fears not having been realized as yet, my apprehensions began to vanish a little, and I thought Mr. Max might be an honest man, and his company, the sportsmen he had been speaking of, although their language seemed to contradict that opinion: Hope soothed my terrors for some time, 'till at length I recollected the traces of blood I had seen on the pillow, which recalled all my apprehensions with redoubled anxiety.

Sleep, whom 'till now I had carefully kept at a distance, began, by degrees, to steal upon me, and shut at last with his leaden wand my heavy eyes: But I was scarce fallen asleep, when one of my pistols dropped on the floor, and went off. I started up, seized by the chilly fangs of terror, and in the same moment the other pistol slipped out of my hand. I had scarcely picked it up when the door suddenly flew open, and three fellows of a gigantic size entered my room with naked swords. Sleep, the report of my pistol, and the sudden appearance of those terrible men, had stunned me so much, that I, without knowing what I was doing, discharged my pistol, at which one of the villains dropped on the floor with a roaring yelp. A numerous crew, armed with guns, cutlasses, and daggers, rushed like lightning into my chamber, and, before I could unsheath my sword, I felt myself in their clutches, bereft of all power of self defence.

A tremendous voice roared like thunder from the adjoining room, "Hither with the rascal."

Before I could recover my recollection I felt myself dragged out of my chamber, and beheld in an instant a man of the most terrible forbiding aspect, who, with a rough thundering voice, menacing looks, and sparkling eyes, asked me if I could not have patiently awaited my doom.

"Tie the daring wretch," added he in a rage, "and throw him into the cellar, until sentence shall be pronounced against him." His commands were obeyed, and Mr. Max himself assisted; I was seized with a despairing stupor, and uttered not a word; I was shut up in a damp cellar; how long I remained in my dungeon I cannot tell, having been in a situation which suspended all my powers of reflection.

After a long interval of the most desponding agony, I was at length dragged forth and brought before the tribunal of that terrible looking man. The villain whom I had wounded was stretched on the bed, his head tied up, and his associates standing round him, bemoaning his hapless fate, and amongst them a venerable old man, whom I at first had not observed.

Now the grim judge began to speak, and the whole assembly to dart furious and bloodthirsty looks at me: The old man likewise turned his face towards me, and it cannot be expressed by words what my sensations were when I discerned the features of Volkert: A poor culprit cannot feel greater joy, when, under the hangman's merciless fangs, his guardian-angel appears to save him from his impending doom. I did indeed not know whether he could save me or not, however the sweet soothing voice of hope silenced all my apprehensions; I had saved him once from ignominy, and perhaps from death itself, he had promised me to prove his gratitude, how could I therefore doubt that he would save me from destruction. "Volkert!" exclaimed I, in a supplicating accent, "Volkert!" The terrible man staggered back, staring by turns at me and him.

"Volkert!" exclaimed I, again lifting up my fettered hands; he knew me, and without the least delay took a knife out of his pocket, and cut asunder the cords my hands had been tied with. The whole frightful assembly was fixed to the ground, seized with wonder and astonishment.

"Thou hast saved me," began my guardian angel now, in a solemn awful accent, "thou hast given me liberty, take back thy gift, and life into the bargain."

"Friends," said he, addressing the gaping crew, "Friends, he is the preserver of my honor and my liberty, what may he expect?"

"Pardon, pardon," was the unanimous cry, "pardon, pardon, he shall live."

"Bravo, my boys," said now their formidable Captain, who was sitting in judgment upon me, "bravo, my honest lads, you are noble fellows: Farewell, Andrew," added he, addressing his dying companion, "Farewell, Andrew, thou art avenged, art doubly avenged by the generosity of thy companions!"

At the same instant the whole crew hurried out of the room, leaving me alone with Volkert. "Farewell, Lieutenant," said he, shaking me by the hand, "you have wisely acted, in leaving F—, like the Austrian, I shall never return to that town: If any similar sinister accident should happen to you, need but pronounce my name and you will be safe."

I was going to embrace, and to assure him of my warmest gratitude, but he tore himself from my arms, and hastened to join his associates. Soon after I heard a confused noise before the door of the cottage, and, ere long, the whole band rode away in full speed. Now I was surrounded by midnight stillness, interrupted only by the groans of the dying robber. Max did not dare to enter the room while I was there.

I was no longer able to remain in the house, the roaring of the tempest was hushed in silence, and the dawn of morn peeping through the windows; I found my horse sleeping in a corner behind the cottage, got on his back, and rode away in a slow pace.

The morning sun rose in all his dazzling splendor, and still I was bewildered between trees and bushes, straying about two tedious hours without being able to find an outlet, 'till at length I was so fortunate to meet a countryman, who, for a small reward, directed me to the road leading to N—.

Warned by my dangerous adventure, I now inquired at every village for the route I was to take, and thus reached at last the place of my destination without having met with any farther misfortune. Before I arrived at N—, an accident happened, which being connected with my adventure at the Haunted Castle, I cannot omit mentioning.

Coming to a village about three miles distant from N—, a great noise struck my ears, proceeding, as I soon could distinguish, from a great number of recruits, carousing and singing at the inn. I alighted and entered the residence of merriment and intoxication, in order to inform myself who the commanding officer was, in hopes to meet with an old acquaintance, but I was disappointed. Two serjeants, entirely unknown to me, conducted the transport, and, inquiring after their officer's name, I found that he was an utter stranger to me.

Having surveyed the recruits, I was going to leave the room, when my eyes by accident fell on a man, standing in a musing attitude by the fire-side, his looks fixed on the floor. Thinking to recollect his features I advanced nearer to him, he started up from his reverie, and seeing me standing before him, staggered back with evident marks of astonishment; however, his terror soon gave way to rapturous joy; he ran towards me, caught me by the hand, and exclaimed, flushed with pleasure,

"Dear, dear Lieutenant, is it you? God be praised that you are still alive! God be praised that I have once more the happiness of seeing my kind old master!"

His voice, his accent, and his transport, gave me no room to doubt that he was my late servant, whom I had lost in the Castle.

The honest fellow could find no words to express his joy, at my not having been famished with my companions in the cellar, as it had been the intention of the robbers: He expressed his joy in so noisy a manner, that we were soon surrounded by the recruits. I begged the serjeants to indulge me with a private conversation with my honest servant, which they granted me with great politeness: I called for the host, requesting him to let us have a room to ourselves, that we might converse without being interrupted by the curiosity of his noisy guests.

As soon as we were in private, I requested John to give me a brief account of what had happened to him after we had left him snoring in the great hall of the Castle; he was very willing to satisfy my curiosity, and related as follows:

I was roused from my sleep by a violent shaking, and, recovering from my drowsiness, saw myself seized by two ill-looking fellows, who were employed to drag me forcibly away. Fear and terror bereft me at first of all power of utterance and resistance. I attempted several times to cry, but I could not pronounce a single word, and, as much as I could observe through the midnight darkness, saw myself carried down the spiral staircase, over the courtyard: When we were arrived at the gate, I was tied upon a horse, and surrounded by a numerous crew, who took me between them and rode away in full speed. My feet being tied together under the horse's belly, it was out of my power to stir, which rendered my situation exceeding painful.

The dawn of morn appeared, but not a single ray of hope cheered my desponding soul, being in the power of those merciless ruffians, who were still sweeping the field with all possible expedition, not caring for the excruciating pains I suffered, and forcing my horse to leap over hedges and ditches.

The swiftness of the race and my uncomfortable situation, deprived me, at length, of all power of recollection, and threw me into a kind of stupefaction which prevented me from observing how long our journey had lasted. I was seized with a fainting fit, and when my recollection returned, observed that I was shut up in a subterraneous dungeon, an old hag was rubbing me with onions, and, when I recovered from the state of stupefaction, occasioned by the cruelty of my leaders:—She fetched a bottle of brandy, admonishing me, in a rough uncouth dialect, to drink plenty of it, which I declined, requesting her to rub my lacerated limbs with it.

Having performed my request with great alacrity she left me, and I had full leisure to contemplate the horrors of my dreary abode, the walls of which were blackened by the hand of time, and overgrown with moss; muddy straw spread on the damp ground served me for a couch, and the faint glimmering of a lamp heightened the horrors of my dungeon; the thick corrupted air made it difficult to fetch breath, to which were added most excruciating pains, not in the least alleviated by the use of brandy, but rather increased on account of the sores my poor frame was covered with; only the agony of my tortured mind surpassed the sufferings of my body; futurity stared me grisly in the face, and the consciousness of being in the power of a set of villains, who would either sacrifice my life, to their thirst of blood, or force me, by threats and exquisite torments, to commit deeds of the most atrocious nature, filled my mind with dreadful apprehensions.

I remained two days in a state of unspeakable despondency; although my bodily pains had abated, and I could move my limbs with more ease, yet the fear of futurity had weakened me so much, that I could not stir from my miserable couch; my misery was augmented by the troublesome officiousness of the old hag, who every instant came to torment me: One time she wanted to apply to my sores poultices of roasted flour, and at another she would make me swallow a spoonful of disgusting nauseous drops; now she would force down my throat a soup of a most uninviting appearance, and a few minutes after she brought straw, which was half rotten, to place it under my head; in short, she tormented me so much by plying me with her unwelcome officiousness and kindness, that the gloominess of my mind hourly increased, and my little remaining strength was entirely spent by my efforts to resist her torturing care for my health and ease.

On the fourth day of my confinement I was taken out of my dungeon, and my apprehensions were realized. The infernal villains intending to make me one of their associates in wickedness, ordered me to mount a horse, and forced me to follow them in full speed through fields and forests, notwithstanding the weak state of my body. My conductors, at first only three in number, and clad in linen frocks, blackened with coal dust, rode ahead, looking back now and then; their black faces and sooty hands evidently foreboded their dark design.

After half an hour's ride my infernal guides stopped at a lonely public house, alighted, and bade me take care of the horses until they should return.

I obeyed their stern command with gloomy silence, tied the horses to a tree, and sat myself down upon a bench before the house. The haunts of my disordered fancy made the time pass quickly on, I revolved in my afflicted mind my former occupation, the happy hours I had spent in the service of a kind indulgent master, and the horrors of my present situation, the briny drops of sorrow and affliction moistened my palid cheeks:—"What will become of thee?" said I to myself. "A robber, and perhaps a murderer too." A chilly trembling glided through my veins, I started up, and was resolved to mount one of the horses, and make my escape, but the want of strength reminded me soon of the utter impossibility of the execution of my rash design. I sunk down upon the bench, imploring heaven rather to put an end to my miserable life, than to suffer me to become an associate of these hell-born fiends. After I had ejaculated this fervent prayer, I felt my despondency abate a little, awaiting with impatience the re-appearance of my fell conductors.

A short time after they came, accompanied by three more ruffians of a most frightful aspect, who, with the greatest expedition fetched their horses from an adjacent stable, mounted them without delay, and rode away like lightning, my conductors did the same, ordered me to follow their example, and galloped over the fields as fast as their coursers could run; coming up with our ill looking companions we pursued our journey with all possible swiftness.

Having by accident mounted the wrong horse, which was the fleetest of all, I kept always ahead, and could distinctly hear every word they spoke, though I could not understand a syllable of their conversation. After it had grown dark we alighted again at a solitary public house, the horses being once more committed to my care, and I awaited with patience the end of an adventure that boded no good.

I had been standing in the chilly air of night above an hour, musing on my deplorable fate, when the inn-keeper brought me a piece of bread and butter, and a mug of beer, but I could neither eat nor drink, shaking with cold.

The night was dark and the sky overcast, a thick dampish fog had wetted my cloaths, and not one friendly star was to be seen in the firmament, which was as gloomy as my mind. After I had been exposed half an hour longer to the inclemency of the chilly air, my conductors reappeared, their number being increased to twelve, and their sooty dress exchanged for green hunting coats; every one of them was armed with a gun, a brace of pistols and a cutlass.

The feelings which were rushing on my mind at that sight admit of no description; the blood froze in my veins, my soul was harrowed up in dreadful suspence, and I mounted my horse more dead than alive, gallopping over the heath with my conductors in senseless stupefaction, like a poor culprit who is dragged along to be delivered to the merciless fangs of the grim fiendly-looking executioner, 'till I at length was roused from my stupor by the sound of horns assailing my ears from afar, and the loud clamorous shouts of our troop.

The sound of horns drew nearer, and my conductors answered it by blowing theirs. Now I perceived a powerful troop of horsemen sweeping the heath like a hurricane. In an instant I was surrounded by a numerous crew on horseback, and rough dismal voices vibrated in my ear in a confused manner: One of them struck fire, a number of torches were lighted, and I beheld, with amazement and dismay, a large troop of terrible beings around me.

Whithersoever I turned my eyes I was frightened almost out of my wits by stern threatening looks: They soon perceived the workings of my desponding mind, laughed at my fear, and uttered terrible execrations. One of them who bore a more tremendous aspect than the rest, came forth, the noisy crew was awed in solemn silence, and the terrible man began to address them thus:

"You know, my brave companions, that this rascal here," (pointing at me) "is the servant of the wretch who has dared to watch in our Castle with armed numbers. The daring scoundrel and his two associates are punished; famine and thirst have seized their victims with merciless fangs, tormenting them with excruciating pains, with agony and black despair; on our next nocturnal visit to the Castle, we shall see them lifeless on the ground. You know how the daring fools have been vexed, teazed and tormented by Father Francis. It was glorious fun, we have been amused with their foolish credulity, and are now amply avenged on these bold disturbers of our nocturnal assembly.

"The villagers are not yet punished," continued he, "for having assisted them, but they shall not escape their doom. Our future safety demands the destruction of the village, and its environs; but, tell me, what shall we do with that fellow there? He is well fed, and seems not to be without strength, my advice is to make him our companion."

"We will, we will," roared the whole troop.

Then their terrible leader resumed, "He must give us to-night a specimen of his dexterity."

"He shall, he shall," was the universal cry. I trembled like a wretched culprit who hears his sentence pronounced, when the speaker addressed me thus:

"Fellow! thou hast heard what an honor we have conferred on thee, we expect that thou wilt be faithful to us, oaths are as little valued among robbers, as they are in hell, and a hand-stroke will satisfy us, give me thy right hand as a token of unshaken fidelity."

Trembling did I obey his stern command, and he bade me to take courage, to abandon all fear, and to follow him. The torches were extinguished, the robbers began to converse in an unintelligible accent, the horns were sounded, the whole troop set spurs to their horses, rushing over the fields like a midnight tempest; I felt myself seized by the arm, and my horse pulled by the bridle after them. After a short ride the voice of the terrible leader ordered us to halt.

"Here," said he to me, "is a gun and a whistle! The former thou art to use in case of necessity, and the latter as soon as a waggon or a coach passes the road."

This said, he rode away, but methought I heard another horseman not far from me.

Now I began to consult with myself what I should do, whether I should betray the innocent traveller, or suffer him to escape: My mind shrunk back from the horrid idea of becoming accessary to the destruction of a fellow creature, but how could I avoid it if I would not myself fall a victim to the cruelty of my infernal companions? Life is the sweetest gift of heaven, and not easy to be parted with.

While I was in deliberation with myself, what course to take, I heard the rattling of a coach within a little distance from me, and a violent trembling seized my limbs: The coach came nearer and my trembling increased. Without knowing what I was about, I was going to apply the whistle to my lips, my hand trembled, a sudden stupor seized me, the whistle dropped to the ground, and the coach passed by in full speed; at the same time I heard somebody whistle behind me, soon after the report of three guns, accompanied with cries and lamentations, struck my ear; a female voice was praying for mercy, loud acclamations filled the air, and soon after all was hushed in profound silence.

I was sitting on my horse in dumb stupefaction, when, on a sudden, I perceived somebody laying hold of the bridle of my steed, and pulling her forcibly after him. After a few minutes I saw at a distance a glimmering light shining through the bushes; as we came nearer to the spot, I beheld in my conductor the terrible leader of the band, and we at length arrived at a place surrounded with bushes, where the robbers were seated round a fire, dividing the spoil; they all gave a loud shriek, as if they already knew how badly I had acquitted myself of my first task.

"Let us pronounce sentence against the rascal!" exclaimed my conductor, with a thundering voice.

"Let us knock his brains out," roared one of the robbers.

"Send him to the dungeon," exclaimed a second.

"The latter we will do," resumed the Captain. "Punishment may, perhaps, recall him to reason."

Having said this, he ordered two of the gang to carry me to the place of confinement; they mounted their horses, took me between them, and hurried away with me at a furious rate. We arrived with the first dawn of day at the bottom of a hill, where I forcibly was dragged through the bushes and thorns fettered with heavy chains, and carried through a narrow passage into a dark dungeon; gropeing about I found myself surrounded with straw, the muddy smell of which left me no doubt that it was half rotten.

Having lingered many hours in that terrible abode of misery, without either hearing or seeing any body, I at last was hailed by the distant hollow sound of approaching footsteps, dying away sometimes, and then vibrating again faintly on my ear; at once they grew more and more audible, and the glimmering of a light began to illuminate the subterraneous cave.

Turning round with much difficulty, I perceived that it emerged from a deep grotto behind me. The glimmering grew lighter, and the sound of footsteps drew nearer; at length I beheld a figure more frightful than the robbers themselves; the old hideous hag adorned with all the graces of hell, ascended with alacrity from the gloomy abyss, panting for breath; and now I had a full view of the horrors of my den: The faint rays of my lamp were reflected in a grisly manner from the lofty walls, hewn into the solid rock, and mixed with the midnight darkness, which was hovering beneath the high vaulted ceiling. My dungeon was of a small circumference, but appeared to be far removed from the surface of the earth; the dreadful abode of horror was infected by a damp pestilential air, through which the light was glimmering as if through a bluish fog.

The antiquated scare-crow began to pity and to bemoan my miserable doom, exhorting me to obey more strictly the commands of my masters, and, having put a pitcher with water, and a piece of bread before me, unfettered my hands, admonishing me to submit patiently to my fate, and never to attempt an escape, which not only would prove abortive, but at the same time prolong and increase my punishment. I uttered not a syllable, and she left me to muse in solitude on my forlorn and unhappy situation.

Three gloomy days of misery and dismay were now elapsed, since I had been thrown into that terrible abode of silence and melancholy, before I saw any body except the old witch, by whose visits alone I could guess the progress of time. No year of my whole life has ever appeared to me so long as those three days of woe; I strove in vain to loosen the fetters which chained my feet, the lock that confined them together baffled all my endeavours, and, after many fruitless efforts, I was obliged to bid a mournful adieu to every ray of hope of making my escape from the fangs of my cruel tyrants; black despair hovered over me with sooty wings, the greedy tooth of grief was gnawing on my vitals, and the recollection of former times of ease and tranquillity served only to heighten my misery.

The fourth day brought me the visit of the Captain, who entered my dungeon with a lighted torch.

"Well, rascal!" exclaimed he, "how dost thou like this beautiful apartment? Art thou tired of thy sepulchre, or dost thou prefer to be entombed alive for ever to the honor of being one of our brave party? Art thou sensible of the foolishness of thy stubborn disobedience, and may I expect that thou wilt be more obsequious in future?"

I groaned a lamentable *yes*, the result of my resolution, which I had been driven to by despair and my forlorn situation.

"Well," resumed my tyrant, unfastening my chains, "I hope thou art sensible that it is more eligible to be a gentleman of the high road, than to be buried alive, amid spiders and toads; I will try once more whether I can make thee a worthy member of our society, rise and follow me!"

I attempted to get on my legs, but I sunk down again upon my damp couch; my legs, which were become quite useless by the pressure of the chains, were now pierced with most excruciating pains, and unable to support my miserable carcase. The robber seeing me struggle in vain to obey his command, seized me with a powerful arm, and dragged me forcibly over the rocky ground. I was trailed along the winding passages of the subterraneous fabric, like a victim to the altar, where it is to receive the finishing stroke. I was every now and then forced to crawl on my knees through narrow holes, and to climb with much difficulty over gaping chasms in the rock, 'till at length an iron door obstructed our passage; my conductor opened it, and I beheld a spacious lofty hall, illuminated with a great number of torches, where some of the robbers were seated at table, eating, drinking, and conversing merrily with each other, and some cleaning guns and pistols, and charging them.

They all spoke kindly to me, inviting me to partake of their blithsome meal, and congratulating me on the wise resolution I had taken to become a sharer of their fortune. I relished the roasted meat, the turkies and hams exceeding well, and swallowed plentiful draughts of most delicious wine. Though I was not remiss to ply briskly the knife and fork and the cheerful goblet, and strove to do honor to the table; yet the robbers chided me every now and then, finding fault with my tardiness.

The exhilerating juice of the grape spread mirth and cheerfulness around, the spacious cavern re-echoed their jocund songs, the tale of their exploits gave variety to the entertainment, and it seemed as if the sting of conscience had entirely lost, with them, its pungent point. The cloth was at length removed, the beldam, who had been waiting at table, began now likewise to eat, and the robbers made themselves ready to leave their subterraneous haunt.

"To-day," said the Captain to me, before they departed, "thou shalt stay at home, but to-morrow thou art to be of our party, and thy deportment must decide whether we can enlist thee in our noble company, or shall knock thy brains out."

Then the whole crew sallied forth through the iron door, without giving me time to answer, and left me alone the old woman, who was very assiduous to amuse me, relating, with much garrulity, many stories of the dear gentlemen, as she called the robbers, and extolling their generosity to the skies.

Perceiving that I did not relish her tiresome tales, she fetched books, cards, and dice, leaving it to my choice what sort of amusement I should fix upon. I preferred reading to a tête-à-tête with the old witch, and endeavoured to dispel the gloom of my mind, by perusing an old book of chivalry.

At night my rusty companion wanted me to sit down to supper with her, which I refused, requesting her to shew me to my bedroom: Vexed by my refusal, she mumbled something between her few remaining teeth, and opened the door of a small side room, where I found a couch, made of clean straw, and covered with a blanket; throwing myself upon it, I slept for the first time sweet and soundly after eight painful nights of horror.

The next morning the old woman thundered at my door, telling me it was broad day, and past nine o'clock, and that our gentlemen would soon return to dinner: I got up much refreshed, and assisted her in the kitchen, which pleased her so well that she promised to recommend me to the good graces of the Captain.

Thus far had my servant proceeded in his narration, without having been interrupted by me, though he had been very circumlocutious, and spoken above an hour: It gave me great pleasure to hear a circumstantial description of the robbers and their cave, and honest John's simplicity afforded me great amusement, which proved a very seasonable relief, in my then gloomy state of mind, I therefore was very much vexed when one of the serjeants entered to tell him that they were waiting for him to proceed on their march, and bade him make haste, just as he was going to give me a full account of the robbers' deportment towards him after their return, of the splendid dinner which the old woman had prepared, assisted by him, and of their discourses at table.

I entreated the rough son of Mars to resign this recruit to me, and to accept from me double the binding money he had given him, but he did not relish my proposal, and John himself was little inclined to enter again into my service; at last I prevailed, by fair words and a small present, on the serjeant to wait a quarter of an hour longer, and he left the room after we had promised to be as expeditious as possible.

When he was gone I asked John, why he would rather be a soldier than enter again into my service.

"What else would you advise me to do?" replied he, with weeping eyes, "my life is exposed to the greatest danger in these parts, and would you like to have a servant who has been a robber?"

"You have not been a robber," interrupted I the poor fellow, but recollected soon that he had not finished his narration, and perhaps might have been compelled at last, by menaces, to become a member of the gang, I therefore requested him to continue his tale, and to be as brief as possible, which he in vain strove to do, going every now and then astray: The substance of his confused continuation was as follows:

The robbers returned, treated John again with kindness, ate, drank, and left him once more, without mentioning a word about his going with them, which did not in the least displease him; he amused himself with reading, and, when night invited him to sleep, he went to his couch with a much lighter heart than when he had left it in the morning. That manner of life he led eight days, during which time the robbers always returned to dinner, in greater or lesser number; the whole gang consisted of twenty-four stout men besides the Captain.

On the ninth, tenth, eleventh, and the three succeeding days, the robbers did not return, but on the fifteenth they all appeared in high spirits, though with empty hands; John concluded, from this circumstance, and from what he could gather from their mysterious discourses, that they must have had several other haunts, where they hoarded up their spoils, the old Castle on the skirts of the Black Forest, seemed, however, to be their usual residence.

After dinner was over, and the goblet had freely circulated, the Captain recollected that John was to give them a second sample of his capacity, ordered him to mount a horse, and conducted him, accompanied by two of his associates, to the high road leading thro' the forest, where he commanded him to lay in ambush, and to rob the first traveller he should see coming along the road.

Poor John was thunderstruck at the stern command of the Captain, fell at his feet, and entreated him to have mercy on him; but the ruffians laughed at him, and their leader repeated his order, swearing he would kill him on the spot, if he did not instantly comply with his desire. The hapless fellow seeing there was no alternative, but to be killed, or to prey on his fellow creatures, concealed himself in a thicket, and the robbers posted themselves opposite to him, behind some bushes, taking the three horses along with them. The first travellers that passed by were two monks, and John thanked God in his heart that they were two. A little while after a ruddy countryman appeared, he was on horseback, as it seemed returning from the market, carrying two empty sacks behind him, and counting money. That will be an easy task, thought John, but when he was going to leave his hiding-place, his knees trembled, he was unable to stir, and the clown pursued his way without being disturbed.

The robbers began to hem, and poor John seized with terror, was going to run after the swain, but, thinking him too far advanced, resolved to wait for the next traveller, and to attack him vigorously.

He had waited a good while for another opportunity to acquit himself of his task, 'till at length a travelling journeyman appeared: John rushed out of his hiding-place before his prey was near enough, and as soon as the frightened traveller saw a man running towards him with a pistol, he took to his heels and luckily got out of his reach.

The Captain and his companions, seized with a fit of roaring laughter, exhorted their awkward pupil, in a low accent, to have a little more patience in future.

Before John could reach his lurking place, a Jew made his appearance; the sight of the poor Israelite fired the novice in robbery with an unusual courage, he rushed upon the terrified Hebrew like lightning, and, having seized him by the collar, demanded his money with a thundering voice: The petrified Israelite feeling himself thus roughly handled, shrieked and lamented most ruefully, and stoutly refused at first to deliver up his mammon, but when he saw his life at stake, and John put his pistol to his breast, yielded at last, with a woful visage, to the uncouth demands of his aggressor, exclaiming in the height of fear and despair, "I will give—I will give—all the money I have about me." So saying, he untied a leathern bag with money, fastened round his waist, and offered it to the greedy robber, who, transported with joy at his success, was thrown off his guard, and the cunning Jew taking hold of an opportunity to recover his treasure, seized, with much adroitness, the pistol, wrested it from poor John's trembling hand, and ordered the affrighted fellow, who was almost petrified, to return him his money instantly, if he would not have his brains blown out; John hesitated not a moment to submit to the Jew's demand, restored him his bag, and took to his heels, but the two robbers sallying forth from their hiding-place, retook him soon, while the cunning Israelite got clear off with his money and John's pistol.

The unfortunate fellow was instantly carried back to the robbers' den, and shut up again in the subterraneous dungeon which he had but lately left. Having been confined there some weeks the robbers took him one day out of his hole, and gave him his liberty, and a small sum of money, after he had sworn a dreadful oath never to reveal the least thing of what he had heard and seen in the cavern during his stay with them, and to leave the country as soon as possible.

This is the substance of my late servant's narrative; he had entirely forgotten his oath 'till he mentioned it, yet he silenced soon his murmuring conscience, persuading himself not to have committed perjury, because he had been intimidated by dreadful menaces to make it, and an oath of that nature could never be binding; he at the same time alledged, that the Captain himself had declared that among robbers swearing was of no importance, and thus soothed his conscience.

I did not think it necessary to undeceive, but gave him a handsome sum of money as a token of my gratitude for his faithful services, and bade him an affectionate farewell. He thanked me with weeping eyes and left the room. When he was gone I mounted my horse, and arrived after a few hours at N—.

Now I come to the last and most important incident I ever met with during the whole time of my recruiting business, which will clear up all the above related events, and dispel the clouds which are still hanging over some parts of my wonderful tale.

Two years were now elapsed since my last adventure, and I had heard nothing farther either of the Necromancer or his associates: The frequent unwelcome visits at the Castle and their alarming consequences, very likely had made both parties more circumspect, which appeared to me to have been the principal motive of those ruffians to release my servant, lest I might be induced to make a strict search after him; whatever may have been their motive for doing so, I had no farther trace either of the robbers or Volkert, and even at F—, the Necromancer's principal place of action, whither I went shortly after, even there, every thing relating to our former adventures was entirely forgotten—the haunted inn had been sold to a new master, the apparition was frightened away, and the house was a respectable auberge.

I also began, by degrees, to forget the adventures which I partly had heard related, and partly experienced myself, being only now and then reminded of those incidents, when, in the lonely hour of solitude the recollection of the Austrian stole on my mind.

My long overclouded serenity had resumed its wonted brightness, and the remembrance of my ever regretted friend was no longer accompanied by gloominess and melancholy sensations; I could again partake of the pleasures which smile at us wherever we are, and could relish again the innocent sports of merriment.

In that state of mind I arrived towards the end of summer at A—, when the expectation of every inhabitant was engaged by the approaching scene of a bloody execution, which was to take place within a few days.

A church having been robbed about six months ago, several suspected persons had been imprisoned and put to the rack, but could not be brought to confession, upon which the magistrates had been obliged to set them at liberty for want of such witnesses as the law requires, and to give up the inquisition until further proofs should be found. Many months elapsed before the enraged priests, aided by the eagle-eyed assistance of the magistrates, could trace out the sacrilegious robbers of their hallowed treasures, and feast their ruthless vengeance on the throes of the victims of their foaming ire, expiring on the flaming pile, 'till at length an accident delivered into their holy fangs the perpetrators of that daring deed, whom they in vain had endeavoured to discover by advertisements, tortures of the rack, and the promise of reward.

There lived in a suburb of A—, an old unsuspected man, named Peter, loved by the children of the place, whom he oftentimes amused with little tales, and bribed with sweetmeats, but dreaded by the aged, who firmly believed him to be on an intimate footing with his Satanic majesty, because he now and then displayed, when in good humour, proofs of his juggling skill, which they beheld with gaping terror. This hoary man, who lived in a mean cottage, in apparent indigence, and could not be suspected of possessing ill-gotten goods, went oftentimes abroad, but whither he journeyed, or what called him so frequently from his abode, nobody could tell with certainty; some said he went a begging, others, more superstitious, pretended to have seen him, through the chinks of the half-decayed window shutters, stretched lifeless on the floor; and some insisted upon having seen him riding through the air on a broomstick, to pay, as it was supposed, his court to his infernal master, to whom his soul and body was said to be mortgaged.

Very fortunately this man was not at A— when the church-robbery was committed, to the greatest satisfaction of some who thought him to be an harmless man, and to the greater mortification of others, who pretended to have suffered many a malicious trick by his sorcery; for if he had not been absent at that time, his ill wishers would certainly have forged a pretext to deliver him up to the civil power, as a suspicious person, because he never went to church, although he was supposed to be a roman catholic.

Some days after the above mentioned prisoners had been set at liberty, he returned to A—, on a holiday after sun set. The children playing in the streets no sooner espied him, than they ran towards him, hailing their hoary benefactor, with loud shouts, searching his pockets for sweetmeats, and teazing the poor old man so unmercifully, that he at last grew angry, and threatened to chastise the troublesome crowd with his staff; however, their demands grew still more clamorous, and some of them began to prick him with pins, which at length obliged him to put his threats in execution.

When the mothers of those ill-mannered boys saw the old man plying the backs of their darlings with his staff, they attacked him like furies, to revenge their children's wrongs and the prophanation of the holiday, and by their vociferations alarmed the whole neighbourhood: The husbands of the enraged dames came soon to their assistance; the children began terribly to roar when they saw their old friend in danger of being torn to pieces by their parents, and poor Peter was glad when he got out of the clutches of the merciless multitude, after having sustained many a hard blow, and hastened with all possible speed to shelter himself from farther insult in his humble cottage.

But who can describe the terror he was seized with, when he perceived that he had lost his wallet in the scuffle! Raving like a madman did he rush out of his hut, to recover his property, which was carried away in triumph by the victorious party: He exhausted all the rhetoric he was master of, entreated them, whined, and swore, but alas! his adversaries had hearts of flint, and stoutly refused to give up their booty, and when he at last, half frantic with despair, endeavoured to regain it by force, a violent shower of stones drove him back to his humble abode, leaving his dear wallet in the ruthless hands of the furious and inexorable mob.

The principal motive that had induced the assailants to retain the wallet, was an impulse of curiosity, to see what the old sorcerer, so they called him, had got by his journey; and the attack of the children was, very likely, a preconcerted matter, in order to provoke his anger, and thus give them an opportunity of satisfying their curiosity.

The wallet having been opened the first object meeting their prying looks was an old pair of breeches, a tattered shirt, and some pairs of stockings, then followed a large book and some unknown instruments, and at last they found at the bottom a heavy leathern bag, the knot by which it was fastened, baffling all their endeavours to untie it, was at length cut asunder, and the amazement of the gaping multitude rose to the highest pitch, when their eyes beheld a great number of gold pieces.

At first the whole crew was struck dumb with astonishment, but their silence was soon interrupted by a voice, exclaiming, "We have entrapped the sacrilegious robber of our church!" which was the signal for the enraged multitude to break out in curses and terrible execrations against the old man; the air resounded with the universal cry, "church robber! church robber!" and some of them, hastening to the justice of peace, roared with a bellowing voice, "we have found him out! we have found him out! we have detected the sacrilegious robber of our church!"

The justice was astonished at the unexpected tidings, but his amazement increased still more, when he saw the large heaps of gold coin, which had been found in the wallet of the old beggar, and instantly sent the beadle to seize poor Peter; mean while the rest of the furious mob had stormed the defenceless hut of the old man, dragged him forth, and conducted him towards the judge's house amid numberless blows and curses. He was now delivered up to the grim catchpole, who instantly carried him to the town prison.

His trial began the following day, and he was ordered to give an account of himself, and how he had got such a large sum of money. Refusing to answer that question, and pretending to have earned the money by honest means, he was put to the rack; yet he stoutly maintained his first declaration, and the justice, being unable to convict him of the charge he stood accused of, was obliged to set him at liberty, retaining, however, his money, until he should have proved that he had got it by lawful means.

Peter promised to prove his deposition within a short time, and returned to his hut, which, during his confinement, had been closely searched by his busy neighbours, who, however, had found nothing in it but some tattered coats, and broken pieces of furniture.

The justice, being a prudent man, dissembled to have dropped all farther inquiry, but secretly appointed some trusty people to watch all his motions. Their vigilance was fruitless a great while, until at length one of Peter's neighbours observed him, one morning, leaving his house with a wallet on his back, and a staff in his hand, setting off in full speed.

The people of the justice, whom he informed of what he had seen, followed Father Peter in different directions, in disguise, and saw him at noontide enter a lonely public-house: Having waited in vain for his reappearance, they began to conceive suspicion, and concealed themselves behind some bushes within a small distance from the house, until it grew dark.

As soon as night had spread her dun mantle over the face of the earth, they heard a distant trampling of horses, bending their course towards the spot where they were hidden, and, ere long, a numerous troop of horsemen alighted at the public house and entered it, upon which the spies crept forth from their lurking place, and stole softly to the windows of the house; there they had not listened six minutes, when they heard a jingling of money, and, peeping through the chinks of one of the shutters, beheld a table covered with dollars, and surrounded by a number of armed men, among whom father Peter was, feasting his looks on the money which was spread before him.

Having now got every information necessary, they mounted each of them one of the horses which the robbers had fastened to some trees, and hurried back to the town with all possible expedition. The public house being distant from A— only two leagues, they arrived there after an hour's ride, and having informed the justice of every thing they had heard and seen, were instantly sent back with a great part of the town guard, well armed, and mounted on the fleetest coursers that could be got.

The whole troops arrived a little before midnight at the public house, where the robbers were seated round a table, eating and drinking in the greatest security, and almost bereft of the use of their senses by frequent libations. They all started up as if roused by a sudden clap of thunder, when the town guard rushed into the room, seizing their arms, and threatening to blow their brains out if they should attempt the least resistance.

Their hands having been tied, father Peter, the landlord, who had concealed himself under the bed, and all his servants were seized, and, having been properly secured, carried off in triumph.

The robbers, amounting to ten, were clad in hunting coats, and their purses well stored with gold and silver coin; the whole train marching slowly on, with lighted torches arrived at A— before it was light, and the prisoners were safely lodged in the strongest dungeon.

Their trial commenced early in the morning, and the youngest of the robbers, who was questioned first, refusing to confess, was put to the rack; his stubbornness being soon subdued, by the torments of the torture, he made evidence, that their gang was very numerous, and scattered all over the country, where they had a great many hiding-places under ground; their chief residence, he said, was the old Castle, on the skirts of the Black Forest, where a great part of their spoils was concealed: He farther confessed, that Father Peter was in close connexion with all the different numerous gangs; that he had no fixed abode, but resided sometimes in this, and at other times in that town, and enjoyed the burghership in several cities, where he possessed houses and estates. He firmly denied to have had any share in the church robbery, but pointed out three of his fellow prisoners who had been concerned in it; whether Peter had been accessary in it or not he could not tell.

The day following the three robbers charged with the sacrilege were brought to the bar, but none of them would plead guilty. Being put to the rack, the first of them, an aged man, bore the three degrees without uttering a word, and died a few hours after he had been re-conducted to the prison. The second confessed at the third degree, that he had been accessary in the church robbery; but declared that the third was innocent, and that he himself had been persuaded by Father Peter, to commit the sacrilege.

Now the hoary dissembler was ordered to the bar: Having heard the charges of the justice with a firm countenance, he replied, with great equanimity.

"Yes, I am guilty, and wish to God, I had no other crimes on my conscience than that which I stand accused of. The sluggish gluttonous monks, who in honor of an image of stone, have ruined, and expelled from their own country a whole innocent family to beg their bread in the streets; these vile villains are far greater felons than myself, and I rejoice at having been an instrument in the hand of providence to avenge the wrongs of the hapless objects of their rapacity, and to restore to those innocent sufferers their property. If this action deserves punishment, you may tear my old limbs asunder, break these withered bones, and reduce to dust and ashes my poor outworn frame, I will not complain, nor utter a groan.

"The grim avenger draws near—I feel the hand of the Supreme Judge; he, and not you, poor mortals, force me to confess my transgressions. I can brave the ire of men, and deride all bodily sufferings; but I must bend my aged knees to him, who dwelleth in heaven, and the pangs of conscience are not to be trifled with."

The Judge and the Sheriffs gazed at each other in dumb silence at these words, and none of them were inclined to question him any farther. Seeing this, he informed them voluntarily of every particular of the sacrilege, and of the family which had been plunged into want and misery, by the rapacious monks, whose church and convent had been robbed, by means of a forged will: He at the same time confessed where and in what manner the jewels, and the gold and silver furniture, had been turned into money, and by what means the sums those articles had fetched had been conveyed to the family, without acquainting the innocent sufferers with the names of their secret benefactors.

The astonishment of the whole court increased with every word the old man uttered, and as soon as he had finished his confession, he requested the jailor to reconduct him to the prison. It lasted a good while before the dread arbiters of life and death could recover from their astonishment, and debate on Peter's doom, which they unanimously agreed to mitigate as much as possible.

According to the rigour of the law he should have been burnt alive, but he and the robber who had been convicted of sacrilege, were sentenced to be beheaded first, and then burnt. The rest of the gang were ordered to close confinement for further examination.

When father Peter with his fellow sufferer was called to the bar, in order to hear his sentence pronounced, he behaved with the same firmness of mind as on his trial, and comforted him who had betrayed him.

Having heard his sentence pronounced with the greatest equanimity, he thanked his judges for their clemency, and left the court, supporting with his arm his companion, who exhibited a ghastly picture of dismay and despondency. Father Peter did not lose his courage during his confinement, and took all possible pains to sooth the grief of his fellow sufferer, and to inspire him with sentiments superior to black despair.

He was to be executed two days after my arrival at A—, and I hesitated long whether I should go and see this extraordinary man or not, although I was much solicited by my friends to do it; having a secret boding, that this reverend old man, who faced the grim spectre of death so cool and undaunted, could be no other person than Father Francis, alias Volkert, and thinking it disingenuous to distress, by my presence, a man who had saved my life two years ago.

Curiosity and sensibility struggled a great while within my breast, until the last day before the execution, when an ardent desire of having cleared up the mysteries of former events got the better of my generous sentiments, and prompted me to see him early in the morning.

Having mustered up all my fortitude I went to the prison at six o'clock: Perhaps, thought I, the old man may now be more willing to dispel thy doubts than formerly, being on the awful brink of eternity, and disclose the mystery of his former impenetrable transactions, and thy presence may not distress the unhappy man so much as thou thinkest! Yet I could not get entirely rid of my apprehensions of increasing the sufferings of my benefactor, or being perhaps disappointed in my expectation.

In this state of mind I arrived at the prison, which was opened by the gaoler after a violent knocking. I requested him to favor me with a short interview with the prisoner, but was denied access, because it was against the common rule to introduce company to the convicts the day before the execution. I offered him a dollar, entreating him to make an exception with me, being a stranger, and having reasons of moment to wish for an interview with the old man: The sight of the money seemed to have more weight with him than my words; he mused awhile, and then said, "since you are a stranger I will make an exception from the common rule, but I must insist upon your telling nobody of this indulgence."

So saying, he conducted me without farther ado to a narrow staircase, leading to a long and narrow passage, at length we came to a small black door, marked with three red crosses, through which I followed him into a dark gloomy room; the entrance was guarded by two men half asleep, and in the background close to the wall I beheld two human figures, of a ghastly woe-worn aspect, and, drawing near with a beating heart, saw that one of them was Volkert: His countenance was pale and emaciated, but still stamped with his usual dignity of mien; his head reclining against the wall, and his hands resting on his knees.

He seemed not to perceive that a stranger was in the room until the gaoler said to him, "Well, Father Peter, there is a gentleman who will be glad to speak to you and to your comrade."

Hearing this, he slowly lifted up his head, staring at me.

"Volkert!" exclaimed I, "Volkert!"

His looks grew wild, his head sunk back, and he heaved a deep groan; whilst I was standing before him like a statue, thrilled with horror and pity.

As soon as the gaoler had left us, Volkert began with a trembling voice, "Lieutenant, are you come to embitter my last hours, or to speak comfort to my afflicted mind?"

"The latter, good Volkert," replied I.

"Then," said he, "you are welcome; sit down, if you please, perhaps I may be able to be useful to you some how or other, before I fall a victim to my crimes. I can caution you at least against cheats like myself."

"No idle curiosity has prompted me," said I, "to see you, nor am I come to distress you by illiberal reproaches, for having once endangered my life; that would be ungenerous: You have saved me once from eminent destruction, and that atones fully for all former injuries; yet, you will not be offended if I earnestly request you to clear up some late events, which have happened to myself and the Austrian, who—"

"Has been imposed upon by me," replied Volkert, "like yourself, whom I had given the lie at F—, in your and your friend's presence: I will give you all the information you desire, and at the same time a short sketch of my life, as well as it is in my power in my present deplorable situation. I wish most ardently I had done what I always intended to do, and set down in writing those events, and the memoirs of my life; they undoubtedly would be very instructive, and greatly lessen the number of impostors, and those that are imposed upon."

Here he stopped, and, having mused a while, began his narrative, which, indeed, was very defective, but satisfactory enough for me.

"I am," thus Volkert began, "a native of England, my father died when I was not quite ten years old, and left me an helpless orphan, without either fortune or near relations: A rich Dutchman being moved by my helpless situation, took me in his house, and, leaving England the year following, carried me over with him to the Hague.

"This worthy man gave me a very liberal education, and when I was thirteen years old took me in his 'counting-house, but, alas! he died before he could establish my fortune as he intended to do.

"His son, who carried on the father's business, had never been very partial to me, and forged a pretext to quarrel with me, and to send me away. A rich nobleman, just going to set out for Germany, wanted a servant, who occasionally would act as secretary, and I was glad to accept his offer to take me in his service: He directed his way to K—, where his father was one of the ministers of state.

"My young master appeared to be little inclined to qualify himself for state business, being possessed of a very small stock of ambition, and entirely addicted to the study of the occult sciences, which had engaged his attention so much, that he was unfit for any thing else. I soon was infected with an ardent desire to become his pupil, and, after a few months' instruction, was as great a fool as himself.

"It would be too tedious if I was to relate all our fruitless endeavours to effect the apparition of a spirit, and I was soon convinced that it lay not in the power of man to lord over these bodiless beings: My master, however, continued his mysterious operations day and night with an indefatigable ardour.

"It is very natural, that it at length came into my head to profit by his superstitious enthusiasm, and that I eagerly seized every opportunity to impose upon a man, who promised to fall an easy sacrifice to art and cunning, having great reason to expect that such an attempt would ensure me his affection, and promote my fortune rapidly.

"One night as he was conjuring up his guardian angel with much impatience, I entered his room, telling him, that all his efforts would be in vain, because he was not acquainted with the proper means of forcing the inhabitants of the other world to make their appearance.

"Gazing at me with wonder and surprise, he inquired whether I had improved so much in the occult sciences that I could effect what he so eagerly desired. I neither denied nor confirmed his question, but told him, that I would give him the next day, a specimen of my skill in Necromancy.

"It was an easy task to impose on my credulous enthusiastic Count, having secured the assistance of a fellow servant. We resided at a country seat his mother had left him, which was the fittest place in the world for the execution of our design. Having succeeded better than I at first expected, I made him my dupe above a twelvemonth, and grew at last so bold and impudent, that the Count could not but perceive my juggling tricks, and instantly sent me away.

"The good credulous man has certainly been convinced afterwards, that the lesson I gave him by my cheats deserved the warmest gratitude.

"I had saved a pretty sum of money during my stay with the Count, and, being used to an idle life, had not the least thought of looking about for another master. I went back to H——, where I abandoned myself to gambling, drinking, and all sorts of dissipation, until all my money was spent, and no other means of getting an honest livelihood left, than to try my fortune in the army.

"A recruiting officer paid me a hundred dollars for my liberty, and I cheerfully enlisted under the banner of Mars.

"I had received the promise to be made a serjeant, but saw myself at first very much disappointed, being forced to serve as a common soldier: Being however a good penman, well skilled in casting accounts, and leading a sober and regular life, I soon rose so high in the good opinion of my superiors, that I was appointed serjeant after nine months service. I certainly should have been promoted higher if I had continued to be zealous in the service, sober and attentive to my superiors, but my patience was exhausted, and I relapsed again into my former dissipations.

"A dissolute life requires money, and the desire of getting it plunges him who has once been led astray from the path of virtue, soon into his former errors. I had once more recourse to my juggling tricks, pretending to possess a supernatural skill, in detecting thefts, in tossing up the cup, and in telling people's fortunes; I conjured up spirits, dispelled the power of witchcraft, and raised up the dead: In short, I did every thing in my power to drain the purses of the weak and credulous.

"This trade was profitable, and very advantageous in many respects; but it lost me the esteem of my superiors, stained my character, poisoned my heart, and reduced me at last to that despicable sort of people, whose heedlessness bids defiance to every obstacle, and who have nothing more at heart than how they may enrich themselves to the detriment of their fellow creatures: In short, I became a rogue of the blackest die.

"It was natural that my cheats now and then miscarried before I arrived at that degree of skill, which, in later years, has crowned with success most of my roguish tricks. My superiors, who had warned me many a time against commiting such villainous actions, became at last tired of admonishing and correcting me by words, and a spirit which I had conjured up played his part so bad, that they found themselves obliged to make an example of me, and to banish me the country.

"An healthy well-made man of my age had no need to be uneasy about getting into the service of any foreign power. I had taken a liking to the life of a soldier, and found soon an opportunity of enlisting under the banners of Austria.

"A few days after I had began my peregrination, I met with a recruiting officer of that country, who proposed me to enter into the Austrian service, but, being grown wiser by experience, I at first feigned to dislike the military profession, and succeeded so well, that the officer at last threw a hundred ducats upon the table, assuring me, upon his salvation, that he never had paid such a price to a recruit.

"Now I thought it high time to strain the strings a little lower, agreed to his terms, and told him, that I had been serjeant in the H—n service: Having given him a specimen of my skill in penmanship, I requested him to recommend me to his commanding officer: He promised it and was as good as his word. The general received me exceeding well, and I occupied my former post, as serjeant, before a year was elapsed.

"Having been sent away with disgrace from H—, I had taken a firm resolution to abstain in future from all fraudulent juggling tricks, and kept my resolution firmly a long while, behaving eight years as it meets a good soldier.

"I abstained entirely from art and fraud, minded my duty, and thus ingratiated myself with my superiors to such a degree, that I kept firmly my ground in spite of many complaints which afterwards were made against me. An unhappy accident induced me to have recourse again to my former juggling tricks, and thus to acquire once more the title of a Necromancer.

"I will tell you all the particulars of that adventure, in order to enliven a little my tedious narrative, and to convince you, that nothing but necessity could tempt me to engage once more in rogueries, which already had destroyed my fortune once, and deprived me of my good character and an honorable employment.

"I was quartered in a house that was said to be haunted: It was rumoured about, that time out of mind it had been haunted by a spirit, who disturbed the tranquillity of the inhabitants, though he never had injured any body: He had now, for about six months, alarmed very much the people that lived in the house, and the report of that extraordinary perturbance had caused such a general fear that most of the rooms were unoccupied.

"Tempted by the cheapness of the lodgings, and desirous to get at the bottom of the alarming apparitions, which had given so much uneasiness to the inhabitants of that house, I went to the owner, and agreed with him to pay five dollars a year for the best room; I instantly took possession of my apartment, and, to my greatest surprise, perceived a long while not the least trace of any supernatural inhabitant.

"My landlord always disappointed my inquiries by vague ambiguous answers, and his daughter, who, as it was rumoured, had suffered most from the dreadful apparition, replied with nothing but a deep sigh, when I interrogated her about the nocturnal phantom.

"That girl had attracted my attention in a high degree, as soon as I had seen her, being adorned with charms which conquered every heart almost irresistibly, because she seemed to be entirely unconscious of their winning powers. Her face was rather pale, her constitution weak and sickly, and although she could not be called a beauty, yet I thought her very amiable, and more bewitching than any woman my eyes had ever beheld; I never had tasted the heavenly bliss of innocent virtuous love, before my thirty-ninth year; but I must confess this girl had infused into my heart, at first sight, sensations I had always been an utter stranger to.

"Helen, this was her name, her father and myself, occupied the first floor of the haunted house, and the second floor was inhabited by a young secretary; all the other rooms, a back parlour, on the ground floor, where the servants lived excepted, were unoccupied.

"The secretary seemed to have no concern for what was passing around him, his whole attention being engaged by his writings, and I happened only now and then to see him in the company of my landlord and his fair daughter, whom he treated as utter strangers: However I watched my opportunity better than him, and was never so happy as when I could spend a few hours in conversation with the charming maid: I always pretended to have something to say to the father, taking care never to come to his apartment but when he was abroad.

"However, all my anxious endeavours to make a tender impression on my charmer's heart proved abortive, Helen neither seemed to take the least notice of the attention I paid her, nor to be pleased with my eager zeal to engage her favor. The discourses I addressed to her consisted mostly in monologues, interrupted by frequent pauses; and her replies in a pantomime, composed of a silent shaking or nodding of the head, accompanied every now and then by a gentle sigh, which, of course made me, by degrees, tired of conversing with her, though my heart at first shrunk back at the thought of giving up such a lovely object.

"I had now been many weeks in the house without either hearing or seeing the least thing of the phantom, the tranquillity of the mansion not having been interrupted for a single moment. The domestics of my landlord were highly surprised, ascribing the peace which they enjoyed to me; even my landlord thought that I had chased away the dread phantom, and oftentimes thanked me warmly for having restored the tranquillity of his house.

"Dear friend," said he one evening to me, shaking me by the hand with evident marks of satisfaction, "to you I owe the peace and tranquillity I now enjoy; if the nightly phantom shall continue to stay away, my house will not longer remain unoccupied, and you shall live in it without paying rent as long as it shall be in my possession."

"These words he spoke in the presence of his daughter, who fetched a deep melancholic sigh.

"A few days after that trifling accident, as it appeared to me, I came home late in the night, and was going to lay myself down to rest, without calling for a candle, every body being gone to bed, when I heard gentle steps before my door: I started up, and the steps advanced nearer and nearer: Now they seemed to retreat, and silence reigned around a while.

"I listened with eager expectation, and, at once heard again the sound of fearful steps, and somebody moving the latch of my door, which now was opened slowly and shut again. I was just going to see what these strange proceedings meant, when a white figure entered my apartment.

"Who art thou?" exclaimed I, with a furious voice, seizing the phantom with a powerful hand.

"Jesu Maria!" groaned the apparition, "for God's sake be quiet."

"Methought I knew the voice, and, asking again who it was that dared to disturb my rest, the ghost whispered, in a faltering accent, "be quiet, dear Sir, I am Helen!"

"Half frantic with rapture I pressed the trembling girl to my panting bosom, printed a glowing kiss on her sweet lips, and asked her, what fortunate accident had procured me the happiness of seeing her so late in the night.

"Oh!" sighed the lovely girl, "you shall save me from destruction."

"With all my heart," answered I, "if it is in my power."

"It is in your power," resumed my sweet visitor, "my father confides in you; O, save me! save me!"

"I entreated her to tell me the source of her affliction, and how I could be serviceable to her; upon which she sat herself down and began as follows:

"The apparition which has lately disturbed the tranquillity of our house is my lover, Henry—is the secretary in the second floor: Last Autumn he asked me in marriage from my father, who refused to comply with his suit, and the unhappy man has been hurried by despair into a resolution which has destroyed the peace of my mind, and has made him likewise miserable.

"Our house has been reported to be haunted by a ghost these many years, because it was formerly a cloyster: My Henry took hold of that superstitious rumour, turning it to his advantage, and, alas! accomplished his design without difficulty. My heart was thrilled with terror at first, and several nights elapsed in unspeakable horror, before I knew that my Henry was the spectre that visited me every night, and made my blood run chill with awful dread. At length he undeceived me, but, alas! it was then too late; my virgin honor was gone for ever: I feel the dreadful consequences of my guilty connexion with the unhappy man, and disgrace and ruin will seize me with merciless fangs, if you do not save me. O, Mr. Volkert! do not refuse your assistance to a poor helpless girl."

"During this woful speech I had been standing before the lovely maid, holding her by her trembling hand, and bending my ear close to her lips, as she was whispering her woes to me. When she had finished her plaintive tale, she pressed me to her heaving bosom, her burning kisses thrilled the very pulses of my heart with voluptuous rapture, her lily arms encircled my neck, her whole lovely form seemed melted into one with mine—but you may easily guess what was the consequence!

"When the crowing of the cock announced the dawn of morning, she left me in high spirits, because I had given her the most solemn promise to procure the consent of her father to her marriage with the secretary, might it cost whatever it would. Her gratitude knew no bounds, she almost suffocated me by her endearments, and left me with these words:

"My happiness, my life, and my honor, are in your power; without your assistance destruction will seize me, and eternal misery will be my dreadful lot."

"As long as my blood was heated I thought no obstacle too arduous, but after a more cool deliberation, I soon grew sensible that I had engaged in a very difficult undertaking: By what natural means could the father of the seduced girl be persuaded to sanction her love? How was it possible to shake the firm resolution of a rigorous headstrong man, if a medium congenial to his manner of thinking was not to be employed, which might surprise and prompt him to come to our terms, for the sake of his own interest.

This medium was no other than what he himself had suggested to me—his belief in the supernaturalness of the apparition, and the power he supposed me to have over it.

"I could not get a wink of sleep during the remainder of the night, racking my brain and tormenting my imagination in vain:—Whenever I fancied to have hit on a feasible expedient, it soon vanished like a deluding dream, as soon as I applied the undeceiving torch of reason, and I saw but too clearly that nothing would extricate me from the maze I was bewildered in but the magic wand.

"I was engaged for three days in a most distressing conflict with my rebelling conscience, and several times on the brink of shifting quarters, and taking a house far enough removed from my then abode but my resolution was always shaken as soon as it was formed, when the doleful situation of the poor distressed girl recurred to my mind, imploring my assistance with a pallid ghastly look.

"It is true, the lover of the afflicted disconsolate girl did not deserve my assistance; however, I could not deny it to myself, that I had greatly injured him—common justice required some atonement, and poor Helen would certainly have been lost without my assistance. These considerations conquered at last every hesitation which reason and honesty had suggested to my troubled mind.

"The fourth night Helen paid me a second visit, entreating me more pressingly than at first; yet I remained firm and unpersuaded a good while; however, when she reminded me of my promise, and of ——, I could no longer maintain my ground, renewed my former promise, and went, without delay, the next morning to work.

"I entered at nine o'clock the apartment of my landlord and could not but observe, that Helen's cheeks were tinged with a crimson hue of inward satisfaction; her aspect and her looks supported my resolution.

"Sir," said I, "the tranquillity of your house is dear to me, and I have had the good fortune, last night, to hit upon means, the application of which will certainly secure it for ever."

"The simple superstitious man embraced me with visible marks of gratitude, exclaiming in an ecstacy of joy, "O, tell me, tell me, what must I do?"

"Then he ordered his daughter to fetch a bottle of Hungarian wine, pressing me to drink; but I declined it, resuming,

"Sir, the ghost that disturbs the peace of your house—"

"Have you seen him?" he interrupted me, with a ghastly look.

"I will see him," replied I, "he is a malicious being, and has given me much trouble; yet I trust I shall be able to get the better of him by the assistance of the occult knowledge which I possess."

"How! how!" stammered the simpleton, "then you are indeed the man I always took you for; then you are really one of those great mortals who understand the wonderful art of necromancy. How happy I am, to meet at last, so unexpectedly, with the man I have always most ardently wished to find out. Tell me, dear friend, what must we do?"

"Nothing in the world," answered I, "but conjure up in due form that turbulent spirit."

"And will you undertake to perform that difficult dangerous task?"

"Why not?"

"And when, dear Sir, do you intend to do me that inestimable favor?"

"The ensuing night if you will consent to it, for without your leave I can do nothing."

"O, that you have! that you have! You may do whatever you please; I will consent to any thing if I can get rid of that infernal disturber of my nocturnal rest."

"I left the credulous man with sensations which sprung from pity rather than exultation, at my easy gotten victory. I instantly made every preparation for executing my roguish plan, being assisted by the secretary, and having won over to my purpose the servants of the house, every thing succeeded to admiration.

"A little before twelve o'clock all the inhabitants of the house resorted to my room, and an intimate friend of mine acted the ghost admirably well: Benumbing perfumes deprived the spectators of the proper use of their senses, and the landlord had previously been made unfit for investigation, by a powder mixed with his wine.

"The ghost appeared, or rather stepped forth, from behind a partition of paper, which I had contrived to make.

"When I asked why he had dared to disturb the tranquillity and the peace of the house, he answered, in a tremulous hollow accent, "Out of resentment against the female sex."

"On my farther inquiries, he related, in short answers, that, a century ago, the cruelty of a lady he had been in love with had driven him to despair, and hurried him into the rash resolution to shut himself up within a cloister's hallowed walls; but, having prophaned his holy order, by entering into it with a worldly heart, polluted by the loose desires of sensual love, he had been condemned to purgatory until a certain condition should be fulfilled.

"All these queries and answers, previously set down in writing and got by heart, produced the desired effect on the blinded mind of the credulous father, who, at length, stammered out the question, "By what means he could be relieved from his torments?" The ghost replied, that he was doomed to suffer the agonies of purgatory, and to haunt his former abode in the midnight hour, until an unhappy couple, separated by a parent's cruel tyranny, should be united in holy wedlock.

"Having related his fictitious tale he disappeared behind the partition of paper, under the cover of a thick smoke, leaving my landlord in a state of mind, which seconded our design to the utmost of our wishes.

"When the credulous man had recovered a little from his astonishment, I asked him, if he could explain the meaning of the ghost's answer, and whether it was in his power to perform the condition he had hinted at: Upon which he silently nodded to me, and promised to pay me a visit early in the morning, which he did at six o'clock, confessing his cruelty towards his daughter, which he believed had provoked the resentment of the monk, and pleaded the poverty of the young man, and the cool indifference he had treated his daughter with ever since his offers had been rejected.

"Now," added he, "I see every thing in its proper light; the ghost has entirely opened my eyes, blinded by avarice: God be

praised that the young man has not yet left my house, as he intended to do, for it would then give much room for scandal, if he
should marry my daughter, which I am very well convinced cannot be avoided, if the tranquillity of my house shall be restored."

"In short, the secretary was married to the girl, and the ghost
appeared no more.

"This beneficial fraud, for so may I justly call it, the honor, and
perhaps the life of the father and daughter, having been saved by
it, and the young man, who was sober and industrious, proving a
very tender and affectionate husband: This beneficial fraud was
the first step, which afterwards led me to ruin and disgrace.

"Possessed of a large stock of knowledge of the human heart,
of experience, and art, I was no longer satisfied with confining myself to trifling juggling tricks, but I soon began to act after a more
extensive plan: In spite of all the precaution I had taken to keep the
above mentioned transaction from the knowledge of the public, it
soon transpired with the usual additions, and every body thought
me to be a sort of supernatural being, and so many opportunities
of preying on the credulity of mankind were thrown in my way,
that I could not stand the temptations which frequently occured,
to profit by the superstition of my fellow creatures.

"I hope you will spare me the distressing task to relate all the
transgressions I committed afterwards: Suffice it to say, that a
complete account of my frauds would swell many volumes. The
few remaining hours of life allotted me, prevent me from relating
all the subsequent cheating tricks which I committed, I therefore
shall confine myself to the two criminal transactions, by which
your friend, the brave Austrian, has been imposed upon; they will
afford you ample means of forming a proper idea of those I am
obliged to bury in silence.

"I had, for the space of six years, carried on my juggling tricks
with so much secresy, that few of my criminal deeds were known.
Although I had been betrayed several times by my associates, and
reprimanded by my superiors, yet I always suffered myself to be
blinded by the two powerful charms of gold and false ambition,
and was ever ready to lend my assistance to deeds of the blackest
hue.

"One day the widow of an honest citizen sent for me, and, having bribed me by some pieces of gold, requested me to assist her in the execution of a most criminal design.

"Her husband, lately deceased, so she told me, had promised her daughter in marriage to a man, whom she could not suffer to become her son-in-law, because he had behaved very disrespectfully towards her while her husband had been living, and scorned to apply for her consent; moreover, she told me, he was a lazy drunkard and a gambler; in one word, a good-for-nothing fellow.

"I know, Mr. Volkert," added she, "that you are in high favor with the Devil, and entreat you to raise up one of the angels of darkness, commanding him to appear to my daughter, and to threaten her to carry her to hell if she will not desist from her intended marriage."

"Shocked at that infernal proposal I was going to throw the money at her feet; would to God I had done it! but three ducats more soothed my indignation, and allured me to promise that I would take the matter into consideration, and inform her of the result of it the following day.

"I kept my promise, enjoining the woman to tell her daughter, as a secret, that her deceased father had, on his death-bed, compelled her to make a solemn promise, never to consent to that marriage: She readily executed my order, and the poor girl was overwhelmed with grief.

"Then I bade the inhuman mother assume a melancholy aspect, to treat her daughter with more kindness than ever, to mingle her tears with those of her child, to inveigh now and then against the caprice of the deceased, to inflame the girl, by degrees, with a desire of knowing the reason her father might have had to forbid, on his death-bed, her union with a man he had always seemed to be fond of; and, after these preparations, to mention, as if by accident, my name, and my skill in necromancy, yet to take care, not to betray her design of having conjured up her deceased husband.

"The cruel unnatural mother executed my orders with all possible dexterity and art, wept with her afflicted disconsolate child, and, by these means, beguiled the unsuspecting heart of her unhappy daughter. The poor victim of a mother's infernal cruelty listened eagerly to the deceitful speeches of her artful parent, and her curiosity was soon raised to so high a pitch, that she one evening came to my lodgings, trembling and shivering, to acquaint me with her woe, and to implore my assistance, which I instantly promised to grant her.

"The rest you very likely know, from the relation of your friend: One of my comrades, who was always ready to execute my commands, acted the ghost, and every thing succeeded, alas! too well.

"But suffer me to drop the dreadful horrid tale; this black infernal deed lays heavy on my conscience, for it has rendered me guilty of the murder of two innocent persons.

"Your friend requested me, soon after, to give him a specimen of my talents, which I readily promised to do as soon as an opportunity should offer; but, God knows, I did not then mean to perform my promise.

"However, the quarrel between the two officers afforded me very soon such an alluring opportunity to display my skill, that I could not stand the temptation to perform the most cunning and subtle trick. The whole transaction bears such strong marks of the marvellous, that you will expect a long explanation, but the contrivance was so simple that a few words will suffice to unfold to you that strange affair.

"One morning a foreign officer sent for and requested me, to compose an ointment, which would make him invulnerable. I stared at him with wonder and astonishment; however, when he covered the whole table with gold, I was tempted to profit by his folly, and asked him who his antagonist was: Being told it was Lieutenant C—, I would not run the risk of exposing myself to his resentment, and left the valiant son of Mars without listening to his proposal.

"The succeeding day your friend visited me: "Volkert," said he, as he entered the room, "I have a job for you: I can give you an excellent opportunity to favor me with a proof of your skill, and to get a handsome sum of money into the bargain."

"I pricked up my ears, made a few faint objections, and at length suffered myself to be persuaded.

"As soon as your friend had left me I went to Baron T—, who was still in bed, without having the least inclination of fighting a duel.

"Baron," exclaimed I, as I entered his room, "give me the money, I am ready to execute your orders; you shall not only be invulnerable, but also leave the field of battle and this town as a man of honor, provided nobody knows that you are returned from your journey."

"That is charming!" exclaimed the undaunted Baron, "nobody besides you and my landlord know that I am returned, and him we can easily silence if secresy is necessary."

"Then he jumped nimbly out of his bed, and gave me the money. I laid my plan before him, and he joyfully submitted to every thing proposed. His landlord and the owner of the house where the conjuration was performed, were bribed: The Baron, who acted the ghost, was concealed in a small closet, to which he, when the whole transaction was finished, retired, under the cover of a thick benumbing smoke, which concealed his retreat, and left the town that very night. The postman had likewise been bribed to deliver the letter, composed by me and copied by the Baron. The certificate of the surgeon-major was forged, and every thing succeeded to our satisfaction.

"As to the duel, every thing was effected by natural means: I cleaned and charged the pistols of Lieutenant C—, and took care to spoil the locks of one brace, and to charge the other with wrong bullets. I informed the governor of the duel, that Baron T—'s courage might be known, and he returned, for the same reason, to town, as soon as the duel was fought, delivering himself into the hands of the soldiers, who had been ordered to arrest the combatants.

"That he might be thought generous, he supplicated for the enlargment of his antagonist, and procured him the governor's pardon.

"The heinousness of this deed of mine will be lessened in your eyes, if I tell you, that the bullets in the Baron's pistols were likewise too small, so that Lieutenant C— could not be wounded dangerously, and the Baron took care not to hurt him materially.

"Volkert had, as yet, spoken with great hilarity, and it almost appeared as if he had entirely forgotten his impending doom; but suddenly he grew more serious and solemn: Gloomy clouds of sorrow were gathering on his brow, the paleness of his countenance increased, his lips were contorted, he gave a deep groan of anguish, and after an awful pause of inward agony, he went on in a faltering accent.

"O that I here could conclude the dreadful tale of my transgressions! O that I had not to relate deeds more glaring and abominable! deeds which thrill my soul with anguish, and pierce my guilty heart with a thousand daggers, pointed by unutterable pangs of a polluted conscience: However, I promised you a sketch of my whole life, and will be as good as my word: Although I shall not be able to give you a full narrative of deeds which fill my soul with horror, yet I will go on as well as I can.

"The intercession of Baron T— in my behalf, had so much weight with the governor, that he suffered me to escape without punishment, and sent me on the recruiting business, in order to get rid of me without provoking my anger: O that he had rather loaded me with his resentment, than with his bounty, and punished me as I deserved: perhaps it would have opened my eyes and brought me back to the path of honesty.

"My ruin was now completed: I began my recruiting business with great alacrity and cheerfulness, and found but too many opportunities of exerting my plotting skill, which I did with so much success, that my comrades were astonished, and my superiors so highly pleased with my zeal, that they put the greatest confidence in me, and intrusted me with sums which enabled me to abandon myself to all manner of dissipation; the few remaining sparks of honesty and virtue were extinguished by degrees, and I was hurrying with rapid steps into the abyss of destruction.

"My dissipations tempted me to defraud my superiors, and soon intricated me in a maze of embarrassment, where I found myself entirely bewildered. I got acquainted and intimately connected with the most dangerous sort of people, with robbers and their infernal associates: Allured by my cunning and artful tricks, they did every thing in their power to gain my confidence, and to win me over to their party, which, alas! laid the foundation to my ruin: I became a spy, a traitor, and, at last, their accomplice in the perpetration of the most shocking crimes.

"My recruiting business was neglected, and my superiors were going to call me back: Being not able to give an account of large sums that had been intrusted to me, I could not appear before my commanding officer, and no other means were left me to escape the impending storm, but to disappear entirely, which I effected in such a manner, that every one firmly believed I was no more.

"I conducted ten robbers, disguised as recruits, through a large town, where many of my profession resided, and, as soon as we had reached the adjacent wood, they took to their heels: I ran to the next village, raving like a madman, related my misfortune, wept, cried, and then returned to the wood, dissembling to be in the greatest despair.

"The robbers, who were waiting for me, made me pull off my uniform, dressed a dead man in it, who, perhaps, had been murdered for that purpose, put a pistol in his hand, and disfigured him by blowing his brains out.

"Now I was no longer Volkert the serjeant; I was Volkert the robber and murderer; I painted my face, feigned to be twenty years older than I really was, and thus escaped being known by my former acquaintances; I soon became famous under the name of Father Francis, bought houses in several towns, and every body took me for what I appeared to be, an old harmless man. Yet I was known at length by one of my former messmates, when in the H—n service, who was recruiting in the empire, and forced me to assist him in his business.

"The cunning rogue had not forgotten my skill in executing deceitful plots, and his expectation, that I should be of great service to him by my artifices, did not deceive him. I never spread my nets in vain when I wanted to catch a well-made young fellow, and we had enlisted within a short time a great number of recruits. How easy I could remove every obstacle I will prove by a single instance, which will give you a true notion of my intricated artifices.

"A well-made, young, and amiable Livonian, lodged with me, at the same Inn, at T—, and my associate took such a liking to him, that he offered to acquit me of all farther services, if I could ensnare this young man.

"I promised to do my utmost, and went instantly to work, ordering some of the gang I was connected with, and who then resided at T— on account of the great fair, to purloin his ring, snuff-box, purse, and watch, returning him the latter in a public place, telling him that I had detected the thief.

"This done, I left him suddenly, without giving him time to make farther inquiries, my sole view being to excite his curiosity and to gain his confidence, in which I succeeded admirably well.

"The Livonian became very anxious to get acquainted with me, watched my return to the Inn several nights, and attempted to converse with me; in short, he was very impatient to draw from me an information of the means by which I had detected the thief, but I always shunned him, and baffled his endeavours a great while, until, at last, I found it necessary to pay him a visit, in order to console him about the loss of a bill of exchange, which my myrmidons had got in their power, along with his pocket-book.

"This bill having contained all the little wealth he had got about him, he was under the necessity of either remaining some time longer at T—, or of selling his linen and every thing of value, and thus return to his own country, in a most distressing condition: I gave him two notes, each of a hundred dollars, the binding money from the recruiting officer.

"My unexpected visit and my seeming generosity, put him into the greatest astonishment, and I left him again abruptly, without entering into conversation with him.

"He was now enlisted without suspecting it, but I did not, as yet, know how I could put him into the power of my employer; however, my inventive genius soon suggested to me the proper means of effecting my purpose. By some letters from his mother, which I had found in the pocket-book, I had learned, that she had died a little time before, very ill satisfied with his conduct, on account of his dissipations when at university.

"The characters engraved on the inside of the ring which I had taken from him, being the same with those the letters of his mother were signed with, put it out of doubt that the miniature

picture of an old lady it was adorned with, must be the likeness of
his mother.

"One of my associates, whose features had by accident some
resemblance with those of the picture, concealed himself at the
inn, painted his face with chalk, wrapped himself in a sheet, and
went at midnight into the room of the young Livonian, who
seemed to wait for my return, to inquire, as I suppose, some particulars about the two notes I had given him the preceding day,
and was not a little frightened when he saw the ghost of his deceased mother entering his room. The phantom walked through
his apartment, looked at the watch which was on the table, to signify that it wanted rest, sighed, gave him a menacing look, and left
him thrilled with horror and amazement.

"The day following I ordered my myrmidons to watch every
step of the Livonian, and was informed that he was gone into a tea
garden, after he had changed the two notes.

"I hastened after him without delay, and found him sitting in
a lonely bower; he did not see me, though I was standing close
by him, being bewildered in gloomy meditations, and talking to
himself. Suddenly he exclaimed, "No, it was a dream!" "It was no
dream," replied I instantly. He looked up, seized with terror and
surprise. I promised to unfold, at ten o'clock at night, all the mysterious accidents which had happened to him at T—, and, having
appointed him to meet me at the city gate, which was within a
small distance from our inn, disappeared suddenly.

"My spies continued to watch all his motions during the remainder of the day, and one of them carried every thing that he
had lost to the landlord of the Inn where we lodged, that he might
be the more eager to meet me and to satisfy his curiosity, which
had the desired effect.

"He kept the appointment very punctual, but I made him wait
above an hour. Just when he was on the point of going home I
came walking towards him with hasty steps, and conducted him
to a lonely public-house within a small distance from the town,
which was the usual haunt of the recruiting officers and their associates.

"Having conducted him into a pleasure-house in the garden,
built over a cellar, to which a trap-door led from the room where

we then were, I asked him what he desired to know? and seeing him hesitate to fix on a question, I inquired if he should not like to know his benefactor, who had interested himself so much for him? He consented to it, and, having drawn a circle round the trap-door, which could be let down from below, I placed him to the centre of it. Some of my associates, who were concealed in the cellar, imitated the roaring of thunder, during my conjurations, opened the trap-door and caused him to sink down into the cellar: He who already had acted the ghost of his mother appeared again in his former disguise; some blew powder of calophony through the windows of the pleasure-house, and every thing succeeded as well as I could wish.

"The poor young man was stunned with wonder and surprise, and, seeing the ghost of his mother as he was sinking down into the cellar, lost all power of recollection. He was instantly carried into a coach, one serjeant of the recruiting officer seated himself by his side, and another mounted the box, driving on with all possible speed, but being a very indifferent coachman, the vehicle was suddenly overturned and one of the unhappy young man's legs was broken.

"When the serjeants saw it they disengaged the horses from the coach and rode away. This was indeed a great disaster, but still it turned out very fortunate for the young man, for a neighbouring nobleman, who saw him in his deplorable situation as he passed the road, took him to his castle, sent for proper assistance, and took so much care of the young man, that he, after a few months, was able to return to his native country, where he safely arrived without having met with any farther sinister accident.

"The recruiting officer, vexed at the miscarrying of our design, now dropped all connexion with me, and I abandoned myself entirely to a life of rapine and plunder.

"You will now expect me to unfold your adventure at the ruinous Castle, on the skirts of the Black Forest, but I hope you will spare me the disagreeable task of enlarging on the particulars, since you have a clue, by the assistance of which you will easily extricate yourself from the maze of mystery and wonder in which you have been bewildered.

"As to the strange apparitions in the subterraneous vaults, they have likewise been effected by the assistance of the robbers. Some of them were concealed in the vaults joining to the principal cellar, and the burying vault, blowing the artificial flashes of lightning through the chinks in the wall, and others being concealed in the hidden recesses of the subterraneous fabric, produced the thunder by means of large kettle drums. The lid of the coffin was opened by a cord, which the darkness concealed from your sight; the female figure was the son of a neighbouring publican, closely connected with our gang, who already had acted the ghost several times, when curious travellers had visited the castle: The light shooting from the coffin was effected by a dark lanthorn, which previously had been placed to it: The bluish glimmering you saw in the other vault, came from a lanthorn composed of blue glass, and placed on the staircase of the cellar.

"The second ghost was one of the robbers; his fractured disfigured head was made of an hollowed pumpkin. Our sudden retreat we effected through the iron doors, and the ruinous side building opposite the cellar door.

"The stench you smelt was effected by some brimstone we had left burning on the staircase: The extinguishing of the light in the lamp, hanging over the cenotaph, and of that which you had taken with you, was caused by a certain spirit I had poured in it as we descended the staircase: Perhaps you will recollect that I took it from you before I began my juggling tricks, as I was leading the way into the cellar. The spirit in the lamp over the cenotaph had previously been poured into it by one of my associates; and the smoke caused by the artificial lightning smothered the light until it evaporated in the arched vault. After the second apparition had disappeared, I overturned the lamp; and the rest you will be able to unravel without my assistance.

"Now I come to the incident which gave you and your friend an opportunity of seeing me in my real character, and of detecting my juggling cheating tricks. Every thing has been carried on and executed under my direction, here is the key to it. Ever since the H—n recruiting officer had known me at T—; I visited that town very seldom, though I possessed a house there, and was esteemed by my neighbours and fellow citizens.

"An acquaintance of mine who kept a public house within a small distance from T—, took a large Inn at that town, and expected to do very well, but an adjacent Inn which was in great renown, disappointed all his hopes, and reduced him soon to very distressing circumstances. He disclosed his distresses to me as I once happened to come to T—, and I advised him to ruin the neighbouring Inn by the introduction of a ghost.

"The owner of the house had died a little time ago, and his son, a young unexperienced and simple lad, carried on the business. We bribed some of his servants to make a noise in the night, and to spread the rumour about, that the house was haunted, and that the late possessor of it appeared at midnight, frightening the guests in a terrible manner.

"This artifice succeeded to the utmost of our wishes, and when I left T—, a few months after, the Inn of my friend, which always had been empty, was crowded with travellers, while that of his neighbour was the lonely haunt of the disguised spectres.

"Having great reason to apprehend that our machination would be detected, sooner or later, I promised my friend, who dreaded the same, to return within a twelvemonth, and to procure him an opportunity of purchasing the haunted Inn, on reasonable terms. I was as good as my word, returned to T—, and what farther happened you know.

"At first I was rather uneasy that the foreign officer had taken lodgings at the haunted Inn, and prohibited every nocturnal disturbance, apprehending the whole artifice would be detected, but just as I was going to leave T—, without having attempted any thing, the cowardice of that officer gave me an opportunity of executing my design.

"His comrades, chicken-hearted like himself, proposed to watch with him in the haunted house, and their imagination played them a trick which, most unexpectedly, favored the execution of my plan.

"They had watched already three successive nights, without either hearing or seeing any thing uncommon; the fourth night a tempest was raging, without their perceiving it, being prevented from doing it by the great quantity of punch they had swallowed, and the roaring noise which was the natural consequence of their inebriation.

"When they entered the room, after having been frightened by the howling of the storm, on their return from the search they had been making, the tempest ceased a few seconds, and it was natural that one of them, who very wisely looked out of the window, could perceive nothing. Being chilled with dread and apprehension, he forgot to bolt the window; his companions had, from like reasons, neglected to shut the door, and the first gust of wind finding no resistance, threw the window and the door suddenly open, the lights were extinguished, and their disordered fancy effected now, what I perhaps would have attempted in vain, with all my juggling skill. Flashes of lightning illuminated the room, the tremendous roaring of thunder shook the house, one of the company overturned the table, in his fright, and they really fancied to see a phantom, which only existed in their disordered imagination, harrowed up by fearful apprehensions and superstitious terror. What farther happened I need not tell you.

"My spies informed me of the departure of the officer, who had resided at the haunted Inn, and of the route he had taken; they likewise apprised me of his return. I hastened to meet him on the road, and the conjuration of the ghost was agreed on.

"Being no stranger to the cowardly disposition of his friends, I apprehended not the least danger from their being present at the experiment, and willingly consented that he should bring with him some of them.

"However, I was very much mistaken, because two of them were gentlemen for whom I was not prepared, and who had been already once deceived by Volkert; yet I did not entirely miss my aim, and the haunted Inn was sold, soon after, to my friend, on very low terms; the simpleton, who had been the owner of it, and who believed still in the reality of the apparition, in spite of what he had seen and heard, when I conjured up the spirit, and in spite of reason and good sense, having no peace nor rest until he disencumbered himself of the possession of ill-gotten wealth.

"The apparition itself was effected by means of a camera-ob-scura,[1] in an apartment beneath that where I performed the cheat, some boards in the floor having the night before been sawed through, after we had made a hole in the ceiling of the lower chamber. The boards which covered the opening close to the wall were replaced in such a manner, that they could be removed from below, by means of which, the smoke could ascend from the lower apartment, and represent the picture in the machine—smoke and darkness put the finishing stroke to the deception.

"I left, like your friend, T— the next morning, with the firm resolution to return no more, apprehending to be delivered up to the vengeance of the civil power, in spite of your generosity, and having lost my good character for ever. On my journey I happened to come to the house where you was confined, and felt the highest satisfaction when I had it in my power to make you some atone-ment for the many wrongs you had suffered by me. My intention was to live here in A—, in solitude and retirement, and to dedicate the rest of my miserable life to repentance, and thus to make my peace with God: But my former lawless companions soon found out my retreat and forced me to renew my crimes, and to assist them in their infernal deeds.

"The crime for which I am confined here you very likely know: All I can say, in order to palliate this last transgression, is, that it is one of the noblest deeds I ever performed, and it would not give me the least uneasiness, if the execution of it had not brought de-struction on other people beside myself."

Here Volkert stopped, fatigued and exhausted by the long narrative: I conversed a good while longer with him on his con-

---

[1] Literally a "dark room," the camera obscura is a forerunner of the camera in mod-ern photography. Using a darkened chamber and a pinhole into which light from outside entered, exact images, though upside down, shimmered and moved on the walls of the chamber. According to Robert Leggat's *History of Photography*, the cam-era obscura was associated with magic, for in the early sixteenth century, Giovanni Battista della Porta used the camera obscura to entertain his guests, and they fled in panic, eventually causing a charge of "sorcery" to be leveled against him. The camera obscura becomes, therefore, merely another of Volkert's technological ma-nipulations, but entirely in keeping with the folk superstitions surrounding the use of such an instrument.

jurations, and could not help mentioning, that I was very much surprised that his deceptions could have been kept so concealed, though he had always been obliged to rely on the assistance of other people: To which he replied,

"Your observation is very just, but your surprise will vanish, if you consider, that my assistants in cheating people, bore their share in the frauds I committed, and, of course, would not have escaped punishment, if they had not kept secret all transactions of that nature.

"It is more surprising," added he, "that one is always certain to find people who will lend their assistance in cheating their fellow citizens, and it is almost incredible how willing every one is to assist any impostor in deceiving others. Yet I do not think that the source of that intriguing disposition, so common among all classes of men, springs from the depravity of human-nature, I rather would attribute it to the pleasure every one feels, when he can prove the superior powers of his genius, which is the head spring that animates us as well to good as to bad actions, and, if guided by a benevolent heart, and good principles, raises us above the common herd, and leads us to honor and glory."

As I rose and was going to leave the prison Volkert squeezed my hand, and said, with a faltering voice,

"To-morrow at this hour I shall be no more; to-morrow, at this hour I shall have seen the Supreme Judge of human kind: I shudder when I think that I must appear before his awful throne; yet there is still one consolation supporting me, one consolation that, as yet, has warded off the deadly arrows of despair, and, I trust, will comfort me in my trying hour, and when he who dwelleth in heaven shall speak to me. This consolation, friend, give me leave to call you by that sacred name, this consolation is not the vain groundless expectation that I shall atone for my sins, by suffering the punishment that awaits me; No! If I had a hundred lives to lose, I could not atone for my manifold crimes: This consolation consists in the persuasion that I shall be made a warning example of the dread consequences attending the criminal abuse of the intellectual powers the great ruler of the universe has given us, and that the world will be warned against impostors like myself."

When he had finished I bade him a last farewell, in a faltering accent, and left the unhappy man, who said to me, as I opened the door,

"Come to-morrow to the place of execution, your presence will give me comfort!"

I left the prison lost in gloomy thought, and with a bleeding heart. The dismal idea of the awful scene which was to be exhibited the next day, haunted me where ever I went, and I struggled in vain to chase it from my mind: The solemn stillness of the night rather increased than diminished my uneasiness, and sleep entirely fled from my weary eyes. The dawn of the rosy morn cheered the whole creation, but my soul was pierced with horror when the first ray of the rising sun hailed me on my couch.

At length the solemn sound of bells announced the approaching hour of execution; I wrapped myself in my cloak, and repaired with trembling steps to the place where Volkert was to atone for his crimes. The streets were crowded with a noisy multitude: Haunted by secret awe did I arrive at the place of execution, and horror made my blood run chill as I beheld the dreadful pile, which soon was to reduce to ashes the preserver of my life.[1]

A gaping multitude was standing around, awaiting with cruel insensibility, and with more than beastly satisfaction, the dreadful catastrophe which was to terminate the life of their fellow creatures.

Without recollection was I standing amid the crowd, when, suddenly a confused noise was heard, and every eye directed to *one* spot: Lifting up my downcast looks, I beheld the funeral procession drawing near with slow solemnity: Volkert was walking in the front with firm and manly steps, followed by his ghastly looking fellow sufferer: The procession stopped at the enclosure, encircling the scaffold, and Volkert's eyes were anxiously looking

---

[1] England had severe penalties for hundreds of offenses throughout the 18th century; indeed, there were an enormous number of capital crimes, even for minors, such as being a pickpocket. Readers of *The Necromancer* would have been well informed of the public's desire for public crime and punishment, particularly executions, and the "entertainment" it afforded to the masses. See Clive Emsley, *Crime and Society in Society in England, 1750-1900* (Pearson Education, 2005) and Edward P. Thompson, *Albion's Fatal Tree: Crime and Society in Eighteenth-Century England* (Knopf, 1975).

around; at length he saw me, nodded to me, with a grateful smile, and entered the enclosure.

His trembling fellow sufferer was first sacrificed by the avenging hand of justice. I cast my eyes to the ground until I perceived by the murmuring noise around, that his sufferings were over. Now I directed again my melancholy looks towards the dread place of execution, and beheld Volkert undressing himself, and approaching with firmness the stool stained with the smoking blood of his friend. Now he was seated, the sword of the executioner lifted up—now it glittered in the morning sun, ready to strike the fatal blow. I shut my eyes involuntarily—a sudden hollow humming told me that Volkert had conquered. Awful sensations thrilled my palpitating heart, and I forced my way through the gaping multitude without looking once more towards the horrid place where Volkert had expired.

At the city gate I looked back and beheld with horror a thick column of smoke ascending aloft and darkening the pure serene air; I could not stand the horrible sight, and hastened to my apartments, determining to leave a place immediately, in which my peace of mind had been so much disturbed.

But being informed that the Captain of the gang would be examined the following day, curiosity got so far the better of my impatience to leave as soon as possible a town where every object recalled to my mind the hapless fate of my preserver, that I resolved to stay one day longer, and very glad I am that I took that resolution: The account this man gave of himself being so singular and remarkable, that I was amply repaid for the melancholy and grief which haunted me with unabating fury, whilst I tarried within the walls of the town where my benefactor had been executed.

The trial began at six o'clock in the morning, and I took care to be in the town house, before the terrible leader of the robbers had made his appearance at the bar. Every one present seemed struck with terror when he entered the hall.

He was of a gigantic make, near seven feet high, his robust limbs corresponding with his extraordinary size; his black and bushy hair covered part of his sunburnt face, which was disfigured by two gaping scars across his left cheek. His eye, for he had but one left, flashed like lightning when he beheld the dread arbiters of life and death eager to pronounce his doom. The judge exhorted him to speak the truth, and not to aggravate his guilt by stubbornness. However nobody expected that a wretch of his appearance would pay the least regard to gentle admonitions, and perhaps remain silent even under the tortures of the rack. His savage look and lofty mien seemed to betoken an haughty spirit, not easy to be subdued. I at least had entertained not the most distant hope of having my curiosity gratified in so satisfactory a manner as he really did. Imagine therefore my astonishment when contrary to all expectation, he began.

"My Lord and Gentlemen,

"I am in your power, and well aware that nothing can avert my impending doom, I scorn the tortures of the rack and bid defiance to every human effort, to force me to a confession of my crimes: You might tear my limbs asunder, and kill me by inches, and yet would never extort a single word from my lips, if I had no other reasons to deal candidly with you. However I will spare you that trouble, and honestly confess my crimes, their origin, and their progress; being strongly persuaded that the history of my life will afford a useful lesson to judges, and teach the guardians of the people to be careful how they inflict punishments if they will not make a complete rogue of many a hapless wretch, who would have been recalled to his duty, and preserved to the human society, by gentle treatment: I never should have become a robber, had not the too great severity of the laws made me an enemy to the human race, and hurried me to the brink of black despair. I know my doom is fixed; however, if your heart is no stranger to pity, you will at least not refuse a tear of humanity to a poor unhappy man, who has been dragged by dire fatality into the path of vice, and forced to commit deeds his soul abhors."

Here he stopped. Awful silence swayed around, and my curiosity was harrowed up to the highest degree, when he began nearly in the following strain.

"I am the son of an Inn-keeper at A—, whose name was Wolf, and who died when I had reached my twenty-fourth year. I succeeded him in his business, which being but indifferent, many of my hours were unemployed: Being an only son, I had been spoiled by my parents, who were delighted with my wanton pranks and indulged me in every thing. Grown up, girls complained of my impudence when I was but twelve years old; and the boys of the village paid homage to my inventive genius. Nature had not dealt niggardly with me in respect of bodily endowments; however, an unfortunate kick from a horse disfigured my face in such a manner, that the girls of the village shunned me, and my play-fellows took frequent opportunities to make me an object of their merriment. The more my female acquaintances avoided me, the more the desire of pleasing took root in my heart. As I grew up, I was given to sensuality, and persuaded myself to be in love. The object of my flame treated me with scorn, and I had reason to apprehend that my rivals were more successful than I; however the girl was poor, and I had reason to hope that her heart, which was inaccessible to my vows and prayers, would yield to presents, which I knew not how to procure, the small income my business afforded me being entirely swallowed up by the vain efforts I made to render my person less disgusting. Being too much addicted to idleness to exert myself in amending my circumstances, and too ambitious to change my expensive mode of life, I had only one mean left to improve my fortune, which thousands before me had tried with more success.

"The village in which I lived gave me an opportunity of committing depredations on the game, and the money I raised in that way wandered regularly into the hands of my mistress. Robert, a game-keeper to the Lord of the Manor, was one of the admirers of Jenny, which was the name of my paramour; he soon observed the advantage which my presents procured me over him, and being spurred by envy and jealousy, he watched me closely: By degrees he began to resort to the Sun, which was the sign of my Inn, more frequently than ever, and his prying eye soon detected the source of my liberal gifts.

"A very rigorous law against game-stealing had been renewed not long before, and Robert was indefatigable to find an opportunity of getting rid of his rival.[1] He succeeded but too soon; I was

---

[1] Game stealing was one of the capital offenses that connoted class differences, since those impoverished by the changing British economy during the 18th century were those who committed this class of crime. Wolf's confessional statements are criticisms of a rigid class structure, whether German or British, which oppressed

caught in the very act of shooting a deer, and condemned to be sent to the house of correction: It cost me all my little remaining fortune to buy off that punishment. Robert had gained his aim, and Jenny's heart was lost to me.

"Glowing resentment rankled in my breast and I was determined to be revenged as soon as a proper opportunity should offer. Poverty and want, hunger and despair, tempted me once more to have recourse to game-stealing, and Robert's watchfulness surprised me a second time. Being reduced to the lowest degree of poverty, it was not in my power to gild the hands of justice a second time, and I was committed for a whole year to the house of correction in the residence. Every lash of the gaoler's whip gave new strength to my resentment, the separation from my mistress increased my passion, and I hastened on the wings of love and revenge to my native place, as soon as I had been set at liberty. I flew to Jenny, but was denied admittance and treated with scorn. The pinching want having subdued my pride and laziness, I offered my services to the rich, in the village, but nobody would employ a fellow who had been imprisoned in the house of correction.

"Pressed by hunger and dire necessity, and foiled in all my attempts at getting an honest livelihood, I renewed my depredations on the game, and was entrapt a third time through Robert's watchfulness. The repeated infringements on the game laws had aggravated my guilt: The judges looked into the records of the law, but not into the heart of the transgressor, paid no regard to the plea of want and dire necessity, and sentenced me to have the mark of a gibbet burnt on my back, and to work three years in the fortifications.

"At the close of that term I recovered my liberty a second time, and here begins a new period of my life.

"I was entirely changed, having entered the fortress as a common transgressor, and left it as a consummate villain. I was not entirely divested of all sentiments of honor when I was confined;

---

the lower classes through the extreme enforcement of property laws. One of the most interesting literary thieves of this type is Lionel Verney, the protagonist of Mary Shelley's *The Last Man* (1827), a born aristocrat-turned-thug, who in his youth scornfully preys upon the livestock of the nobility as part of his vendetta against those who destroyed his father.

however the few remaining sparks of ambition were soon extinguished by ignominy, being confined in one room with twenty-three malefactors, two of whom were murderers, and all the rest famous thieves and vagabonds. I was laughed at, when mentioning the name of God, and urged every day to utter blasphemies against our Holy Redeemer! My fellow prisoners sung obscene songs to me, which I could not hear without disgust and horror, and committed actions which I could not behold without blushing. Every day new rogueries were related, or wicked designs fabricated.

"At first I avoided the company of that abominable set of wretches as much as possible, hiding myself in the remotest corners of the prison; however, I wanted a companion in my solitude, and the cruelty of my gaoler had refused me even the poor consolation of taking my dog with me. My labour was hard and my health declining: I wanted assistance, and, to be sincere with you, I was in need of comfort, which, scanty as it was, I could not obtain without sacrificing the last remains of my conscience.

"Thus I used myself by degrees to hear without disgust, the most horrid language, and to behold without aversion, and at length with secret pleasure, the most shocking actions; before the termination of my confinement I was superior in wickedness to my instructors in villany, and began to thirst with increasing impatience for liberty and revenge: I hated the whole human race, because every one of my fellow creatures was either happier or less wicked than myself; I fancied to be a martyr to the natural rights of man, and a victim of glaring injustice. I rubbed my chains against the wall in a fit of frenzy, grinding my teeth when the sun was rising behind the rock on which the fortress stood, and experienced with unutterable agony, what a hell an extensive view creates in the bosom of a prisoner.

"The free air whistling through the iron grates of my window, and the swallow perching on the massy bars, seemed to mock me with their liberty, and rendered my imprisonment more hateful and horrid to me. Seized with the burning fangs of despair, I vowed unrelenting and burning revenge to the whole human race, and have been as good as my word.

"The first idea which rushed upon my mind as soon as I saw myself at liberty, was that of my native village. I had indeed not the least glimmering of hope to meet there with the smallest assistance in my distress; however I entertained sanguine hopes to glut my revenge, which gave wings to my steps. My heart beat violently when my impatient eye beheld the steeple of the village; however, it was not that sweet satisfaction which I had felt on my first pilgrimage, which was now heaving in my bosom. The recollection of all the misfortunes and cruel persecutions I once had suffered there awakened me suddenly from a kind of stupefaction; all my wounds began to bleed anew: I quickened my steps, anticipating the pleasure it would afford me to strike my enemies with terror by my sudden appearance, and to feast my eyes on the pangs of the devoted victims of my vengeance.

"The bells were ringing to summon the inhabitants to the church when I made my appearance in the market-place: I was soon known by the inhabitants, who were going to church, and every one who met me started back at the sight of me. Having always been very fond of children, I could not resist the involuntary impulse of giving a penny to a boy who was skipping by; he stared at me for a moment and then threw the money in my face. If my blood had not been heated so much, I should have recollected that my long and bushy beard had frightened the poor boy; however, my polluted heart had infected my reason, and tears, which I never had shed in my life, were trickling down my cheeks.

"The boy does not know who I am, nor whence I came," said I, half loud to myself, "and yet he avoids me like a wild ferocious beast: Is my black heart marked on my brow, or have I ceased resembling a human being, because I am sensible that I hate all human kind?" The contempt of that boy grieved me more than my long imprisonment, because I had treated him kindly, and could not accuse him of personal hatred.

"I seated myself on a large stone opposite the church: What intention I had I do not know, however I remember very well that I rose up in a fit of burning rage when I saw that all my former acquaintances passed by with visible contempt, and scarcely deigned to look at me.

"I left my station in an agony of vexation, to find out a lodging, and as I was turning round the corner of a street I met my Jenny. 'My dear Wolf,' she exclaimed, and offered to embrace me, 'God be praised that you are returned at last; I have shed many a bitter tear during your absence!' Hunger and misery were marked in her face, and I beheld with horror that she was infected with an ignominious illness: Her tattered raiment and her whole appearance told me plainly what a miserable wretch she was. I soon guessed the origin of her abject situation, concluding by the sight of some dragoons that soldiers had been quartered in the village. 'Soldier's strumpet!' I exclaimed, and turned my back to her with an exulting laughter. It gave me some satisfaction to see her infidelity rewarded in so shocking a manner. I never had loved her sincerely.

"My mother was dead, and my house had been sold for the benefit of the creditors: I had no friend, no money, except a few groats; everybody fled me like a mad dog, however I was dead to shame and disgrace. After my first imprisonment I had shunned all human society, because I could not stand the contempt I met with every where. Now I intruded upon them, and it afforded me a malicious satisfaction to drive them away by my appearance: It gave me a pleasure, because I had nothing farther to lose, and nobody to care for; I had no farther occasion for the least good quality, because nobody believed I had one left; the whole world was open to me, and perhaps I should have been able to recover the character of an honest man in a distant province, however I had no courage to assume even the mask of honesty; despair and disgrace had forced these sentiments upon me, and I persuaded myself that every sense of honor was useless to me, since I had no claim to the smallest share of it. If my vanity and pride had maintained their dominion over me, I certainly should have put an end to my existence; I did not know myself what my intentions were, I wanted to do mischief so much I knew: I wished to deserve my fate. 'The laws,' said I to myself, 'are the guardians of human happiness, and therefore I will do whatever is in my power to subvert them.' Necessity and thoughtlessness had once compelled me to sin, but now I did it voluntarily because it gave me pleasure.

"I had again recourse to game-stealing, for hunting had always been my chief passion, and life called for support: But this was not the sole motive which prompted me to reassume my former favorite occupation; the desire of bidding defiance to the laws and to infringe the prerogatives of the prince was an additional impulse; I had no apprehension of being taken up once more, for now I had a ball in readiness to stop the mouth of my informer, and was sure I could not miss my aim.

"I killed all the deer which came in my way, selling only a few pieces on the frontiers, the remainder I left behind to rot. I lived very sparing in order to be able to afford the expences for powder and shot. My depredations and the havoc I made in the forest, caused a great alarm, but nobody suspected me, my miserable appearance screened me from suspicion and my name was forgotten.

"This mode of life I continued for several months without being detected. One morning I was rambling through the forest pursuing the traces of a deer. Having hunted without success two tedious hours, I began to give up every hope of coming at my prey, when I saw it at once within the reach of my gun. I took my aim and was going to fire, but started suddenly back, when I saw a hat upon the ground not far from me. I looked around with great circumspection and beheld Robert, the game-keeper, standing behind the trunk of an oak, and aiming at the same deer which I intended to kill. My blood froze in my veins as I beheld the author of all my misfortunes; and this very man whom I hated most among the whole human race, was within reach of my fusee: Infernal joy thrilled my whole frame, I would not have exchanged my gun for the universe; the burning revenge which 'till then had been rankling in my bosom, rose up into my finger's end, which was going to put an end to my adversary's life; however an invisible hand seemed to retain my arm to prevent the horrid deed: I trembled violently as I directed my gun against my foe—a chilly sweat bedewed my face—my teeth began to chatter, as if a fever frost had seized my frame—methought I felt the icy fang of death upon my heart, and every nerve was quivering.

"I hesitated a minute—one more elapsed—and now a third. Revenge and conscience were struggling violently for victory— the former gained and Robert lay weltering in his blood!—

"My gun dropped on the ground when Robert fell—Murderer, stammered I with quivering lips—the forest was as silent as a church-yard, and I heard distinctly the word murderer. Creeping nearer to the spot where my enemy was swimming in his blood, I saw him just expire. I stood a dreadful minute of grisly horror before my murdered foe, as if petrified—a yelling laughter restored me to the use of my senses: 'Wilt thou any more tell tales, good friend,' said I, stepping boldly nearer, and turning him upon his back. His eyes were wide open, I grew serious, and every power of utterance fled; strange and horrid sensations chilled my heart.

"'Till then I had been a transgressor of the laws on the score of the disgrace I had suffered, but now I had perpetrated a deed for which I had not yet atoned. An hour before that horrid action, no man living would have been able to persuade me that there was a more abject being upon earth than myself, but now I began to fancy that I had been enviable an hour ago.

"Not the most distant idea of God's judgments came in my mind; however I had a confused notion of halter and gibbet, and of the execution of a murderer which I had witnessed when a boy. The idea of having forfeited my life froze my very soul with dreadful fear: I wished ardently that it might be in my power to restore to life my slain enemy, and racked my brain to recall to my recollection all the injuries he had made me suffer, but, strange to tell, my memory seemed to be entirely extinguished, I could not recall a shadow of all the ideas, which, but a quarter of an hour ago had filled my soul with glowing revenge; I could not conceive how I could commit such a horrid deed.

"I was still standing by the corpse in a kind of stupefaction, when I was roused from my desponding reverie by the cracking of whips, and the creeking of waggons on the high road, which was about a mile distant from the spot where I then was.

"I went mechanically deeper into the forest, and, recollecting on the way that Robert had been used to wear a watch, I wished to get it in my possession. I wanted money to reach the frontier, and yet I had no courage to return to the place where the corpse lay, the idea of the devil and the omnipresence of God rushing suddenly on my mind. I struggled a few moments, and having summoned all my boldness, determined to go back and fetch the watch in defiance of God and the devil.

"I found what I had expected, and in a green purse a little more than a dollar, silver coin: As I was going to put both in my pocket, I started suddenly back and considered whether I should take it or not. It was no fit of shame, nor was it fear to aggravate my crime through robbery; it was rather scorn, which prompted me to fling the watch upon the ground, and to take only one half of the money. I wanted to be thought an enemy of the game-keeper but not his robber.

"Now I fled deeper into the forest. I knew that it extended itself four German miles[1] towards the north, where the frontiers of the country began. I fled on the wings of fear 'till noon; the swiftness of my flight had dispelled the agony of my conscience; however, it returned with redoubled violence as my strength began to be exhausted; a thousand grisly phantoms tortured my fancy, and filled my soul with dreadful bodings. I had no other choice but either to put an end to my wretched existence, or to drag on a life embittered by a continual fear of dying under the hand of the executioner: I had not the courage to rid myself of a painful existence, and shuddered at the idea of leading a life of never-ceasing torments.

"Hemmed in between the certain tortures of life and the uncertain horrors of eternity, equally averse to life and to death, I finished the sixth hour of my flight, an hour abounding with agonies, which no living man can form an idea of.

"Gloomy and slow I had pursued a narrow foot-path, which led through the darkest thicket, when suddenly a rough commanding voice ordered me to stop. The voice was not far off; agony and the horrors of despair, which had assumed their dreadful sway over me, had made me entirely regardless to the objects around me, my eyes were cast to the ground, and I had covered part of my face with my hat, as if that could have hidden me from the eye of the lifeless creation. Starting and lifting up my eyes, I saw a savage-

---

[1] A German Mile is Five and a Half English. [Translator's Note].

looking man coming towards me: He was armed with an enormous club, his figure was of a monstrous size, my first surprise at least had made me think so, and the colour of his face was of the mulatto hue, which gave to the white of a squinting eye additional terrors. Instead of a girdle he had his green buttonless great coat tied with a thick cord, to which an enormous knife and a brace of pistols were fastened. I had quickened my steps when his terrible voice assailed my ears, but he soon came up with me and stopped me with a powerful arm. The sound of a human voice had filled my soul with terror, however, the sight of a ruffian raised my spirits: In my miserable situation I had full reason to tremble at the sight of an honest man, but none at all at that of a robber.

"Who art thou?" thundered the frightful apparition in my ear.

"Thy equal," was my reply, "if thou really art what thy appearance bespeaks."

"This is not the right way. What business hast thou here?"

"And what right hast thou to question me?" I replied in a determined accent.

"The terrible man measured me with his looks from tip to toe: He seemed to compare my haughty answer with my defenceless situation—

"Thou art impudent like a beggar," he resumed at length.

"Very possible, I have been one but yesterday."

"He laughed, exclaiming with a horrid grin, "My honest friend, I hope thou doest not presume to be thought something better."

"That is nothing to thee," so saying I wanted to pursue my way.

"Fairly and softly, my dear boy, why in such a hurry? What weighty business is it which makes thee run so fast?"

"I mused a moment, and cannot conceive what prompted me to reply in a slow accent, "Life is short and hell everlasting."

"He stared at me with a ghastly look, "I will be damned," he resumed at length, "if thou hast not stumbled against a gallows on thy way."

"It may come to that one time, farewell, comrade."

"Stay a moment longer," he exclaimed, taking a tin bottle from his hunting pouch and offering it to me after he had swallowed a large draught: The hurry of my fright and the dreadful agonies of mind I had undergone had reduced my strength very low, and my parched lips had not been moistened with one refreshing draught that whole unfortunate day. Famine had already stared me horribly in the face, in that extensive forest, where three miles around no refreshment could be procured, you may therefore easily think how joyfully I accepted this offer. I swallowed greedily the contents of the bottle, and new strength animated my whole frame, my heart was expanded with new courage, and hope and love for life returned in my desponding heart; I began to fancy that I was not wholly miserable; so much relief afforded me that welcome draught, and I must confess that my situation began to appear less dreadful to me, since I, after a thousand miscarried hopes, had found at last a being that bore some resemblance with me. In the desponding situation in which I was, I would not have hesitated to pledge the health of an infernal spirit, in order to have a confidant.

"Meanwhile my new companion had stretched himself upon the grass, and I followed his example.

"Thy brandy has given me new life," said I, "we must be better acquainted with each other."

"He struck fire and lighted his pipe.

"Is it long since thou hast carried on this trade?"

"He stared at me—"What means that question?"

"I took the knife from his girdle, resuming, "Has this instrument done much execution."

"Who art thou?" he roared in a terrible accent, flinging his pipe on the grass and starting up.

"A murderer like thyself— but only a beginner."

"He gazed at me and took up his pipe.

"Thou art no inhabitant of these districts," he resumed, at length.

"I am; hast thou heard of Wolf, the innkeeper, at A—?"

"He started up as if frantic, exclaiming in a rapturous accent, "Wolf the inn-keeper, who has been punished so severely for game-stealing?"

"That very man I am."

"Welcome, comrade, a thousand times welcome!" he exclaimed, shaking me joyfully by the hand, "how glad am I that I have found thee at last, I have been many many months in search of thee; I know thee very well, know all what thou hast suffered, and have been longing for thy assistance this great while."

"For my assistance? To what purpose?"

"Every body speaks of thee: Thou hast many enemies, hast suffered glaring injuries, hast been entirely ruined and persecuted with unheard of severity."—He grew warm.—"They have immured thee in the house of correction, have treated thee like a galley-slave at the fortress, have stripped thee of thy fortune, and reduced thee to beggary, because thou hast killed a few paltry deer, which the Prince suffers to prey on our corn, and to rob us of the fruit of our diligence. Is it come to that, brother, that a human being is valued less than a hare or a boar? Are we not better than the wild beasts of the field? And a fellow like thyself could brook such injury."

"What could I do?"

"That we shall see: But pray tell me, whence dost thou come, and on what errand?"

"I related my whole history to him, and, without awaiting the end of it he jumped up with joyful impatience, pulling me after him with all his might.

"Come along, brother," he said, "now art thou ripe, art the very man I wanted for my purpose. I shall reap great honor by introducing thee to our common wealth. Make haste and follow me."

"Whither art thou going to conduct me?"

"Don't ask questions but come and see;" so saying, he dragged me forcibly after him.

"As we proceeded the forest grew more and more intricated, impenetrable and gloomy: None of us spoke a word until I was suddenly roused from my apathy by the whistle of my leader: I looked around and beheld myself at the declivity of a steep rock, projecting over a deep cavern. A second whistle answered from the womb of the rock, and a ladder rose slowly from the abyss, a thundering voice hallooed from the deep, and the winding cavern echoed to the sound. My leader descended, first bidding me to wait 'till he should return. 'I first must secure the mastiff which guards the entrance to our abode,' he said, 'thou art a stranger, and the ferocious beast would tear thee to pieces.'—So saying, he disappeared.

"Now I was standing alone before the precipice, and was well aware of it. The imprudence of my leader did not escape my notice: It would have cost me no more but a resolute effort to pull up the ladder, and I would have been restored to liberty, and effected my escape without the least danger of being overtaken by the inhabitants of the cavern; I cannot but confess that I had some temptation to do it: Looking down into the abyss I was struck with an obscure idea of the bottomless gulph of hell, from whence there is no redemption to be expected. I began to shudder at the new course of life which I was going to commence. A sudden flight only could have saved me. I was half determined to effect my escape, and already stretching out my hand to pull up the ladder, when suddenly I fancied to hear a thundering voice as if from the womb of hell, 'What has a murderer to risk?' and my arm lost its hold, and every power of motion. My doom was fixed, the time of repentance past, and the murder I had committed was towering behind me like a mountain shutting up for ever my return to the path of virtue.

"My leader reappeared the same moment, bidding me descend into the cavern. I had now no other choice left but to submit to necessity, and climbed down. Having advanced a few steps under the excavated rock, our passage grew larger, and I beheld some huts at a distance, and as I approached nearer, a round spot covered with grass appeared to my view. About twenty people were sitting round a blazing fire. 'Here,' my leader exclaimed, 'here I bring you a new member of our society, whose name is not unknown to you, rise and welcome the celebrated Wolf, of A——.'[1]

---

[1] Though Teuthold does not use the word, banditti (a society of robbers) become a commonplace in Gothic writing after the publication of Ann Radcliffe's works (See Jack Voller's note on the subject in his edition of Radcliffe's *The Veiled Picture*, p. 24, n. 2), but there may also be a connection to Friedrich Schiller's *Die Räuber* (*The Robbers*), which Kahlert clearly had read, particularly given the social and political content of this passage.

"Wolf," they all exclaimed with one voice, starting up and forming a circle around me, men, women and children: Their joy was unfeigned and cordial; confidence and even respect was marked in their looks; one squeezed my hand, the other clapt me on the shoulder, in a confidential manner; all seemed sincerely rejoiced at seeing me, and the scene was not unlike the meeting again of an old beloved acquaintance.

"My arrival had interrupted their dinner, they retook their seats and pressed me to partake of their inviting meal, which consisted of venison of all kind and stewed fruits. The goblet filled with delicious wine wandered from hand to hand, and spread merriment and joviality around; plenty and concord seemed to reign in that little society, and every one strove to manifest his joy at my presence.

"I was seated between two females which was the place of honor at table, and having expected to meet with the refuse of their sex, how great was my astonishment when I found amid this gang of robbers the most beautiful female figures my eyes ever beheld. Margaret, the eldest and handsomest of the two, was called Miss, and could not be much above eighteen; her language was very licentious, and her looks still more so. Maria, the youngest, was married, but had run away from a husband who had treated her ill; her form was superior to that of my other neighbour, however she was pale and of a delicate constitution, and in the whole less striking at first sight than the lively Margaret. They seemed to rival who first should kindle my desires; the beautiful Margaret strove to dispel my timidity by wanton jokes, however I soon conceived an invincible dislike to that woman, and the modest Maria fettered my heart for ever.

"You see, brother," said the man who had been my conductor to that place, "You see how we live here, and every day passes like the present: Is it not true, comrades?"

"Yes, every day passes like the present," the whole gang exclaimed.

"If therefore you think you can accustom yourself to our manner of life, then stay with us and be our captain: Do you consent to it, comrades?"

"An unanimous *yes* rent the air.

"My imagination was fired with wine and loose desires, my reason fettered, and my blood heated: Human society had banished me—and there I found brotherly affection, good living and honor. Whatever might have been my choice, I could not escape the hand of punishing justice; however, in a situation like that which was offered me, I could at least sell my life dear: Voluptuousness was my ruling passion, and I had 'till then always been treated with scorn and contempt by the other sex, but here I could expect to satisfy my desires, and to be received with pleasure: My resolution cost me but very little, and I exclaimed, after a moment's consideration, "I will stay with you, comrades, if you will cede to me my beautiful neighbour."

"All of them agreed to consent to my request, and I became unexpectedly the avowed possessor of a w—e, and the chief of a gang of robbers!

"To be revenged on the prince, in whose dominions I had suffered so much disgrace, was the chief desire of my heart, and to effect that purpose the first use I made of my new acquired authority. Our gang consisted in eight stout fellows besides myself, the rest was composed of women and children: My new associates had contented themselves 'till I was joined to their society, with clandestine depredations in the pantries and cellars of the rich peasants, and game-stealing, and never had recourse to violent means. My views went farther: I proposed to declare open war against the game, which had brought on my disgrace and ruin, and to rob the houses of the judges who had punished me so severely.

"To effect our purpose we wanted horses, the frontiers, where the dominions of my former sovereign terminated, being three miles distant. By means of house-breaking and some highway robberies we soon got possession of a sufficient sum of money, with which we dispatched one of our associates to a distant town to buy four horses, firearms, powder, and ball. The houses of the hated judges were pillaged in a tempestuous night, and whenever the face of the earth was covered with midnight darkness, we sallied forth from our den to destroy the game in those parts where my misfortunes had commenced, and I took care to let my persecutors know that it was Wolf who committed these depredations.

"Meeting with success in our nocturnal rambles our temerity increased, and we waylaid the traveller on the high road, however I took great care not to perpetrate a second murder. The terror of my name soon spread itself all over the country, and the neighbouring magistrates tried every means to get me in their power; a great reward was promised to him who should take me, dead or alive, and, if one of my associates, a full pardon; however, I was so fortunate to elude the watchfulness of my pursuers for a considerable time, and to frustrate every attempt on my liberty.

"I had carried on this infernal trade a whole year, when I began to be tired of it. The gang, whose leader I was, having disappointed my sanguine hopes, I soon perceived, with terror, how much my fancy, heated by wine and loose desires, had been imposed upon, when I consented to become the captain of my associates. Hunger and want frequently supplied the place of superfluity and ease, which I had expected, and I was necessitated many a time to risk my life in order to procure a scanty meal, which hardly sufficed to appease the violent cravings of my empty stomach. The visionary image of brotherly concord disappeared, and envy, suspicion, and jealousy stepped in its place, loosening the ties of our society; the solemn promise of a full pardon to him who should deliver me into the hands of justice, was a powerful temptation to lawless robbers, and I was well aware of the dangers which surrounded me. I became a stranger to sleep, a victim to never ceasing apprehensions; the phantom of suspicion pursued me every where, tormented me when awake, laid down with me upon my couch, and created frightful dreams, when my weary eyes were now and then closed by the hand of slumber. My conscience, which had been lulled asleep, recovered its power by degrees, and the sleeping viper of remorse was roused by the general tempest which was raging within my breast; the hatred I bore the human race turned its dagger against myself—I was reconciled to human kind, and cursed nobody but myself: The dreadful consequences of vice stared me grisly in the face, and my natural good sense dispelled at length the delusions which had led me astray from the blessed path of virtue; I felt how deep I had fallen, and gloomy melancholy stepped in the place of gnashing despair: I wished, with weeping eyes, to have it in my power to recall the times past, and was convinced that I would make a better use of the hours I had dedicated to the vile service of guilt; I began to hope that I yet would reform, being sensible that I should be able to effect a reform. On the highest summit of depravity I was more inclined to tread in the steps of virtue, than before I had committed the first lawless deed.

"A war had broken out in Germany at that time, and recruits were raising every where, which gave me some hopes to retreat in an honorable manner from my associates, and turn a useful member of human society: I wrote a letter to my prince, the copy of which you will find in my pocket-book."

The letter was produced and read by the clerk, the purport of it ran, as much as I can remember, as follows:

"If your Highness does not think it beneath your dignity to condescend to a villain like myself, if a criminal of my atrocity is not entirely excluded from your mercy, O then do not reject the humble petition of a repenting sinner—I am a murderer and robber, have forfeited my life, and am pursued by the avenging hand of justice, I will deliver myself into the hand of the executive power—but I, at the same time, am going to lay a very strange prayer at the feet of your throne: I detest life and do not fear to die, it would however be dreadful to me to die, without having lived. I wish to live, in order to repair my crimes past, and to make my peace with human society, which I have offended. My execution will be a warning example to the world, but not atone for my wicked deeds; I hate vice, and have a strong desire to try the path of honesty and virtue; I have shewn great capacities to become a terror to the state, and I flatter myself that I yet have some abilities to render services to the country which I have injured.

"I am well aware that I supplicate for something quite uncommon: My life being forfeited, it does not become me to propose conditions to punishing justice; however, I am not yet chained in fetters, am yet at liberty, and fear has the least share in my prayer.

"It is mercy that I crave, and if I had some claim to justice I would not attempt now to enforce it; yet there is one circumstance which I have reason to recall to the recollection of my judges. The period of my crimes commences with that rigorous sentence which has deprived me of my honor. If my judges had not been too severe, if they had listened to the voice of equity and humanity, I should perhaps not have been reduced to the necessity of craving the mercy of your Highness—their want of feeling has plunged me in the fatal gulph of guilt.

"Let mercy supply the place of justice and spare my life, if it is in your power to intercede with the law in my behalf, the remainder of my life shall be entirely devoted to your service: If you can grant my humble prayer let me know it by way of the public prints, and I will throw myself at your feet, confiding in your princely word; if not, then justice may proceed as it shall be deemed proper, and I must act as necessity shall require."

"This petition," thus resumed the delinquent, "was not taken notice of, as well as a second and third, and having not the least glimmering of hope left, to be pardoned, I took the resolution to leave the country, and to die in the service of the King of Prussia as a brave soldier.

"I gave my gang the slip, and began my journey. My road led me through a small country town, where I intended to stay the night: A few weeks ago a proclamation had been published through the whole country, commanding a strict examination of every traveller, because the Prince had taken a party in the war, as a member of the German Empire. The gate-keeper of the town which I was going to enter was sitting upon a bench before his house as I rode by; my forbidding countenance and motley dress raised his suspicion, and as soon as I had entered the gate he shut it and demanded my passport, after he had first secured the bridle of my horse. I was prepared for accidents of that sort, having provided myself with a passport, which I had taken from a merchant whom I had robbed. However this testimony would not satisfy the eagle-eyed gate-keeper, my physiognomy being in contradiction with it, and I was obliged to follow him to the bailiffs house: He ordered me to await his return at the door.

"The passport was examined, and mean while a rabble began to assemble around me, attracted by my strange figure; a whispering arose among the multitude and some of the crowd were pointing alternately at me and my horse; the latter having been stolen by one of my former associates, my conscience gave the alarm. The gate-keeper returned with the passport, and told me, that the bailiff understanding that I came from the seat of the war, would be glad to have half an hour's conversation with me, and to get some information of the situation of our army. This message increased my apprehension of being known, and fearing the invitation of the bailiff to be a snare to get me in his power without resistance, I clapt spurs to my horse without returning an answer.

"My sudden flight gave the signal to an universal hue and cry; a thief! a thief! exclaimed the whole multitude, pursuing me with all possible speed: The iron hand of punishing vengeance seemed ready to grasp me, my life was at stake, and I redoubled the swiftness of my flight, goading the sides of my horse without mercy.

"My pursuers were soon far behind me, panting for breath, and liberty promised to gladden my heart again, when the fleetness of my flight was suddenly stopt by a dead wall. My pursuers gave a loud shout when they saw me entrapt, and I had given over every hope of effecting my escape, when a sudden thought struck me, that the wall might be the city wall, and that perhaps I would regain my liberty through a window of one of the houses on the bottom of the street. The door of that on the left side was open, I jumped from my horse, and entered it with a pistol in each hand, bolting the door after me, and hastening up stairs without being seen by any one of the inhabitants. My pursuers were close at my heels, and thundered at the door when I was rushing into a room where nobody was but an old woman: Seeing a man with a brace of pistols, terror fettered her tongue, and she fell in a swoon. I opened the window, and, imagine my joy, when the open field hailed my anxious looks; I bolted the door, placed chairs and tables against it, threw the bed out of the window, and concealed myself in the chimney to await there the setting in of night.

"This was the work of a few moments, and I was safely housed in my hiding-place when the door was forced open with a thundering noise. My calculations had not deceived me, and my plan succeeded as well as I could expect it. My pursuers seeing the window open, and the feather-bed lying in the field, believed firmly I had effected my escape: Some young men jumped boldly down, and others went to pursue me on horseback; the old woman who could tell no tales, was carried to another part of the house, and I was left alone to muse on my awkward situation.

"Soon after the owner of the house came into the room with some of his neighbours, and confirmed by his discourses my hope that nobody suspected my hiding-place. One of the company thought I might be concealed under the bed, but his idea of my still being in the house was, to my inexpressible satisfaction, treated with ridicule. At length my situation became extremely painful to me, and I wished fervently my unwelcome visitors might be gone.

"After two tedious hours I was at length released of my fear to be detected by some unforeseen accident, when the landlord and his friends left also the room where I was hidden. As soon as the coast was clear, and the tranquillity of the house restored, I climbed higher up into the chimney with the intention to get upon the roof; however, on maturer consideration I thought it safer to remain where I was, hearing many voices in the field, which made me afraid of being detected.

"The time crept slowly on, and I thought the wished-for hour of midnight would never set in: Hunger and thirst increased the horrors of my situation, and that ever watchful remembrance of the mortal race, conscience, began to remind me of my wickedness, and the punishments of never sleeping justice, which sooner or later would overtake me: My resolution of leaving the path of vice acquired new strength, and I vowed fervently never to sin again if I should escape once more.

"Amidst these salutary meditations and resolutions night began to set in, and I breathed freer. At length the featherbed was brought back, but nobody came to sleep in it that night, and the room remained unoccupied.

"As soon as midnight silence announced to me that every body was gone to rest, I slided softly down the chimney, tore one of the bed sheets and twisted it in a line to make use of it in getting into the field. No sooner had I touched the ground than I took to my heels to reach, before daybreak, the Black Forest, which I knew was only two miles distant, being well aware that the whole country would be in a hue and cry after me as soon as my nocturnal escape should be known. Fear gave me strength and winged my feet: Fatigued and entirely spent I reached the skirts of the Black

Forest, and threw myself into the first thicket to rest my weary limbs.

"Fatigued by the long journey I had made and the anxiety and fear which continually had harrassed my mind, I fell asleep: I had not slept two hours, as I could guess by the sun, when I was suddenly roused by the distant barking of dogs; I started up and listened, when the hallooing of two huntsmen vibrated in my ear: They seemed to direct their course towards the spot where I was concealed, and no other means of escape were left me, but to climb up an adjoining oak tree, and to hide myself amid its thickest branches, where I fancied to find security.

"However all my fears and apprehensions returned with redoubled force, when the dogs came to the tree which sheltered me and began to bark in a terrible manner; the hunters were close at their heels, but seeing no game, they recalled my new persecutors and pursued their way. Fear of falling into the hands of my enemies obliged me to remain where I was until the dark mantle of night should cover once more my flight.

"Hunger and thirst had hardly left me sufficient strength to keep my situation any longer, when I, to my inexpressible joy, espied the nest of a raven in the top of a tree, and six eggs in it. This unexpected relief gave me new strength, new life, new hope, and I awaited with patience the setting in of night, when I got down, pursuing my way through the forest.

"The night was dark, and a rising tempest shook the tops of the lofty oaks: The distant lightning and the hollow voice of the thunder announced a dreadful night. The thunder soon began to shake the firmament, flashes of lightning illuminated, by intervals, the dark and dreary forest, and to increase the miseries of my situation, a storm of rain gushed down with such violence as if all the flood-gates of heaven had been opened at once. I sought shelter beneath an antient oak, but, alas! a flash of lightning which shivered to atoms a lofty beech tree, not above fifty paces from the spot where I was standing, made me soon quit my dangerous asylum, and drove me to an open spot where I was exposed to all the violence of the storm: I was soon wet to the skin; my teeth began to chatter, and all my little courage fled on the wings of despondency.

"I had stood the fury of the elements two horrid dreadful hours, no sound was heard but the screech of the owl, the croaking of the raven, the roaring of thunder, and the howling of furious winds: midnight was past, and the hurricane still raged with unabated fury: My wounded conscience brought all my crimes to my recollection, I fancied the day of judgment was near, and was seized with a violent trembling. My tortured soul divined a thousand horrid thoughts, and I vowed fervently to pursue the steps of virtue.

"My whole frame shaking with cold I began to run without knowing whither I was directing my course, in order to warm my blood, which was almost chilled, when suddenly the ground gave way beneath my feet, and I fell into a deep pit. My fall was violent, however I received no other hurt except a few bruises, my coat being entangled in the roots of a tree about four yards from the bottom of my subterraneous dungeon: I strove to climb up the wall, which appeared to be horizontal, but all my endeavours were fruitless, and the dreadful spectre of famine stared me grisly in the face: I sat down upon the damp ground and began to muse on my forlorn situation, when a sudden flash of vivid lightning illuminated my prison, and disclosed to my eyes a narrow passage; I groped along the winding passage with fearful steps, not knowing whether it would lead me upwards or downwards.

"I had walked above half an hour and not yet found an outlet, the little hope I had to extricate myself from my subterraneous dungeon began to die away by degrees, and seemed to be entirely frustrated, when a massy iron door suddenly obstructed my way; I exerted all my little remaining strength to force it open, however the impenetrable darkness which surrounded me rendered all my labors abortive: The punishment of my crimes seemed to be arrived, and I sunk down upon the damp ground in a fit of despair entirely spent, and incapable to attempt any farther efforts to open the fatal door; cold drops of sweat bedewed my wearied limbs, and I began, the first time in my life, fervently to pray.

"At length a thought struck me, that perhaps the flash of the powder would disclose to me an outlet, if I was to fire a pistol. I hastily took one out of my pocket and discharged it; my hope had not deceived me entirely, and I beheld another passage to the left, which I instantly pursued with alacrity. 'Ere long I came to a second iron door, which however soon yielded to my efforts to open it, and let me into a spacious vault.

"Having groped about half an hour longer I was thrilled with unutterable joy when I discovered, after many fruitless researches, a narrow staircase, which led me into a roomy hall, faintly illuminated by the rays of the moon, who was peeping through the lofty windows, composed of stained glass."

Here the robber gave a full description of the Haunted Castle, on the skirts of the Black Forest, which you, my dear friend, know too well to require a repetition of the faithful picture he drew.

"Having explored every corner of the antient fabric," thus he continued, "without meeting a living soul, I descended into a spacious court-yard, from whence a lofty gate-way led me into the open field. The dawn of morn began to break in the East from the purple clouds, and I heard the crowing of cocks within a small distance. He only who has been in a situation like mine can form an idea of the rapture which rushed on my soul when I perceived myself to be so near an inhabited spot.

"Quickening my tottering steps I saw two country wenches with baskets on their heads coming from the adjacent village, which seemed to be not above a quarter of a mile distant: I was just going to enquire of them the name of the village, when both of them raised a dreadful scream, running back as fast as possible. Being desirous to know, previous to my entrance into the village, where I was, lest I might unknowingly run into the hands of my pursuers; I summoned up all the few remains of strength, which hunger and fatigue had left me, in order to come up with them, but when the frightened girls perceived me close at their heels, they threw down their baskets, and fled with the swiftness of an arrow.

"Fearing to be known, and apprehending the wenches would alarm the village, I was obliged to desist from my pursuit, and to seek a hiding-place 'till I should be able to continue my journey, for I found it utterly impossible to advance a mile farther. No place promising a safer asylum than the desolated castle, I resolved to return, but previously to examine the baskets the girls had dropt, whether they might not contain some victuals to appease the pinching hunger which tormented me.

"It seemed they had been on their way to the market, their baskets containing some lumps of butter, two earthen jars with milk, some small cheeses, and two large pieces of coarse bread. The milk, which was not all run out of the earthen vessels, quenched my thirst, and the bread and cheese I took with me to the castle to satisfy the pressing demands of my stomach.

"On my arrival in the great hall of the castle I struck fire with the help of a steel I had in my pocket, and the flint of one of my pistols, and soon was seated by the blazing flame drying my wet garments and appeasing my hunger. Casting my looks accidentally on my hands, I saw that they were as black as those of a coalheaver, from the soot of the chimney where I had sheltered myself against the first onset of my pursuers, and having every reason to believe that my face must be the same hue, I easily could account for the sudden flight of the two girls, who, very likely took me for the devil: This idea silenced my fears of a visit from the alarmed villagers tolerably, and the soothing hand of sleep began to close my eyes."

Thus far the captain of the robbers had related his extraordinary tale, when the chief Justice commending the apparent sincerity of his voluntary confession, broke up the court, ordering the prisoner to be reconducted to his dungeon until the day following, when he would hear the continuation of his adventures. My business not allowing me to stay a day longer, I departed reluctantly at four o'clock in the afternoon: However, before I left N— I obtained the promise of a friend of mine whom I accidentally had met, that he would send me the continuation of the robber's farther confession, and four weeks after I received the following letter, which contains every thing you may wish to know.

CONTINUATION OF WOLF'S CONFESSION, AND THE FINAL ISSUE OF HIS
TRIAL.

My worthy friend,

It is with the sincerest satisfaction I am going to give you a
faithful account of the remainder of Wolf's confession, and the
final issue of his trial, according to my promise.

You will remember that he closed the narration of his singular adventures which he gave on the first day of his trial, with
his reluctant return to the castle, where he intended to stay 'till
the darkness of night should shelter him against the pursuit of his
persecutors. The great fatigue he had sustained on his flight soon
closed his weary eyes, and he slept 'till after sun set, when he left
the Castle to pursue his way to F—, where he intended to enlist in
the Prussian service.

Directed by the silver rays of the rising moon he soon found
his way to the high road: At the first well he fell in with he cleaned
his sooty face and hands and then went briskly on. Being well
stocked with provisions, he determined not to enter any inhabited
place before he should be obliged by necessity to do it, lest some
new misfortunes might cross his military scheme. With that view
he left the high road whenever it led through a village, walked all
night long and slept in the day time. Thus he travelled onward
two nights without having met with any accident, when he, at the
close of the third day, was obliged to direct his course to a small
hamlet in order to provide himself with provisions: As soon as it
was dark he went with fearful steps to a baker's shop, to purchase
some bread, but great was his terror when he wanted to pay for
the small loaf of coarse bread he had bought, and could not find
his purse, which must have dropt out of his pocket when he dried
his garments in the hall of the castle.

Being entirely destitute of money, he offered one of his pistols,
which he took out of his pocket, in lieu of payment: The baker
viewed him from tip to toe, and after some hesitation agreed to
the bargain. Unfortunately the house of this man had been robbed
some weeks ago by a gang of thieves, and Wolf's savage look
joined with his singular appearance rendered him suspicious to

the baker, who, ever since the robbery had been committed in his house, took every ill-looking stranger for a thief.

Prompted by that notion he ordered one of his people to follow Wolf at some distance as soon as he had left the house, and went instantly to the bailiff to inform him of his suspicions, and the strange bargain he had just concluded.

The magistrate who had been indefatigable in his researches after the daring robbers, without succeeding in his endeavours to find them out, soon fell in with his opinion, and ordered some stout fellows to follow the suspected robber, and to secure him by surprise.

Wolf, who had mean while struck again into the forest, seated himself behind some bushes by the banks of a rivulet, and began to appease the demands of his grumbling stomach, not observing that he was followed, when suddenly four sinewy arms seized him from behind.

The unexpected surprise, the continual fatigues he had undergone, and the strength of his adversaries rendered it impossible to disengage himself from their powerful grasps, and he was dragged before the magistrate of the hamlet who demanded his passport: Having been obliged to leave it behind when his alarmed conscience had drawn upon him his late disaster, he had no other choice left but to pretend being an Austrian deserter, who wanted to go into the Prussian service. The bailiff mistrusting his veracity, ordered him to be searched, when a loaded pistol and a large knife were found upon him, which increased the suspicion of the zealous magistrate, who, without farther ado, sent him to the prison.

New apprehensions of a dreadful nature assailed now the unhappy man. The fear that all his former crimes would be detected filled his desponding soul with black despair; however his lamentable situation took soon a turn more favorable than he could have expected. A transport of Prussian recruits passing thro' the village in the afternoon, the bailiff ordered him to be delivered to the commanding officer, thinking this to be the most commodious way to rid the country of a fellow whose whole appearance bore evident marks of his thiefish profession, and to spare himself the trouble of a tedious examination. His size and the robust make

of his limbs rendered him a very acceptable acquisition to the recruiting officer, and he was enrolled as a Prussian soldier to his
unutterable joy.

Wolf the robber was now at once appointed to fight the battles
of Frederic the Great,[1] and made a solemn vow to fulfil cheerfully
the duties of his honorable calling.

The transport arrived safe at Magdeburg,[2] and the new soldier
was with his companions instructed in the art of killing lawfully
his fellow creatures. The Corporal who was appointed to instruct
him in the manual exercise, was famous for his severity, conform-
ing strictly to the military principles of his royal master, who, as
it is universally known, had it laid down as a rule to inspire his
martial bands of heroism by the frequent application of wooden
arguments. Wolf who was not in the least partial to that sort of
reasoning, found it very difficult to brook the brutality of his drill-
ing master, who seemed to have a particular predilection for him,
plying his back so frequently and so severely, that the new soldier
was soon rendered too sensible of his instructor's partiality for
him.

Wolf exerted himself to the utmost of his ability to please
the rigorous corporal, and to shelter himself against the frequent
heavy showers of blows and cuffs, but not being able to attain his
end, resentment and hatred began at length to rankle in his heart,
his whole stock of patience was exhausted, and he began to have
frequent recourse to drinking, in order to dispel the gloominess of
mind which haunted him incessantly, and to drown the recollection of his forlorn situation.

One day as he came half intoxicated to the parade, he acquitted himself so badly of his task, that his military mentor plied his
back most unmercifully. Wolfs anger was roused, his blood was

---

[1] Frederick the Great (Friedrich der Grosse) is the famous "enlightened" ruler of
Prussia (1740-1786) who wished to unite Germany. His main opponent was Austria,
and his strongest ally was England.
[2] During the Thirty Years' War, Imperial Forces destroyed the city of Magdeburg,
and 25,000 of the city's 30,000 inhabitants perished as a result of the attack and by
fires that broke out during the attack. Interestingly, following the Reformation and
until the reign of Frederick the Great, no Catholics were "admitted" to Magdeburg. See entry on Magdeburg in *Catholic Encyclopedia*, http://www.newadvent.
org/cathen/09524b.htm.

boiling, and he called his chastiser a savage beast, a blood-hound, and many other names of the same stamp. The fury of his tyrant being raised to the highest degree by that language, he inflicted his blows with so much violence, that Wolf, in a fit of despair struck him to the ground with the butt end of his gun. He was instantly seized, carried to the prison, and sentenced by a court martial to run the gauntlet.

The day of execution appeared, the soldiers were drawn up, and his back was bared, when lo! the mark of his ignominy was seen between his shoulders. It being evident by the sign of a gallows, which was seen between his shoulders, that he had been under the hands of the common hangman, he was declared unworthy to receive military punishment, and sentenced to work in the fortification.

Confined with the dregs of human kind, and ever in company with the basest of villains, his weak virtuous resolutions died away by degrees. He once more began to consider himself as the sport of injustice and barbarous cruelty, his belief in the providence of the benevolent ruler of the world soon gave way to atheistical principles, and his former desire for doing mischief returned with redoubled force, when he saw his sincere endeavours to become an useful member of human society were thwarted again in a most cruel manner: He began to think that he was doomed to be a villain, and being driven to despair by hard labour, and frequent blows, he concerted plans of effecting his escape.

One of his fellow prisoners, a most consummate ruffian, joined with him in devising means of regaining their liberty, and after many fruitless efforts they at length effected their escape, assisted by an impenetrable fog which covered their flight. As soon as their escape was known in the fortress, the cannons were fired, and the country roused: However they happily eluded their pursuers, and reached at the close of day a wood where they resolved to conceal themselves in the tops of the trees 'till the heat of the pursuit should have abated.

In this uncomfortable situation they remained as long as their small stock of provisions lasted, consulting with each other by what means they could best procure an independent livelihood, and at last agreed to resort to the Haunted Castle in the Black

Forest, and there to commence robbers. After many fatiguing rambles and alarming fears, they arrived at length at the wished for asylum.

Wolf's inventive genius begot the scheme to render that desolated fabric more secure against the intrusion of unwelcome visitors, by raising an idea in the fancy of the neighbouring villagers of its being haunted by evil spirits. In order to accomplish their design, they set up a dreadful howling and doleful lamentations whenever they perceived some of the villagers near the environs of the castle. The gloomy appearance of that half decayed fabric, aided by the superstition of the credulous peasantry rendered their artful schemes successful, and in a short time none of the villagers dared to approach their lurking place, from which they sallied out every night disguised in the skin of goats, which they had stolen and fleeced, and committed numberless robberies in the village. Having procured a sufficient stock of money, Wolf's associate was dispatched to a neighbouring town to procure fire-arms, powder, and ball, and then they began to prey on the unwary wanderer. To relate the numberless robberies they committed before they were joined by new associates would swell volumes: As their numbers augmented they became more daring, and extended their depredations many miles over the country, 'till after a series of thirty successful years their infernal society sustained a deadly blow by the nocturnal surprize which delivered them into the power of punishing justice. Wolf has since confessed that they have a great number of hiding-places besides the solitary castle, and that their gang consists of fifty-three ruffians, who are dispersed all over the country. The useful information he has given to his Judges has enabled them to secure a great number of innkeepers and publicans, who were leagued with that infernal set of ruffians, of whom six more have been taken up since you have left me, however their money and the great booty they have hoarded up, has not been detected as yet, and is supposed to have been removed on the first alarm by the rest of the gang. Wolf's life will be spared on account of his faithful confession, and the great assistance he has afforded his Judges in putting a final stop to the depredations which have been committed for a series of years in the environs of the Black Forest; he is to be committed for life to the house of correction where he will have ample scope to reflect on his life past, and to prepare to meet that eternal Judge who sooner or later overtakes the wicked in his vile pursuits. Thus I have executed my task as well as it was in my power, and trust you will kindly overlook the defects of my narrative, and always believe me to be with the greatest sincerity,

Your affectionate friend,

P—.

FINIS.

CONTEMPORARY REVIEWS

The Monthly Review, April 1795, p. 465.

Art. 38. *The Necromancer:* or the Tale of the Black Forest: founded on Facts. Translated from the German of Lawrence Flammenburg, by Peter Teuthold. 12mo. 2 vols. 6s. sewed. Lane. 1794.

In the mind of man there is a predisposition to credulity, which too often renders the very means adopted as a remedy, a proximate cause of new disease. The Platonic idea of influencing dæmons or disembodied spirits by human rites and adjurations, of learning secret phænomena from their revelation, and of accomplishing by their intervention important purposes of this world, had scarcely been mentioned, much less credited, since the time of the old Alchemists and Rosicrusians, until some modern novelists chose once more to familiarize the superstition; partly in order to expose it, and partly in order to extract from it new sources of the terrible. The opinion itself now seems again creeping into repute; it is mentioned even by philosophers without a sneer; and it is becoming the corner-stone of a spreading sect of visionaries, whose favoured or impudent proselytes are said to behold by day, and in the very streets of this metropolis, the wandering souls of holy men of other times. It requires perhaps some leaning towards these and the like notions, or at least a sufficient respect from them not to laugh at but to sympathize with the curiosity and apprehensions of those imbued with them, in order to be pleased with this novel. In Germany, no doubt, such doctrines have made a wider impression and progress than in our country; since *raising ghosts* is an operation of frequent recurrence in The Necromancer; although the scene of adventure be laid in a frequented part of the country in our own half-century, and among the informed classes of the people. The prevailing spirit of the fable would best be manifested by extracts; but for these we cannot spare room.

The extraordinary events, which occupy the first volume, are, in the second, not very dexterously unravelled. They chiefly result from a confederacy of banditti; the leaders of which are seized, tried, and executed for their crimes, and die becomingly penitent; leaving behind them the necessary confessions.

Of the style of the novel, we have only to observe that it is not improperly adapted to a work which, we doubt not, will eagerly be perused by those who are ever on the watch for something new and strange.

British Critic, vol. 4 (1794): 194

Art. 35. *The Necromancer; or, the Tale of the Black Forest, founded on Facts, translated from the German of Lawrence Flammenburg,* by Peter Teuthold. 2 vol. 12mo. Lane, 1794.

A stranger farrago of Ghosts and Robbers was never put together. This work calls itself a translation from the German: out of respect to such of our countrymen as are authors, we heartily wish it may be a translation. We should be sorry to see an English original so full of absurdities. Errors of ignorance or of the press occur perpetually, such as affect for effect, adjectives used for adverbs, &c. &c.

Critical Review ser. 2. vol. 11 (1794): 469

The Necromancer: or the Tale of the Black Forest: founded on Facts: translated from the German of Lawrence Flammenberg, by Peter Teuthold. 2 vols. 12mo. 6s. sewed. Lane. 1794.

We are assured that the strange events related in these volumes, are founded on facts, the authenticity of which can be warranted by the translator, who has lived many years not far from the principal place of action. Exclusive of the entertainment arising from this narrative, it has in view an additional purpose, of greater importance to the public. It exposes the arts which have been practised in a particular part of Germany, for carrying on a series of nocturnal depredations in the neighbourhood, and infusing into the credulous multitude a firm belief in the existence of sorcery.

Lightning Source UK Ltd.
Milton Keynes UK
UKHW010641190819
348220UK00001B/119/P